Obloeron:

The Return to Lowbridge

By Sean Sweeney

Obloeron: The Return to Lowbridge

Copyright © 2006, 2015, 2020 by Sean Sweeney

All rights reserved. No part of this book may be reproduced or transmitted in any form or by any means, electronic or mechanical, including photocopying, recording, or any information storage and retrieval system, without prior written permission of the Author. Your support of author's rights is appreciated.

This book, an original publication, was registered with the United States Library of Congress Copyright Office.

Cover designed by Terry C. Simpson

Obloeron:
The Return to Lowbridge

By Sean Sweeney

Chapter 1

Even as the sun dropped from the sky like an elven arrow had punctured it, the temperature had dropped just as quickly. It felt as if the gods had shoved the entire realm into the coldest pit of hell.

Damp, frigid air rushed through the desolate, snowy plains as if it flowed like a raging river. Small drops of crystalline frozen water fell from the heavens, but not in an intermittent flurry—flakes the size of bricks cascaded to the earth—as it was a storm with no signs of stopping. While the sun's rays beat down on the snow, reflecting its light and blinding anyone who happened to traverse those lands during the day, any nighttime wanderers had to deal with weather beyond imagination, weather beyond any nightmarish vision.

Such was the nighttime weather of the frigid northlands.

Here, in the barren plains in the northernmost reaches of the realms, travelers faced brutal windstorms that nipped at their eyes, ears and nose; they faced tremendous snowstorms which buried people alive; they faced hypothermia, they faced insomnia, they faced inevitable signs of claustrophobia. After all, who would want to sleep with the threat of being buried alive or frozen to death closing in all around them?

It was considered brave—yet foolhardy—to walk the frozen wasteland at night. Yet for a group of dwarves, somewhat fresh from battle, going through it was the only way to get back to their precious homeland in the southwest.

Their home was Lowbridge.

The name itself sung with a voice all its own in the hearts of many of the dwarves, calling them to its grassy vales, its mines deep in the mountains.

But for the Twenty-fourth King of Lowbridge, something else—more than those grassy vales and mines—called him back home.

The heir to his kingdom called Radamuck Rosar back home. Much had happened since the Lady Rosar had given birth: Radamuck's son was only a few days old when his closest advisor, Yanos Kingsfoil the halfling, met with the Bastine elves. The elves and dwarves banded together to repel a group of orcs who had tortured and maimed villagers located just outside the elves' realm. After that conquest, Radamuck knew he had to keep going on in his search for the Chalice of Obloeron, which when melted down and mixed with pure melted silver it could make a weapon invincible. Not only that, Radamuck planned to use the rest of the mixture and form another weapon—a weapon that his son, the future Twenty-fifth King of Lowbridge, would wield to strike fear in the hearts of his foes.

He had found the chalice only a month prior to this night, and now, for the past fortnight, Radamuck and his rugged dwarven army were in the process of making the long march home—but they would go no further tonight.

"Ev'ryone, halt yerselves. Rest yer weary bones," he commanded. Everyone did so.

They neared the southernmost borders of the northlands and, while the temperatures in the southern part of the frozen realm were slightly warmer, it didn't mean they were safe from the cold.

As Radamuck looked about, he noticed that the snow had let up slightly, from its near whiteout conditions the day before to a small flurry. The dwarves were hungry, cold, and morale was low. But he had words for his dwarves that kept them going and boosting their morale by a fraction.

"We'll be in sight of Lowbridge soon, me lads! Just keep yer heads up for the next few days, yer eyes forward, and yeh'll be back in yer own beds with yer hairy-faced women 'fore yeh know it!" the king said. Hearty guffaws greeted his pronouncement.

One of the marchers was not in the mood to cheer for this, and Radamuck knew it: the human member of their group wasn't thinking of the grassy vales of Lowbridge or the hairy women they would find when they got there. No, he thought entirely back on the village of his birth, leagues to the north, and the beautiful woman who dwelt there.

For he was Grumpet T. Paddymeyer, and Radamuck knew his dreams—both by day and while he slept—were wrought with despair.

A fortnight ago, he left the township of Kayiko with the Lowbridge dwarves to escort Radamuck and to protect him from harm as he brought the chalice to the southwest realm next to the Enchanted Sea. But it pained him to go, for the woman he loved, the fair Jessica, had been there and he had wanted to spend the rest of his days together with her. But his duty called to him, and he wanted to protect this dwarf who had become as close to a father as he had ever known. With tears flowing down his cheeks, he had bid his new wife good bye and left with the dwarves.

A fortnight later, he had told Radamuck about visions invading his dreams, and it was a vision which had haunted him since before the battle with the wizard of Statuary Tower: Jessica, bloody and beaten, in the hands of that wizard.

But they were only dreams: the wizard, Dramin, was now dead and never again would he hurt Grumpet or his wife. Grumpet had seen to that with a mighty cut with *Flad-rul*, his own sword handed down to him by his grandfather, Krampel Paddymeyer. He had cleaved the head of the wizard clean off, ending his life.

Nearby, the human, in a crouch, got to his feet. He watched as his friend arched his back and closed his eyes, stretching his corded back muscles, relieving the knots from it. He stretched his arms to his sides, turning his waist to the left, then back to the right. His muscles popped. He opened his eyes and looked toward the southernmost borders of the northlands, which weren't so far away. The sun just now crept out from its hiding place to the east, and for some reason, Grumpet's forehead crinkled. Radamuck followed his gaze, and he felt his cheek twitch with recognition as he laid his eyes on the dwelling ahead.

But his attention turned away as he heard the little voice of his littlest companion coming toward him and Grumpet.

Yanos Kingsfoil ran hard, all while yelling to get Radamuck's attention, followed by the king's nephew, Aidan.

"Radamuck! Radamuck! I don't know where it came from, but it looks like it just popped out of nowhere!" said the halfling, his blue eyes wide from shock.

Radamuck held his hands up in a calming gesture.

“We see it, lad. We see it. My only question is where did it come from, and why is it here?”

Radamuck led his friends forward, Grumpet right behind them. The king knew his human companion had many questions, and he figured there were answers forthcoming.

The building was white, melding and meshing with the surrounding snow so well that it could have been here all the time without the company knowing it. It looked exactly the same as Radamuck had seen it the first time, much farther north from this spot in the northlands. It was twenty-five axe-lengths tall, fifty axe-lengths wide and large enough inside to hold the entire dwarf army. Even then he thought it a mirage, but he did not mistake the tree that stood to the left of the doorway. The tree was upside down, its roots visible instead of flowering buds on its branches.

And on the right hand side of the doorway sat a man who appeared nearly unrecognizable from the first time they saw him.

Kirkrik Dannell sat in a chair, his usual robes discarded. He wore short pants which left his spindly legs bare from mid-thigh downward, exposing them to the increasingly brightening sunshine. His chest was also bare and had turned slightly brown, and a white substance covered his nose. He had his long white hair pulled back, and the hair of his beard, which was just as white and newly grown, was flung back over his right shoulder. His eyes were closed.

“I knew you’d come to see me if I popped out of the ground right in front of you. Pull up a chair, Radamuck,” said the wizard, and, with a flick of his hand, conjured four chairs out of thin air.

Radamuck quickly tapped Grumpet’s shoulder; the human only stared at the wizard, with mouth agape. The dwarf knew Grumpet had heard of the previous encounter with Kirkrik Dannell through Aidan.

The four friends sat down—Yanos in a slightly smaller chair than the dwarves and the human captain—as the wizard opened his eyes. The air grew warmer and it looked as though Kirkrik had taken advantage of the warm air for quite some time.

"What are yeh doing here, me friend?" Radamuck asked. "I was hopin' I'd see yeh earlier than this."

Kirkrik Dannell yawned and stretched.

"Well, in answer to your second question first, even though it wasn't a real question, I was off in the southwest, in Grimstead, settling a dispute between ground tillers and a group of mad oxen; if you ever go there, wear shoes. I don't think my feet will ever smell worse after that trip," said the wizard, showing the trio the browned soles of his feet, which did not look like they were browned from the sun—or dirt. The four friends grimaced at the sight of his feet. "But in answer to your first question, I have been tanning here, waiting for you to appear. I had almost given up hope of your coming, but my raven came to me last week to tell me of your approach."

Radamuck took joy at knowing the wizard—despite his sometime kooky behavior—waited for him near the southernmost borders of this dangerous land. As he smiled, Kirkrik addressed Radamuck's comrades.

"Welcome back, Yanos Kingsfoil. I see that you have healed from the pains that Victor Dramin inflicted upon you," the wizard said to the halfling. Yanos looked at the wizard with his eyes wide. "There was no lingering damage done. Had it not been for the work of Kaidenn and Radamuck, you would not have survived that encounter. I for one am glad you are well now.

"I sense you wish to return to your homeland of Deerkin. Relax, for the king will grant you your leave in due time. He knows of your wish, as well. He needs you for some time further. Patience is a virtue, my little friend," he added. Yanos bowed his head, his face burning with embarrassment.

The wizard then addressed the younger dwarf with another one of his warm smiles.

"Young Aidan, I also know what troubles you also," he said, and noticed a flicker of surprise on both Aidan and Radamuck's countenances.

Aidan tried to hide his face from Radamuck, for he had not allowed his emotions to get the better of him before now, as it was unlike a dwarf to show emotions such as these. He was unsuccessful, as Radamuck grew instantly concerned for his nephew; he didn't say anything to him, however. He let the wizard continue.

"Your lady love awaits you in Lowbridge, and still holds true to you. Do not despair, for the flame she burns in her heart for you has given her hope these last months. When you arrive, seek her out and find solitude. You will know what to do then."

Aidan Rosar appeared stunned, but bowed his head and muttered his thanks to the white-haired wizard.

"But don't tell her about the incident with the loaded axe; she may never forgive you for nearly taking your eye out," Kirkrik said with a wink. Radamuck smiled, for he remembered the incident.

Kirkrik then turned his attention to Grumpet T. Paddymeyer, and his smile continued to outshine the rising sun.

"It is great to finally make your acquaintance, Grumpet. I have heard of your exploits as I watched the battle of Statuary Tower from afar, as well as your swordsmanship in the assaults upon your homeland by the wizard Dramin. These last few battles have proven beyond any doubt that you are the rightful heir to the great Krampel Paddymeyer, and that *Flad-rul*, the sword known for its fiery cut, could not have been placed in better hands. I remember your grandfather well, and you are his rightful heir.

"As for your thoughts of Jessica, I want you to know that even though you left her a fortnight ago, you will see her much sooner than you think. I will not tell you the details now," he said, noticing the human's surprise, "for this involves all of you. Knowing too much of your own futures could, for some reason, destroy you prematurely.

"Now, if you will please rouse the company Aidan, I wish to go inside. The sun is doing murder to my skin. However, I do like to look bronze in the winter months. Makes me look slimmer and much younger," the wizard said with a wink to the dwarf.

Aidan sent Yanos to rouse the dwarf army, and minutes later, the company entered the home of Kirkrik Dannell for the second time.

The interior of the wizard's chateau had not changed much since the company's last visit several months ago. He had obtained new toys and gadgets, all with some special magical power. Radamuck looked around and saw swords, axes, and, to his surprise, red-hot chili powder, laying around the sitting room.

"Makes instant dragon breath!" Kirkrik said when he saw Grumpet's quizzical look at the chili powder. "Just three drops into the mouth and any enemies closest to you will run for cover—or get burned in the process of fleeing! Haven't found anyone brave enough to become an instant dragon for only a few seconds. They seem to think they have to guard jewels for the rest of their lives; it's not like they grow scales or anything."

Radamuck laughed, and if he had the ability to pull Grumpet's skin and bone away, he would see his friend now knew why he called Kirkrik Dannell a "silly old mage," for the eccentric wizard took the chili powder and put it in the corner by a stool. There on the stool slept an aged bullfrog, snoring so peacefully and contentedly—Kirkrik was careful not to wake his friend Edison. The dwarf looked intently at the bullfrog and hoped its slumber would continue long until after they left, for he didn't want to hear any more of Edison's legendary wise-cracks. He felt sure the frog would come up with something uncouth to say about Grumpet's manner of dress, as he wore a shirt of chain mail on his torso along with a leather jerkin. He had a leathery skirt around his waist, which was for travel.

Grumpet explored the house—the dwarf company, along with Yanos Kingsfoil and Arrol Goldleaf, their elven general, had already gone upstairs to rest for a long time in comfort—while Radamuck and Kirkrik stayed downstairs.

"So show me your new prize, Radamuck," said Kirkrik, anxious to see the chalice the dwarf had recovered a month ago.

Radamuck grabbed his sack by the door and sat it on the back of the sofa, opening the burlap covering. He revealed the solid gold chalice for the first time in days, and the magical object filled the entire room with light: it was so bright that it jarred Edison awake.

"Turn out that light!" the bullfrog screamed.

The wizard looked at the bright light emanating from the bag and uttered a soft spell, cancelling the light long enough to put his eyes on the chalice. When the light dissipated, Kirkrik sighed heavily.

Radamuck removed the cup from his satchel and offered the wizard an opportunity to hold it.

But Kirkrik Dannell's hands never inched toward it.

"I dare not touch it, my friend," he said softly, "for I do not want my abilities diminished by its powers. Do not worry about yourself touching it; you will not be affected. However, I must not touch it, for my powers would wane, and you will need me at full strength for what approaches."

Radamuck swallowed hard before he put the chalice back into his sack. He then removed another recent acquisition: the orb Grumpet had recovered following the battle with Victor Dramin. He showed the wizard this, carefully removing the cloth from it. It also shone brightly, causing the wizard to take in breath that he nearly forgot to let out.

Kirkrik took the crystal ball from Radamuck and gazed softly into it. Mists swirled inside it, yet Kirkrik didn't say anything. He looked entranced by the new discovery, and his eyes had slightly glazed over as he looked into the depths the orb held. It wasn't until Radamuck had tapped the wizard's chest that Kirkrik awoke, stunned, before he looked back down at the orb with new eyes.

"This is amazing! The orb used by the wizard of the northlands! I will have to study this further, to see what ends we can make of it. With my goodly power, I cannot see how I could not bend it to my will! Thank you for bringing this to me, Radamuck. This could be the key we need to end evil forever!" Kirkrik said gleefully.

Radamuck bowed to the wizard.

"I knew it was somethin' yeh should see, Kirkrik. Yeh'd be the only one I knew that could use it," he said.

Kirkrik Dannell gave a smile to the dwarf.

"Hopefully when I peer into the orb at a later date, I'll see what the enemy saw. And then, if I can see what he saw, that means we can then see what he saw as his truths. And when we see his truths, we can ultimately find out what the consequences were for seeing what he saw as his truths," he said, and as he turned to secure the company's new find, Radamuck looked perplexed, trying to make out what Kirkrik's see-saw battle with words was about. When the wizard returned, Radamuck's face resumed its normal state and felt a hand on his shoulder.

"Let's go outside and talk quietly," the wizard suggested. Radamuck allowed Kirkrik to lead him back outside. There, he found growing plants of various sizes in various types of holders.

"Look at how my garden grows!" Kirkrik gushed in his high-pitched, squeaky voice, leading Radamuck toward the plants and forgetting about the orb for a minute. The dwarf king knew he should keep his distance from them, fearing he may have his feet tangled by vines and hung upside down. But the soft smile of the wizard told the dwarf that nothing would happen to him.

"They all look very interestin'," Radamuck said, and noticed the wizard cried from the dwarf's praise for his plants. Radamuck saw plants with eyes on individual leaves, as well as plants breathing underwater—he saw one shrub in a glass pot that had gills and took in water while expelling it through a hole at the top of the plant. Radamuck offered a slight chuckle, knowing that Kirkrik Dannell watched him for his reaction.

As they walked through the garden, Kirkrik spoke to the dwarf king.

"Let's walk and speak of the battle in the north," Kirkrik said. "I must say that if Arrol Goldleaf did not return with the Bastine elves at that exact moment, then the battle would have been lost, you would have been dead, and Victor Dramin's reign of terror over the northlands would have continued until he ruled all the realms. I could not have foreseen an ending to his rule if you failed."

"If the Snowy Mountains dwarves didn't arrive at that moment to take out the elementals—" Radamuck began to say, but Kirkrik interrupted him with a wave of his hand.

"The dwarves of your friend Kaidenn did exactly as you wanted them to, which proves your presence is commanding and you can bend those weaker than you to your will. I know you do that unintentionally. But had the elves not arrived to help you beat back the trolls, Dramin wouldn't have needed to conjure the elementals.

"It was the elves' presence that forced Dramin to go against his plan; he needed something to combat their swift steeds," Kirkrik continued. "He felt that the earth elementals would do it. But, as you say, it was your dwarf friends from the north who took them out, so I suppose we are both correct in our presumptions."

"Grumpet also fought bravely," Radamuck said. "Dramin had frozen me dwarves; that Caz Axewielder is a fine warmonger!"

"Yes he did, and young Caz will go to the wall for his king. However, you and I did not expect any differently from either of them. As I told Grumpet, he showed that he is the true heir to Krampel Paddymeyer's power in that battle; both of them have taken out two individuals who were destined for domination of the realms, and the entire world shall sing their praises through songs," Kirkrik said, which made Radamuck reminisce.

It had been fifty years ago that the Great Imperial Wars had taken place, and Radamuck remembered the young warrior named Krampel, *Flad-rul* in his right hand, a golden shield in his left. How he wielded both with such power, *Flad-rul* flaming as he cut down enemies, his shield stopping his foes' attacks. It was at that instant he realized he never saw that shield in Grumpet's possession. He wondered what had happened to that beautiful shield, engraved with a flaming dragon on the front and raised fire dancing along the rim. The dwarf king made a note to ask him about it, for he felt that the great sword *Flad-rul* should be paired again with its shield.

And then, his brain became emblazoned with a stunning vision. His eyes focused toward the south. With the gift of foresight that he as king of the Lowbridge dwarves possessed, he saw in his head an image of Grumpet, standing on a mountaintop, victorious after a long battle, surrounded by fallen enemies, shield and sword gleaming in the sun.

***

Radamuck and Kirkrik re-entered the latter's palatial home, only to find the surly bullfrog awake and yapping at Grumpet. Edison must have said something rude to the human, because Radamuck heard Kirkrik telling off his friend as they walked into the sitting room.

"Edison! How dare you use that language against our guest? His clothes are none of your concern! Now apologize to Grumpet, right now," admonished the wizard.

Edison croaked before he spoke.

"I'm sorry for offending you, princess," he said, before he saw Kirkrik's hand swing toward him. But before it made contact, Edison leaped off the stool and out of the way. He got to the stairs before he turned his froggy face toward the trio and roared. "Good to see you again, beard boy! I like your new choice of travelling companions!" He then bounded up the spiral staircase. A slamming door made the chateau shudder for the briefest of moments.

"Rude, I tell you!" Kirkrik roared up the stairs. "I'm sorry, Grumpet. He's usually not like this."

Radamuck turned his head in shock toward the wizard. He remembered his own indoctrination at the hands of Kirkrik Dannell's bloated talking bullfrog and knew that this must be the type of reception the wizard's guests received from it.

"It's okay, Kirkrik. If I can handle Victor Dramin's taunts, I can handle a talking bullfrog," Grumpet said, "however I knew he would say something about my attire. It's all I had that wasn't bloodied from battle."

"Worry not, my new friend. Time for you to sleep in comfort, for you have walked far and now you can rest without fear of blinding snow and mind-numbing cold," Kirkrik said.

Both Grumpet and Radamuck grew sleepy, and before they toddled up the spiral staircase to his stateroom, the wizard turned to the dwarf.

“The usual for breakfast, Radamuck?” Kirkrik said.

Radamuck nodded and the wizard left for his own first floor bedroom, but then Grumpet tugged on the dwarf’s leather jerkin.

“What’s your usual breakfast here?” Grumpet asked.

Radamuck said flatly, “Two eggs, side o’ wisecrackin’ bullfrog.”

Chapter 2

The next morning, after the entire army had eaten, Radamuck wanted to tackle the final leg of his journey back to Lowbridge.

But before he left, the wizard pulled him aside, anxious to speak with him.

"By going the way of the Forest of Purge, you draw less attention to yourself than by going through Briskey Bucktooth. You may or may not run into trouble in the forest; I cannot be totally certain, but less danger should be there than in the city," Kirkrik said, looking into Radamuck's dark eyes with extended purpose.

"Yeh need not worry 'bout us, me friend. The dwarves o' Lowbridge can stand up to anyone or anythin' that wants to get their hands on me treasure, and we'll leave them with a splittin' headache, too," Radamuck said with a grin. "I expect to be back in me realm in five days. I'll contact yeh with yer amulet when I get there."

Kirkrik allowed himself a chuckle. "I was just about to tell you to contact me if you needed me. Are you learning to read minds, too?"

Again, the dwarf king laughed heartily at the wizard's comment.

"No, I just know yeh by now, yeh and yer amulet. I know yeh were tryin' to get a hold of me durin' the trip here. And don't think I never felt it burnin' while me and me kin were at war," Radamuck said gruffly, shaking his fist up into the face of the unflustered Kirkrik Dannell.

"Well, that's good to know you still have it. But that wasn't me who was trying to contact you. That was Edison trying to roast marshmallows while sunbathing. Thought it would be cute to use it to reflect the suns' rays off the amulet and onto the marshmallow. It almost worked, too. I had to stop him; he dripped goo all over it and I had to pry it away from him. I thought you'd never get in touch with me if he dripped any more on it," Kirkrik said.

"And my plan almost worked, too," shouted the bullfrog, this time from the second-floor landing. "But he came back to you, Kirkrik, just like you said he would. Maybe I should try melting chocolate on it next time."

The wizard waved an admonitory finger at the bullfrog, which croaked and then leapt away. Radamuck only chuckled at Edison's antics.

The pair looked at each other, knowing it was time to say good-bye, even though it was, by Kirkrik's own estimation, only for a short while.

"Well, I think I will be seeing you soon, Radamuck. I foresee events that will re-shape your kingdom as well as all the realms. When you see me, or feel the amulet's touch go hot, prepare for the worst. Until then, keep your treasure safe, and keep your friends close to you," the wizard said.

Radamuck felt each hair standing on end as he clamped his hand in Kirkrik's, said his thanks, and made for the door, with the rest of the company behind him. Grumpet, with his beautiful sword next to his hip, followed the king on his heels, while Aidan, Arrol, and Yanos took up the rear guard.

As Radamuck opened the door, he stepped out onto the steps leading to the chateau and looked across the land, fully expecting to see more snow. But for the first time in months, Radamuck's eyes fell on green: not a flake of snow anywhere. Plants grew and flowers were in bloom. The temperature was warmer, the air dryer. He didn't know exactly where he was, that is until Kirkrik pushed himself through the crowd of dwarves to stand again at the king's side.

"Well, you will see, Radamuck, that I have helped you on your way slightly. I knew you all did not wish to feel snow under your feet again," Kirkrik said, "so I pushed the house several hundred miles closer to your goal last night. Lowbridge is now less than a day's march from here."

The dwarves shouted their hearty thanks to the wizard and, as the warm air made them perspire slightly, the company took off their protective wintry skins. They had worn the skins for so long, ever since Lord Baeron gave them to the dwarves following their battle with orcs in the elven realm, that they felt the weight of dirt, grime and sweat lift immediately once they removed them.

***

Grumpet, who had never stepped out of the northlands, immediately felt warmer than he ever did in his life. He quickly took off the leather jerkin, one insulted with wool to keep him warm against the northlands' constantly changing weather. He was now bare from the waist up, and as the sun beat down on his arms, chest and broad back, his pectoral muscles corded and flexed as he removed the garment. He felt lighter without the jerkin and thought he would be able to fight slightly faster without the hindrance of upper clothing.

Radamuck came up to him. He laid his hand upon Grumpet's back and said, "Are yeh ready, me friend? Yeh're already a long way from home. Only a few more days more, and then you'll see the country of the gods."

Grumpet saw a glitter of anticipation in the eyes of the dwarf king, and knew it was an anticipation he had never seen there before. He knew Radamuck longed to see his kingdom, not to mention his wife and his newborn son, and knew exactly how the king felt, for he wished that Jessica were here with him now, instead of waiting for him back in Kayiko.

"Yes, Your Highness. I am ready to go. I made a promise to protect you, and I shall hold myself to that promise, regardless of my own desires. No man or beast will come between you as long as *Flad-rul* has a cut left in it, or as long as the strength of Grumpet T. Paddymeyer remains mighty," the captain said, bowing his head to the dwarven leader in front of him.

Radamuck smiled through his black beard and clapped the man on his extremely thick upper arm. He then turned to his dwarves, his arms raised in a victory stance.

"Aye, me friends! A small march remains, and then we shall see the mountain tops of our land! Fear not, the ale will taste even better when we arrive back in Lowbridge!" Radamuck exclaimed, and again, hearty cheers erupted from the mouths of the dwarf army. He looked back to wave his thanks to Kirkrik Dannell, but in the excitement of feeling warm again and coming closer to home, the dwarves did not notice that the large chateau had vanished from sight.

***

At the peak of the northlands, a heavy gray mist hung near the base of what had been Statuary Tower. Snow had covered the rubble, mainly huge blocks of stone and floorboards. The elements had relentlessly pounded the final resting place of Victor Dramin.

There were orc blades sticking out of the snow, and not far from the blades were mounds of white covering the fallen warriors, the minions who dared to do Dramin's dastardly deeds before the warriors from the south soundly defeated them.

A tree trunk, what had once been a weapon of mass destruction by Dramin's earth elementals and subsequently used as a battering ram, lay among the debris. Pieces of its bark and insides had broken off as the dwarves had used it repeatedly against a wooden door in order to enter the wizard's inner sanctum. What had been the upper most levels of the tower buried it, after it had been blasted off by the elves when they had ruthlessly attacked the tower's master.

But the downed trunk and shattered stone didn't matter to the mist...

Despite the lack of wind, the mist swirled over the grave, never breaking apart and moving across the battlefield. It continued swirling, horizontally and then vertically, until it was the width and height of a human. It was slender in spots and curvy in others. Its head formed slowly, a long nose sprouted from the center of the mist, and the figure's hair shot out in many directions. The two-dimensional figure then shuddered as the mists congealed and solidified, taking on the features of the wizard who had died in that spot.

The wizard, Victor Dramin, had come together in spirit form.

Looking down at his "body," the wizard's moves were exaggerated. He nearly doubled over as he looked toward his feet. Dramin moved clumsily, but as soon as he closed his eyes and concentrated, creating a spell to cause the mists to solidify even further. He swept his hand through thin air, and, thanks to the spell he had conjured, no longer moved like he had drank all of the late Danolf Jenson's prized birch mead.

Dramin looked out over the snowy plains, looking at the mounds of snow that covered his dead army. He looked back at what used to be his home, and saw the rubble that lay there. Just by looking at the stones strewn all over the place, he knew what caused the tower to collapse—the dwarves had removed the Chalice of Obloeron from its base.

Prior to the dwarf attack, he had created a spell that would have destroyed the tower and left none inside alive had the enemy removed the chalice from the dwarven-like idol that guarded it. He had found the irony amusing, so he used it to his advantage. He wanted to taunt the dwarf king who had—in Dramin's opinion—so foolishly waged war with the new overlord of the northlands. With old magic, he left an imprint of himself on the stone dwarf; he wanted to appear returned to life, if only to torment the dwarf king and his followers.

With a wave of his milky-white hand, the wizard removed one stone, then another. Impatiently he flung stone and wood from the ground, anxious to see the frozen corpses of his enemies laying on the circular stair leading to the sublevels of Statuary Tower.

What he found—the lack of bodies—disappointed him. Not one bearded body lay dead along the darkened staircase, however desperately he tried to find one. He had hoped to at least find the remains of the swordsman who had unceremoniously cleaved his head clean off, but again, his hopes were dashed. He waved his hand again, more furiously this time, sending fragments of stone flying into the air, landing in a heap in the snow. Dramin's eyes narrowed, peering into the cavernous passageways that led deeper and deeper into his former stronghold.

Still no bodies were found, and Dramin grew increasingly agitated.

With a grunt, he flung his corporeal form forward as he reached the location of the chalice. He spotted the dwarven deity, toppled over to its side, its head cracked and severed from the stone. The walls bulged inward, as if the force of the tower collapsing had buckled the sublevels to near bursting.

But what he saw at the foot of the dwarven god had been the breaking point. He wanted to wipe his misty eyes clear, so that what he saw was unmistakable.

He saw nothing there.

Despite knowing the result, his anger boiled deep in the pit of what would be his stomach. The wizard flung his head back in rage, bellowing a hoarse growl that echoed throughout the chamber. But then, he tossed his hands toward the sky and uttered an ancient incantation.

The rubble that lay in the snow above exploded and flew into the air, breaking into pebbles as it crashed back to earth. Flames tore through the air, emanating from deep within the hole, melting the snow and creating a soggy circle around the base of the tower.

Victor Dramin stalked up the stairs from the lower levels, the flames tickling what would be his legs and cloak. He paid them no mind; they had no effect on the ghostly sorcerer.

He exited and paced near the base of the tower, his footprints not making a mark on the wet, snow-cleared ground. He wanted to kick something but thought against it, as his misty self wouldn't let him make contact with anything. Dramin had walked several feet and back when he looked toward the far side of the hole.

He spotted an orb laying amongst the scattered pieces of stone, wood and books and knew immediately that this wasn't his usual orb: he knew that if the dwarves had found the one in the ninth level, they would have captured it and taken it for their own.

However, he had locked this orb away on the third level, in the library. He—and Danolf Jenson before him—had used this orb when he wanted to survey his lands while he read the ancient texts. The other orb did the same, yet it also gave counsel to the elder wizard that led to many of Jenson's atrocities.

He, Dramin, had used it, as well, just prior to the attack on Kayiko, an attack which, at the time, had seemed prosperous. However, it urged the young mage to attack again.

Dramin lost that battle.

Despite his anger, he continued using that orb, thinking it could give him enough clairvoyance to defeat the oncoming dwarves. Through it he saw the mountain dwarves give them aid, and while he had decided long ago that his destruction of that mountain would occur, he also saw through it the way to beat the defenders of the south.

Again, he had failed. Those same mountain dwarves and their war engines destroyed his elementals.

For a split second, he felt grateful for the dwarves taking that blasted orb, for it had brought him nothing but grief. With this orb, he knew he could plan against his enemies.

With a wave of his hand, the orb dislodged from the waxy crevice it had become nestled in—Dramin's fire spell, conjured from his ire, had melted several candles and caused the orb to become caught between the melted wax and several large tomes—and brought it toward him. It hovered in front of Dramin, and as he closed his eyes, he saw visions in his head that came from the orb.

The first vision was the Snowy Mountains. He knew he would have to take those mountain dwarves out, especially since they had interfered with his affairs one too many times.

But that would have to wait, for the time being.

As he continued his meditation, Dramin realized he no longer had an army at his disposal. Any chance of recovering warriors in this last war were slim to none—the corpses of the dead had been frozen far too long.

He would need to find an army to flatten the mountain, the orb told him. He saw through the mists the orb showed that the human who wields the Sword of the South would die when he got his army. His army would also stomp all over the dwarf king and his followers.

Dramin sneered at the thought; which seemed, to him, a better thought than going after the mountain dwarves. He had tried to crush the dwarf king under his boot, and he had proved to be an opponent to fear.

But this new version, this dead version, of Victor Dramin did not know what fear was.

The orb showed that he needed a body to inhabit, for the corporeal form would not strike fear into his enemies' hearts.

For that, the orb spoke to him in a language all its own, that he would need to trick someone strong into allowing him to take over their body. An ancient spell would take care of that, Dramin thought simply, and he had one memorized from his earlier teachings.

In addition, despite having his magical powers intact, he was far too weak to fly all the way south, knowing that was where the dwarf king now marched. He could walk like a mortal man, however, he knew he would walk slower than the winds could carry him.

That didn't faze the young, evil wizard, though.

He had all the time in the world; after all, he was already dead.

He had eternity.

***

The company had already marched a quarter of a day and their feet had grown tired from the already long march—some needed to take a pain-relieving potion while at the wizard's residence, and even that didn't help—before Radamuck called for a halt. Some dwarves fell face first into the dwarf in front, causing a domino effect. It only stopped when Caz Axewielder fell sideways just as the forward-falling dwarves reached him.

With the ground littered with anxious and tired dwarves, Grumpet came forward to speak with Radamuck. Stepping over the idle form of Aidan Rosar, who snored, the human warrior found the king sitting on a rock, with his sandals off. He massaged his worn feet.

Taking a seat next to the dwarf, Grumpet took his water bottle out and took a long sip from it. Offering the last few sips to Radamuck, he passed it to the king.

They were in a glade full of pine needles which, for now, served as the bedding for the sleeping dwarves. Pine trees reached for the heavens, dotting the landscape about 20-25 feet apart. The clearing they sat—or lay—in opened to the sky, and the sun beat down. It was nearly midday.

"There's a brook up ahead," Radamuck said, "we can fill our bottles there. There won't be another water source until after we leave the Forest of Purge, and that will take us most o' the rest o' the day to march through."

And, to himself, the dwarf added, *if something doesn't waylay us in there, intending to steal the chalice.*

"Yeh would be best to have yer sword out when we enter the forest, Grumpet, and that reminds me—whatever happened to that shield yer grandfather carried with him?" Radamuck asked.

"I don't know. He never had it in his possession when he died. Only *Flad-rul*," he said, patting the hilt of the famous blade.

Radamuck's brow curled, the lines of his years showing on his face. He did not know for the life of him why the shield would have been separated from the elder Paddymeyer's side. The shield and *Flad-rul* practically went together. He shook the thought from his mind, until Grumpet grabbed his shoulder.

"Is there something I should know, Your Highness?" he asked.

Radamuck looked into Grumpet's eyes and said, "Nay, me friend. Just curious, that's all. I knew yer grandfather had a shield during the Wars and I never saw yeh with it. I wanted to know if yeh had any idea what might have happened to it," the king replied.

They ended up marching through the night, as they came upon the wooden glen known as the Forest of Purge. With trees of all types encased within its limits, the forest loomed ahead like a shadow. Darkness crept toward them, the shadow of the trees cascading eastward as the sun sank behind the trees.

Showing little trepidation, Radamuck urged his dwarves forward. Grumpet, Aidan, Caz, Yanos and Arrol all took flanking positions around the king. All had weapons drawn per the king's request.

As they entered the glade, whatever traces of light that hit the trees ended there. The night enveloped them all, the company unable to see the member in front of them. Radamuck ordered a halt again and asked Arrol Goldleaf, their elf general, to light a brand with a small piece of timber which had fallen from a nearby sycamore tree.

With the kindling lit, its meager light shone around the company. Arrol passed the branch around to the other members, who had picked up smaller branches and proceeded to light them, making torches. When all were lit and able to see, they continued marching, stubbing their toes occasionally on roots and unseen rocks.

They walked through the heavily wooden land for miles and miles, until they came across a small clearing. They had seen the clearing from afar, as a pale light lingered in the trees. On seeing the light ahead, the company's mood brightened slightly, as they were pleased to find more travelers in this part of the realms.

But they weren't with Radamuck when he had spoken with Kirkrik Dannell back at his chateau. He immediately grew wary of the travelers ahead, hoping they were stranded and not pillagers or highwaymen. If they were the latter, they would not have known about their capture of the chalice—unless they had an orb like the one they recovered from Statuary Tower. Radamuck decided on using extreme caution when dealing with this group.

Eventually they arrived in the clearing, only to find a group of eleven humans, all in various states of dress. They stood with their swords drawn, all but expecting the dwarves to attack.

However, one of the men appeared perfectly calm and relaxed in the presence of the dwarves, and it appeared to both Radamuck and Grumpet that he was their leader. Dressed in fine cloth, the man stood approximately one and a half axe lengths tall, the top of his head level with Grumpet's chin. His hair, which lay underneath a plumed hat, was black and neatly trimmed. His face was slightly pale, his nose perfectly straight, the teeth whiter than quartz. He had a distinguished look upon him, accentuated by the short mustache he wore on his upper lip and the goatee along his chin. He also had a cloak upon his shoulders, which went below the knee, a few inches above the ankles. It was cast behind his right shoulder and draped over his left. They noticed that the cloak would have hid any weapon.

The man stepped forward and doffed his plumed hat, before bowing low in greeting.

"Welcome, dear travelers, to the camp of Frampton! I see you have come a great deal and your road lies through us. Perhaps you'd like to stay and enjoy our company and tell stories of your adventures, or perhaps you'd like to continue on your way. If you choose the latter, I would be happy to let you pass. For a tithe, that is," the man said, smirking as he spoke his last phrase.

Radamuck stepped forward, his warriors slightly behind him.

"I am Radamuck Rosar, the Twenty-fourth King of Lowbridge. None may request a tithe from me or me men, so step aside and let us pass or feel our blades in yer heads!" Radamuck said.

The man with the plumed hat bowed to the king mannerly, before he spoke again.

"And I am Frampton, he who leads this group, and yes, Your Highness, I have heard of your recent exploits far to the north. We know what you carry. Would you like to see your homeland again," Frampton said threateningly, "or would you rather escape with your lives minus the Chalice of Obloeron? It is your choice, my friend."

Frampton must be mad, thought Radamuck. *Did he not see the 150 other dwarves followin' me into the clearing, not to mention Yanos, Grumpet and Arrol?*

But then, the human spoke, distracting the king from his thoughts.

"Shall you escape my clutches now, Radamuck Rosar, I will still find a way to capture the chalice. Mark my words, dwarf: I will have it by hook or by crook, and if that means a war on the plains of Lowbridge to end your civilization, then so be it," Frampton spat.

Radamuck grew enraged at the man's pronouncement. None had brought war to Lowbridge—especially if they knew what was best for them! Apparently, this human needed a lesson in couth speech.

Noticing Radamuck's posture, Grumpet lifted *Flad-rul* and shot it back toward his right shoulder, two hands firmly grasping the handle of the Flame Thrower as it came alive, fire springing from the steel. Aidan had his sword-axe out, while Yanos and Arrol had their weapons drawn and ready to use. The other dwarves also had their axes drawn and ready. Caz Axewielder looked like he simply wanted to gore someone.

It had been too long since they had fought the wizard, and Radamuck had hoped they would not deal with enemies for quite some time.

Radamuck hurried forward, his axe held one-handed above his right shoulder. He hurtled after Frampton, but did not dig his blades deep into his skull: the human had disappeared with a swish of his cloak. All that remained was a great puff of smoke—and the ten ape-like humans who stood guard.

They charged at the dwarves, and Grumpet met the first with a parry to the left. Reversing the oncoming man's sword to the right, Grumpet lunged forward and stabbed the human through the gut. A great moan of excruciating pain blasted out of his mouth, but Grumpet slid the sword back out, wound up, and severed the man's head, slicing from right to left through the throat, ending the man's pain and his misery.

Caz Axewielder joined in, rushing with his head down into an unsuspecting human's side as he did battle with Radamuck. The twin horns on the helm of the young dwarf punctured his lung, and Radamuck brought his axe down into the chest cavity of the man as Caz rolled off him with a somersault.

"We can share that kill, me boy," Radamuck praised the young dwarf, who then gave a primal scream and charged after another human.

Aidan's whirling blades had a human confused, the axe chopping from the left, the sword slicing from the right. It was all the human could do to save himself, as he attempted to parry each and every thrust that Aidan Rosar could dish out. One false slip and the life of the human was over.

It did end, soon after he dropped his sword as Aidan's sword side sliced through his wrist. He screamed and rushed away from the battle, only to find Arrol Goldleaf standing before him, his bow drawn with an arrow tucked neatly in the string.

He fired the bolt from close range, hitting the man full in the face. He staggered backward and fell dead into a heap.

The battle finished quickly, ten dead humans to no losses for the company, and none of the dwarves, Arrol or Grumpet broke a sweat while fighting. Grumpet, who had fought from one human to the other, had four kills while Caz Axewielder, who had made a name for himself as the Lowbridge dwarves' new warmonger, notched three gores on his twin-horned helm.

After they collected their fallen enemies' weapons, they supped on salted pork and drank water to sate their parched mouths. Then, Grumpet took another branch, lit it in the flames of the campfire, and, with Radamuck's permission, led the company through the woods with twenty miles to go to reach Lowbridge—and possibly a war, if Frampton's dramatic pronouncement was believable.

Chapter 3

If having survived the battle at Statuary Tower meant having to then camp out in the wild snows of the northlands, then a small group of trolls and orcs wished they had died under their master's watchful gaze.

The survivors huddled together next to a small campfire, with the the vast bulk of trolls taking up most of the space around the tiny conflagration. Finding kindling for a fire had turned out difficult; the orcs—at the orders of the trolls, and from fear of having their limbs torn clean off—had scurried back to the battlefield and had secured enough wood from the floorboards of Statuary Tower to build several fires.

However, they had rationed the wood so it would last for several days. And as the sun had already drifted to the horizon and its light extinguished, the small fire was meant to keep them all warm.

So far, it wasn't working.

And while the embers slowly burned and faded out as the winds howled around them, yet another argument broke out between the two factions of the camp.

"Da war woodah been won if da weezard had leesahned to da trolls," said the troll leader, Grizelda McFrump. "We shoodah attaahked da enahmee along wid da orrks. Tha' way, da enahmee woodah been ovahwhelmt by owah numbahs. Dey woodn't hahve 'ad time to orrgahnize dere reinforrcemahnts.

"Da weezard woodn't leesahn to Grizelda. Da weezard lose battle, da weezard die 'cause he no leesahn to Grizelda," she continued.

The orcs chittered away in their own language, obviously showing their own side of the wars' misgivings.

"We couldn't have won that war, ya ugly frunk," said the orc leader, Pudgy DeSchnair, causing Grizelda McFrump to stand. "If the enemy had all its members fighting in one wave, they still would have slaughtered yer trolls and me orcs."

Pudgy stood after he said that, as Grizelda came toward him. Pudgy quickly slipped his hand down into the snow, and as the troll got closer, the orc flung a handful of powder into the troll's face, confusing it. Wiping the snow out of her eyes, flinging the excess toward the fire—and ceremoniously dousing what remained of the meager flames—the troll bared her teeth and growled deeply at the orc. By then, Pudgy had his long knife out and looked ready to stick it in her if she drew close enough.

The other trolls and orcs all stood, weapons out, standing behind their respective leaders. The growling intensified and each group had tossed threats back and forth, when the fire, which had already been extinguished by the troll, re-ignited and jumped ten feet into the air. The flames curled around and caught the flesh of one of the orcs, who started rushing around, screaming at the top of its lungs.

The flames danced on the panicky orc, until Grizelda McFrump leveled the orc to the snowy ground with a wicked stiff-armed lariat, dousing the flames from the orc's body.

Those standing huddled together on one side of the now huge campfire, the battle lines erased. They looked at one another, not knowing what to do. Their weapons stayed in their hands.

After a minute, the flames had lowered, and out of the fire walked what looked like a man. The flames licked and tucked at the man's flesh, but as they saw, the man didn't have any flesh. His skin looked transparent and they saw the flames behind him as he stepped out of the fire.

"Who ahh you?" Grizelda McFrump demanded, her club firmly in her huge hand.

The misty-bodied human gave what looked to the troll as a sneer, his lip curling on the left side of his face. He eyed the motley assemblage viciously, scanning them for signs of fear.

Seeing none, the ghost decided to put fear into them.

"You ask a question that needs an answer, Grizelda McFrump, and I shall answer you. You are looking at the man you will give your loyalty to, or you shall meet your death!" the man said.

Troll and orc alike laughed at the man's words; Pudgy DeSchnair nearly doubled over with laughter.

But the laughter stopped, as the man thrust his arms forward with his palms up, as blue light streamed from his ghostly hands, colliding with the chest of the troll priestess.

Grizelda McFrump found herself taken off her feet with the force of the blast, flying backward and landing some twenty feet away, her bones cracking and splintering as she hit the earth.

As the remaining trolls rushed to see if Grizelda was dead, the orcs turned to face the intruder, weapons drawn. Pudgy DeSchnair, fully composed, rushed the corporeal form with his knife held above his head. But he got no closer than five feet from the man, as he immediately felt an invisible hand clench around his neck. Pudgy felt the air passages constrict against his will, and he tried to free himself, clawing and pounding at the invisible grip.

Pudgy stopped fighting and soon succumbed to the talons that squeezed his throat. The ghost unceremoniously flung Pudgy into the fire with a wave of his hand, where the flames consumed his asphyxiated corpse.

The ghost man looked at the remaining warriors with hate in his eyes. Then he walked forward, moving slowly, so that all saw him. The corporeal form made no footprints in the snow as it walked, not stopping until it came to where Grizelda McFrump landed.

Looking down at the troll's dead body, the man fell forward, merging its misty shape with the solid flesh. The trolls wondered what had happened, but then they saw Grizelda flutter her eyes.

Her eyes then flew open, the eyeballs misty white and unfocused. Pushing herself up, broken bones and all, the troll priestess got to her feet and looked at both her own warriors and the orcs.

She then opened her mouth, but the voice that spoke was not the troll's voice; it was a deeper voice, seeming to come from the boundless echoes of another plane of existence.

"I am the spirit of Dramin. Swear fealty to me now, and I'll let you keep your miserable lives. Choosing to cross Dramin is folly," it said.

The orcs and trolls looked upon each other in fright, coming face to face with their once-dead master. Each went to their knees, murmuring to the being next to them.

"Quiet!" Dramin's spirit said in a little more than a whisper; the evil warriors complied out of more than just fear. "As you know by now, the dwarf army thinks I am dead, cut down by the mercenary. But they will soon learn Victor Dramin is more powerful than they originally thought, when I come back and destroy their lands! And you, my loyal and noble warriors, will help me in doing so.

"After we leave the northlands, each of you will go far and wide, finding the beings that answer to the call of evil. Gnomes, trolls, orcs, dark elves. Call them all to Dramin, for they will be involved in the greatest siege known to the realms. For I possess the orb," he waved his hand, producing the orb from the flames that he had entered their camp by, "and have foreseen our victory; yes, I say our victory, for you will be my lieutenants in the grand army. You shall go forth and tell them my message. Those that want power, let them seek me. Those that want to destroy, let them swear fealty. Those who want to give their body so that I may walk freely again, let them be one who wants power and the ability to destroy. Those that fail to heed your call, let them be the ones who die!" With another surge of power, the flames of the campfire flew higher and higher, reaching for the heavens.

The orcs and trolls again cowered from the sight of the rising fire, but the reassuring voice of Dramin calmed them.

"I have foreseen an individual who has the ability to provide a surrogate body for me. He is far from here, and he has great skill. He also knows of power and domination, and should suit my needs well. But for now," the wizard said, leaving the body of the troll, letting it fall back to the snow with a thump, "you will take the body of Grizelda McFrump with us; she will be of use. Her body is adequate to possess, but not to do magic. Leave the orc in the flames. It is worthless. Orcs will carry the wood for fires, for we shall have many nights here in the northlands. We walk far to the south, for the dwarven homeland is there. Our war will start when we have all the necessary people, and we cannot start it until we are there. Any additional orcs and trolls in our path, we will collect and bring them with us. But now, we march."

Out of fear for losing their lives, the trolls picked up the deadweight of the priestess and heaved her onto their shoulders. The orcs, scrambling to and fro after Dramin's voice suddenly stopped, prepared the wood for travel.

And, after a long last look into the flames, peering ahead to what he believed what the dwarven kingdom would look like after he was through with it, Victor Dramin set for the south to begin his war—and to look for a body to inhabit.

***

Frampton returned to the clearing where he had left his human servants. The scene wasn't what he expected.

But what he saw didn't exactly dismay him, either.

Dead bodies, with severed limbs and heads, bodies gored and slashed, lay across the ground or leaning against the trees. As he walked through the clearing, he looked at their faces, all of which had contorted forever in pain. He had recognized all of them as being those who had stood with him when the dwarves entered the clearing.

He dismissed the scene with a shrug. It was irrelevant. The dwarves would meet their gods in time—especially the king, Radamuck Rosar, and his human swordsman. He thought he had seen that sword before, cocked back at the shoulder; it was a long time ago, of course.

Frampton quickly stalked off through the trees, dipping into the spy nature which had kept him alive for so long. Looking at the ground, he decided he would follow the many footprints filing toward the south.

It was time to make good on his threats.

***

The trees had thinned and the sun's morning rays had streamed softly into the outer reaches of the Forest of Purge. With the elf general Arrol Goldleaf leading the company through the maze of trees, the Lowbridge dwarves, Grumpet T. Paddymeyer and Yanos Kingsfoil soon looked upon a plateau of grass.

Not needing to adjust his eyes to the sun, Arrol scanned the southern horizon, looking for signs of aggressors that might impede their progress back to the grassy vales of the dwarven kingdom.

Seeing none, the elf turned back to the company.

"My lord Radamuck, there are no enemies to the south, southeast or southwest in your immediate path. The road to Lowbridge is clear, and your path is set before you all," the elf declared, which earned a dwarven cheer. "And as your path is clear and free of enemies, I must depart from your company," Arrol said, and several dwarves murmured. They weren't expecting this, most of all Radamuck. Yanos, standing near the king, looked close to tears within seconds of that announcement. "I regret leaving you as you are so close to returning home, but I am needed back in my realm. I promised Lord Baeron that I would escort you until you were safe, and, as I have seen with my elf eyes, your road is clear, and you are all safe."

Radamuck stepped forward and clasped his elf friend on his strong forearms. Arrol also grasped the dwarf's forearm, a gesture of friendship between elves.

"Me friend, I thank yeh for what yeh've done these long, cold months. Yeh deserve all me thanks and more. Yeh've provided us with protection and friendship, and yeh've taught us to see past the barriers of race. Me dwarves will never forget yeh for that, and yeh're welcome in the caverns of Lowbridge any time," Radamuck said, bowing to Arrol, who returned the bow. "I, the Twenty-fourth King of Lowbridge, give yeh me thanks and yer leave."

With a smile, the elf walked over to Grumpet, who had known the elf the shortest of the company. Again placing hands on the others' forearms, Arrol spoke to his friend.

"Grumpet, you are the greatest swordsman of the age, and you proved it in Statuary Tower. You will have more challenges ahead of you in the future, and I know that your brute strength and pure nerve will get you through any adversity—and any adversary. May the gods bless you in your quest," Arrol said, bowing. Grumpet only bowed in return, speechless.

Arrol smiled, as if to say words were not necessary.

He went to Aidan Rosar next, a dwarf he truly respected. "Young Aidan, we've had the chance to spar together and walk together, and converse on the nature of all things. You are an inquisitive dwarf who seeks knowledge beyond war, and I foresee that you will find the knowledge you seek and become a much powerful warrior for that. I shall never forget the way you destroyed the troll, and how you showed your kin how you handled a new weapon in battle. If I am ever in another battle, I will wish to the gods that I had you next to me."

Aidan quickly grasped the elf in a hug. Arrol patted the dwarf on the back, and Aidan let go, tears brimming in his eyes.

The next and final good-bye was hard for both parties involved. Arrol stopped in front of Yanos Kingsfoil and dropped onto his right knee, looking the halfling in his brown eyes. Yanos' eyes were filled with tears and the elf stared hard at him.

"This is not a time for tears, Yanos Kingsfoil. You and I have formed a bond in many different ways. You are by far the most cunning halfling I have ever met, and I fear for those that must fight against you; the way your eyes were filled with hate deep in the caverns of Bastine as you killed a drow elf, I was glad to be on your side. And yet, even as your eyes grew cold from battle, you proved shortly thereafter that you have a warm heart. The way you grieved for the lost humans touched my heart, and that is what I will never forget about you, my friend," Arrol said, and by the time he was done, both he and the halfling were openly crying.

Yanos did not speak, either, and, like Aidan, grasped the elf in a hug around the neck. When he let go, he ran back toward the forest, but Radamuck's grip kept him close by.

Turning from the company, Arrol stretched his arms out in front of him and closed his eyes, concentrating on the empty air in front of him. He whispered under his breath, and while none heard him, they knew his objective: he called for Sapphire, his magical Pegasus, to return to the realms once more.

Within seconds, a fine pink mist began to appear near the elf's feet, a mist that grew high until it reached his chest. It expanded for several axe lengths, taking shape into the magical flying horse. It solidified and the white horse appeared as the mists dissipated. Sapphire pawed at the ground and gave a horse-like whinny.

Knowing that he was now ready to go, Arrol Goldleaf looked one last time at the company, holding onto the Pegasus's reins. Tears streamed down his elven cheeks, but he smiled at them all before he raised himself onto his mount. Digging his heels into Sapphire's flank, the Pegasus started into a trot before it sprinted. It spread its large wings, flapped them twice and with a large push, leapt straight into the sky. The Pegasus beat its wings, gaining more altitude until it turned into a speck in the sky. It had a 400-mile flight until it reached the Citadel, by which time the Lowbridge dwarves would have closed in on their homeland.

When they no longer had sight of the elf and his flying steed, Radamuck bowed his head and prayed to his gods, wishing the elf a safe and protected flight. As he finished, he looked at his dwarves and said, "We're closin' in on Lowbridge, me friends. Time to go."

The company remained quiet as it departed the Forest of Purge's shadow, and remained that way for quite some time: While the departure of Arrol Goldleaf was a shock, the mood of the company brightened as they came upon a shallow brook that flowed steadily to the southeast. Looking to Grumpet with a smile on his face, Radamuck said, "Welcome to the dwarf kingdom of Lowbridge! This is the Stream of the Dwallows, a cooling waterway that marks the northernmost borders of our realm!"

Turning to his army, the king screamed, "We are home!" and raised his arms in victory. The army cheered mightily and one by one, it splashed through the Dwallows and immediately felt reinvigorated: the stream had healing powers, giving each a new spring in his step. The army laughed and sang, as if they knew their voices would carry all the way to Lowbridge.

Radamuck walked at the army's head with a brisk gait, a smile splashed across his face. He had led the army out of Lowbridge nearly a year prior on his special mission, to find the Chalice of Obloeron and bring it back here. When it was back, he had planned to celebrate with all those involved.

But not all of them returned. And as he thought about those dwarves, all one hundred fifty of them, the sack on his back grew increasingly heavy. Like a conscience, the chalice weighed him down.

They died without knowin' what I was seekin', he thought, and wondered if their deaths were in vain. *They had died protectin' Lowbridge's king, which was the oath they had promised when they began their tours of duty, even though Lowbridge's king was not exactly on a mission to defend the kingdom itself. They were on a quest to find a magical object that would make the kingdom invincible, and*, as Radamuck suddenly thought, *that wasn't always a good thing; Lowbridge would be marked now*. Just then he remembered Frampton's words, and how they now suddenly sounded so prophetic: *Mark my words, dwarf: I will have the chalice by hook or by crook, and if that means a war on the plains of Lowbridge, then so be it*.

The king, as he looked back on the past year, now realized he had been greedy and had only thought about himself. Deep down, he knew he wasn't thinking about the good of Lowbridge or its people. By having the chalice in his possession, and bringing it into Lowbridge proper, he might jeopardize his people's lives.

This only sunk his heart further down into his chest, and made the weight on his back increasingly heavy.

He then made a decision—even though it may kill his people, he would have to bring it into his city, but melt it down quickly so that it may not become a threat.

He had come this far. He had no other choice.

Even though he now had misgivings about taking the chalice as his own, his heart felt gladdened, he and the army back within the limits of his own realm. He missed the winding corridors of Lowbridge, the grassy vales, the large hall where his people gathered to worship their gods.

But most of all, he missed his wife, Lady Rosar, and the first few months of his son's life.

Within minutes he stood in that spot where he had lay with Lady Rosar, discussing with her the plans for the chalice. She never expressed any misgivings for going after it then.

Maybe I shouldn't think twice about it, either, he thought.

Radamuck's pace quickened. He looked back toward his friends, especially Aidan, Yanos and Grumpet, who also picked up their footsteps to match those of the king.

Aidan reached into his pack, removing a small bundle of cloth. Wrapped tightly around a set of connecting rods, Aidan unfurled the cloth to reveal the family crest of Rosar. Connecting the rods together and securing the cloth to it, the King's banner caught the wind and pointed the way home. The army cheered as the banner, a golden shield with an axe and a hammer crossing each other on a field of red, peeled away.

Radamuck looked back, saw his banner waving through the air, and then smiled. Seeing that standard flying through his lands, his heart soared higher, the thoughts of the chalice forgotten for the moment.

***

As Grumpet T. Paddymeyer walked with the singing dwarf army, he now looked forward to seeing the majestic city he had heard so much about. He wanted to see the great hall, its deep mines, and its flowing underground medicinal pools.

Unfortunately, he didn't have his bride, the fair Jessica Paddymeyer, with him to take in the wondrous sights he would behold. And that panged at his heart, for he knew he would have to depart the dwarves soon and return to Kayiko.

As he walked through the tall grass, he wondered what Jessica would think of this land. For all their lives, they saw nothing but snow and a meager existence. Here, the dwarves saw sunshine and green grass and sweet, warm air.

He knew his wife would love this land, and wished he had her here to enjoy it with him. Maybe he would convince her to return to Lowbridge with him to live in serene beauty instead of cold, gray despair.

That is, when he finally saw her again. How he wished for one more look at her fair face, and knew he would see her wonderful visage sometime soon.

Slipping from his reverie, he noticed the top of an approaching mountain, still quite a distance away. When Radamuck shouted, "Lowbridge is near!" Grumpet immediately knew what he saw. The peak burst over the hill they now climbed.

The mountain came into view as the company came over the hill, and Grumpet gasped, immediately taken with its beauty. For someone who lived in the shadow of a small mountain for his entire life, Lowbridge was as the dwarves had bragged about and more. Unlike his own township, Lowbridge was built into the mountain and filled the caverns inside with dwarves, jewels, gallons of ale and practically the largest halls in the world.

Lowbridge stretched for what looked like miles across the northeastern tip of the base of the mountain, with battlements placed strategically on the mountainside. The gate to the city was the substance the dwarves mined from their deep caverns—the precious whitesilver. The gate was several axe lengths high and double that wide, so that when it opened its doors, the entire Rosar army entered and left the city as a unit.

In addition to the gate and the battlements, Grumpet saw many causeways running to and from the battlements and to smaller gates, with dwarves walking about them. They went about their business, not knowing that within a few minutes, their king would be back to rule their fair city once again.

***

At one of the battlements, Lowbridge Home Defense Sergeant Mandrin O. Range looked through his spyglass, keeping an eye on the surrounding hills for potential threats as well as friendly visitors to the dwarven kingdom. It was dull work, searching the skies and the lands all day for threats that may never come. After all, Briskey Bucktooth hadn't organized against their smaller neighbor for decades, and the next closest realm to the dwarves was the old forest, less than a day's march to the northeast, and no one lived there.

But tarry from his duty, Range did not, and at the orders of the king, he would keep his constant vigil to search the hills. But the king was not in the realm, and hadn't been for nearly a year.

As he thought this, the wind blew mightily from the northeast, nearly toppling the dwarf from his perch high above the gates to the mountainous city. But as he recomposed himself, he thought he heard the gruff voices of many beings singing a song Range himself had learned as a dwarfling in these very halls.

It felt like one hundred voices carrying the tune from the heavens, and the dwarf looked up toward the sky. Seeing nothing, he tuned his ears toward the sound, which came from beyond the large hillock. Range leaned forward, pressing his weight against the barricade to near snapping, before he saw it: a splash of red poking from above the hill. It was a small army of dwarves, dwarves who had been born and reared within the hills.

And at the head of the group came a dwarf that no spyglass needed to identify for a Lowbridgian: the rugged exterior and long black beard betrayed him long before the watch tower saw his face.

Range stared, open-mouthed at the hillock: the king had returned!

He quickly turned and handed out orders to those around him.

"Raise the heralds and sound the trumpets! Alert the steward and the Lady of Lowbridge! The king has returned!" Range said, and after the stunned dwarves realized what he said, they rushed off to prepare for the king's arrival. Seconds later, the heralds blasted their trumpets, sending shock waves of music out toward the army. As the trumpets blared, Range felt a tingle of excitement rush through his extremities.

Anytime the king returns home there is a good party, and Range couldn't wait to go off duty to have some of the king's best ales.

***

As the trumpets sounded, the army which had followed Radamuck Rosar to the far reaches of the northlands and through nearly every realm created gave an incredibly loud cheer.

Seeing their city was only the tip of the iceberg, for the heralds calling them home made the journey feel complete. Soon, they would be back inside the mountain, back with their dwarf women and children.

The gate then opened, and filing out of the entrance was the Guard of the King, a group of twenty well-armed dwarves, all dressed in flowing blood red cloaks with full faced helmets and double-bladed axes. Escorting them out was the steward of the city, Fib Niosh, as well as a delegation of the king's advisors. The steward wore robes of brown, which blended well with his brown beard. He was nearly as old as Radamuck, but carried none of the king's wisdom or power. Yet Fib was the smartest dwarf of the king's advisors, and of the lot, he was the only one Radamuck trusted to lead his people while he was on the quest.

With Fib Niosh among the Guard of the King, it was the first step in the transfer of power process from the steward back to the king. Radamuck hated this procedure, which included a running tally of the events which had occurred in the king's absence. It took so much time, but he did see the point of it after returning from an earlier campaign against oppression—it kept the king up to date and also told him of lingering matters that need his immediate attention.

The Guard of the King finally arrived in front of Radamuck, forming two lines on either side of him, giving the king an axe length of distance to meet with the steward. Fib Niosh approached, and, with the delegation standing behind him, stopped to greet Radamuck outside the gates to the city.

"Welcome back to Lowbridge, Yer Highness. A lot has happened since yeh left..." Fib Niosh began. Radamuck rolled his eyes, but paid attention anyway.

He better make it short, Radamuck thought. *There is a dwarf princeling in this city that needs to meet his papa, and he didn't understand politics very well yet.*

Chapter 4

"So other than that, Yer Highness, the kingdom has run smoothly in yer stead," Fib concluded, and by the time the steward had finished, Radamuck had a headache. The list was lengthy, with the greatest trouble being a dispute over cavern rights, which to Radamuck was a trivial matter he would deal with any old time.

But now, Radamuck simply wanted to see his wife, his son, and address his people on his return.

He also wanted to visit with the families who lost loved ones in the battles in Kayiko and at Statuary Tower, but dreaded each and every one of those.

"It's time for yeh to re-enter yer city, Yer Highness. But," Fib Niosh added in an undertone, "if I may say so Yer Highness, is it wise to bring another non-dwarf into Lowbridge?"

Radamuck knew immediately about whom Fib spoke: Grumpet. Radamuck had always been a non-racist dwarf, unlike most of his kind. He had befriended elves and halflings and humans, while Fib Niosh—and the late General Roding, as well—had an issue with those who failed to out-drink him.

"I assure yeh, Councilor Niosh, that Grumpet T. Paddymeyer is no ordinary human. In fact, he may be the reason I am still alive today, for if we did not cross his path, our entire army would have been decimated beyond recognition," Radamuck said in an admonishing tone, look at the dwarf directly in his eyes. "For he wields the Sword O' The South, the weapon that has brought peace once again to the northlands, and soon to all the realms!"

Fib Niosh bristled at being called a councilor again. He had tried to talk the king out of other things before—going after the chalice, for example—but had been knocked off his feet by Radamuck's intense gaze for doing so.

"I was only suggestin' that to Yer Majesty; however, I, and all those who serve yeh, will abide by yer rulin'," Fib said, recovering. "It would be an honor to have the Sword O' The South in Lowbridge again."

"Right," Radamuck said, gesturing to Fib Niosh, the delegation of advisors, and the Guard of the King to move toward the city. He desperately wanted to get indoors, for dark storm clouds were moving in from the Enchanted Sea; tonight looked to be a stormy one and the king had had enough of wet nights out of doors.

As one, the Guard of the King turned around and marched forward, with the delegation and Fib Niosh moving aside so Radamuck led the way in. At Radamuck's insistence, he had Grumpet, Aidan and Yanos follow him, followed by the reluctant steward, the advisors and the rest of the army. With Radamuck's aggressive and purposeful strut, they walked through the gates within seconds, with Home Defense personnel saluting their king as he entered the city's outer corridors.

Minutes later, heralds inside the great hall blared their trumpets. The red cloaked Guardsdwarves led Radamuck and Company into the hall, which was wider than the length of Kirkrik Dannell's chateau. From the entrance to the hall, the Guard walked down the four stairs leading to the floor while the entire kingdom of Lowbridge came to its collective feet to welcome back their king. When the Guardsdwarves came to rest on either side of the aisle, the heralds blew their last notes as Radamuck, Aidan, Grumpet and Yanos walked down the stairs and through the parted crowd. The army followed, as the steward and the rest of the delegation took another route to the dais, located at the far end of the hall. Whispers greeted the army, as the kingdom didn't have trouble noticing the army was now half the size it had been when it left Lowbridge a year prior.

As he walked to the dais, Radamuck's eyes were focused on one person and one person alone: his wife, Lady Rosar, sat to the right hand side of the king's pumice-made and gemstone-laden throne, her small frame looking elegant in robes of lilac. Her hair, which cascaded past her shoulders to the middle of her back, and beard glittered under the torchlight, and as Radamuck clearly saw, she smiled at the sight of her handsome king.

All he wanted to do at that time was order the army and the rest of his kingdom away to have just a moment with Lady Rosar, who made moments stretch to an eternity by just kissing him. Radamuck felt himself growing emotional as he saw his bride, for she was the fairest being in all of Lowbridge, in his kingly opinion. His heart soared into his throat at her smile, his hands became clammy, and his thoughts muddied. He was amazed that after one hundred-plus years of marriage, she still turned his head.

Shaking his thoughts out of his head, Radamuck reached the foot of the dais. Inviting his friends to join him, the Twenty-fourth King of Lowbridge walked up the stairs and turned to face the assembled crowd, his kinsmen. The army walked to the front of the stage and took seats in front. The Guardsdwarves also came to the front to stand in front of the dais, with their axes held in a ceremonial position against their right shoulder.

He faced his stare toward the throng and removed his hood. Fib Niosh came from behind him, carrying a wooden box that was roughly a foot wide by a foot deep. Inside it, as every dwarf in Lowbridge knew, was the last part of the transition from stewardship to monarchy.

Inside the box was the crown of Radamuck Rosar, the one worn by every king the dwarven realm had known for nearly three millennia.

Radamuck stood stoically as Fib Niosh opened the box, and the crowd took in breath. Out came the crown, and the assemblage oohed and aahed, enthralled by the crown's sheer beauty. Made of silver and adorned with a single ruby, the king's headpiece sparkled and glittered as the torchlight splashed upon it. As Fib held the crown above Radamuck's head and then settled it upon Radamuck's brow, the entire kingdom bowed as one, their right hands thumping lightly on their breast. The steward stepped back and pronounced, "The Twenty-fourth King of Lowbridge has returned to his ancestral homeland. His rule will last forever!"

Boisterous cheers echoed throughout the great hall, bouncing joyously off the cavern walls. But as soon as it started, it ended as the king held up his right hand, asking for quiet from his subjects.

He got it immediately.

“We have traveled far and wide, me friends. We have gained,” Radamuck said, acknowledging Grumpet’s presence on the dais, “and we have lost. Many weeks we have been gone from this great land, and many of yer kin will never return to it. For they were defendin’ their king, as well as the oppressed, in a lengthy moment of their king’s lack of proper thought.”

The hall buzzed as Radamuck acknowledged his own faults, and even though they were stunned by this revelation, they respected him even more. They were proud their king had the humility and the courage to stand up in front of them and admit when he was wrong, for they knew that leaders of other realms would pass blame from themselves when they were in the wrong.

“Despite our losses, our kingdom has gained significantly. For starters, we have been fortunate along our travels to reclaim a long-standing alliance with the elves of the Bastine realm,” Radamuck said, to great cheers from the crowd, even though he knew they were just being polite and publicly unquestioning their king. “In addition, we have met the heir to Krampel Paddymeyer in the village of Kayiko, far to the north. Behold, me friends, for the Sword O’ The South has returned to Lowbridge!”

The crowd stood in awe at Radamuck’s pronouncement, and soon everyone looked this way and that, sending hurried whispers to their neighbors.

“So that is who the human is? I hope he can fight like Paddymeyer.”

“By the gods, the Sword Of The South!”

“Where’s ‘is beard? ‘E can’t fight without a beard!”

As the crowd murmured, Radamuck looked toward Grumpet, who had instinctively moved forward, and as the king saw, had a slightly stunned look on his face. Grumpet grasped *Flad-rul* and pulled the gleaming, fiery blade from its sheath, a trail of fire spouting from it as it cut brilliantly through the air. He held it in front of him, the blade bisecting his face from view.

After Grumpet had relaxed and re-sheathed his sword, Radamuck took the pack off his shoulders and placed it on the floor in front of him. He opened the sack, and, like in Kirkrik Dannell's chateau, the cavern filled with golden light; Radamuck had to shield his eyes. With two hands, his removed the magnificent chalice from it, and many dwarven mouths fell open at the sight. Its beauty shimmered throughout the great hall, as Radamuck lifted it above his head, letting the entire world see it.

Again, his dwarven subjects gasped in wonderment, bowing at the knee, genuflecting toward the cup in reverence of its beauty and its multi-realm attraction.

Fib Niosh stepped forward and spoke with the king.

"Yer Highness, yeh may want to put the chalice back in the sack, because yeh may need to use two hands in a minute," the steward said, and the king looked at him quizzically. But then, the heralds' trumpet blared again.

Lady Rosar came forward toward her husband, and as she reached him, a dwarven handmaiden came through a side entrance, carrying a bundle within her arms.

Radamuck's heart leapt into his throat, for he knew what that bundle was. It had been his longing wish to meet the heir to his kingdom, the dwarven princeling which had been in his thoughts for hours.

Taking the baby from the handmaiden and nodding as the handmaiden curtsied, Lady Rosar turned toward her husband and bowed as she presented the baby to him. Fighting back tears, the king gently took the baby into his arms and, for the first time, looked into the face of his son.

The baby looked incredibly precious, Radamuck immediately thought, as he saw a tuft of black hair growing on the top of his head. And, while there was not yet a beard growing on his chin, Radamuck was sure that when it grew in, it would be as long and majestic as his own. The baby's hazel eyes bored holes into Radamuck's own black ones, looking at his father's face and smiling at his papa.

Radamuck smiled at the baby and made slightly cooing noises at him, bringing his hand to the baby's mouth and thibbing the baby's lips with it. The baby then grasped for Radamuck's beard with his pudgy fingers. The assembled kingdom gave an "awwww" at the sight, and Radamuck looked at them all and gave a slight laugh.

Lady Rosar touched his shoulder and leaned in to her husband's ear.

"I still have yet to name him, my dear. I was waiting for you to return to name him. Any suggestions?" she asked. Her voice was melodic for a dwarf, yet firmer then even Radamuck's gruff exterior.

Radamuck looked back to her and thanked the gods that his wife was this thoughtful. Looking into her blue eyes, he smiled and whispered one word to her.

"Radasack."

Lady Rosar smiled at the name and nodded to Radamuck, who also smiled at her. He then turned back to the crowd and held his son in two hands, aloft, for all to see. Then, in his booming voice, he announced, "All hail Radasack Rosar, son of Radamuck, Twenty-fifth King of Lowbridge!"

The hall lowered itself into its knees, bowing their heads. All on the dais, including Yanos and Grumpet, bowed as well. When a king's heir is named and presented to the kingdom, the subjects bow and pray to the dwarf god of wisdom to bless the newborn baby with the knowledge he needs to lead the people in the event of his father's death in battle or of old age. After a minute of prayer, the crowd stood and applauded the princeling's naming and crowning-in-waiting.

Lowering his son and placing him back into the arms of Lady Rosar, Radamuck stretched his arms wide and exclaimed, "Let our celebratory feast begin! Bring out the ale! Let it snow food and let the rivers rush with drink!"

The crowd again gave a cheer, its loudest yet, as the servants busied themselves with kegs, flagons, and serving trays. And as they did that, Radamuck again stood next to his queen, kissed her whiskery lips, and looked down upon the face of his son with a smile.

***

Aidan Rosar had stood on the dais by his uncle, standing in between Grumpet and Yanos, but he hadn't heard a word his uncle said. His eyes searched the great hall for some sign of her. Her face would have been the greatest sight his eyes had ever seen, for he had only seen her face in his dreams for months.

And today, he would finally look into her eyes again.

She wasn't in the front, behind the bulky dwarf soldiers, or in the middle, with her family. He searched frantically to the point of almost giving up.

But then her saw her hair, and then he unleashed the brightness in his heart, and he knew she saw it in his face.

It was the vivid, fiery red hair, matched by an equally red beard, which had attracted him to her in the first place, while she was attracted by his reasonably calm demeanor in the kingdom. They had fallen in love several years ago, and it was the thought of being together forever which kept them going for so long. It was the only thought which guided his sword and axe in battle.

His brown eyes locked onto her green ones.

Aidan Rosar looked at her and saw her bring her hand up to her face, bringing it up to her eyes, where she wiped away the tears touching the brims. His heart broke, for while he knew she felt happy to see him, he never wanted her to cry for any reason. The act of love by her caused his eyes to suddenly brim with tears, but he fought them back as much as possible.

The beauty distracted him so much that he was almost caught standing on the dais when the entire cavern bowed for his cousins' naming; Yanos had kicked the back of his right knee to break his eye contact with his lady love. The halfling looked up at him and nodded toward Radamuck. Aidan caught the cue and, while still looking at her, he lowered his knee politely.

After Radamuck had announced the feast would begin Aidan knew he should have went over to visit with Radasack, but he thought he would have plenty of time to get to know his baby cousin.

There was only one dwarf, just one in the entire kingdom, he wanted to see right now.

Instinctively, he walked down the stairs from the dais to the hall floor and past the Guard of the King, with his eyes focused on her, and her eyes on him. As other dwarves crossed their path, their eye contact never wavered, even though Aidan had passed several kegs of ale. The couple drew closer and closer to each other, when suddenly there was no space between them or their hearts.

They quickly embraced, both mixed between laughter and tears. Each held the other tightly, and when their heads parted from the rest of their bodies, they came together in a kiss which told the realms what they felt about each other.

Pecking her lips twice, Aidan took her face into his hands and looked into her green eyes.

"Oh my dear Prestillia," Aidan said, his chest heaving with emotion, "I've missed you so much. The days without you grew to months, and when we found the chalice, the only thing I could think of was getting back to you."

Prestillia smiled brightly through her beard and pressed her head to his shoulder. She took in his sweet smell and sighed.

"Aidan, I missed you, too. Every day alone in the city felt like a year, every month an eternity. I'm so glad to see you safe and sound again, my love," she said.

"It has been too long for us to be apart. Let us spend time getting to know each other again. I have so much to tell you of our adventures," Aidan said. Prestillia smiled and nodded, clasping her hand in Aidan's and allowed him to lead from the feasts and the drink in the great hall.

The enormous weight which had been on his shoulders for weeks suddenly lifted as he walked with her.

***

Lady Rosar looked toward her nephew and his lady love and smiled. They were so young and she was pleased to see him so happy.

She walked a few steps and placed her hand on her husband's left shoulder. Radamuck took his eyes off his son and saw Lady Rosar looking toward Aidan. When he saw the two lovebirds kissing, he smiled through his long black beard.

"They'll be married soon, Radamuck. And what a happy day that will be in Lowbridge!" Lady Rosar said.

Radamuck looked toward the happy couple and nodded. "Aye, it will. Aidan deserves all the happiness in the world, especially after the way me brother died. I've done me best as a surrogate father to him, but it's time he has the happiness. He's ready to be a father and a husband," he said. "Yeh should have seen him in battle, me love. He has improved so much that it really isn't fair to our enemies. He is such a good swordsdwarf now. And he even showed skills I never knew existed in him."

His wife smiled at him. "Don't be so hard on yourself, Radamuck. You taught him a lot, and there were some things you couldn't teach him. He had to learn a lot of things on his own, especially with a sword. There were none in the land who could teach him that, and I'm sure he could make himself a fine weapons master, if you were to so deem him that title."

"He helped teach the townspeople of Kayiko how to fight 'fore the wizard invaded them a second time. He and Grumpet sparred with each other and I was amazed at how much he had grown, and how he could keep his own with someone who was taller than he and had a longer reach," Radamuck said, just as Grumpet came over to join them.

"Aidan is as good a fighter as any, Radamuck, and you should be proud of him," Grumpet said, before bowing to Lady Rosar. "My lady, my service."

She returned the bow with a nod of her head, welcoming the warrior to Lowbridge.

"Radamuck, I see this is a time for the dwarves to celebrate. I should take my leave now and return to my homeland in the north," Grumpet said, looking at the dwarf king.

"Nonsense, me young friend!" Radamuck boomed so loudly that Radasack cried. Passing the baby to his mother, Radamuck then grabbed Grumpet by the elbow. "Yeh've just as much of a right to be here celebratin' with all of yer friends in me army. They look to yeh and know yeh could lead them in battle alongside me and Aidan. They respect yeh, see."

He gave Grumpet a hard stare, which seemed to cut off any argument.

"I know what yeh're thinkin', especially 'bout me lettin' Arrol go. I'm goin' to need yeh here, Grumpet; Kirkrik said so. He told me to keep yeh close for when the time comes. I'm sure he has his reasons, didn't want to tell me too much. Besides, I still want to talk to yeh 'bout what I said on the dais, but that'll have to come later," Radamuck said softly, so none of the others could hear. He grabbed two flagons of mead from a passing tray and passed one to the captain. "Here, drink up! Yeh'll be payin' a disservice to the king if yeh don't!"

Radamuck drained his mug in one gulp before issuing a loud belch from deep within him. The entire crowd cheered as their king pronounced the mead in good order in his own special way. Grumpet also drank the mead, downing half of it quickly. Also belching, the crowd gave another cheer and waved the human down to join them. He then had mugs thrust into his open hands and soon he was laughing and singing dwarven songs with the rest of them.

Radamuck looked at the scene and laughed. Thinking he should join his people he looked to his wife, who nodded and told him to enjoy himself and that he deserved it.

"But don't have too much fun, my dear. We have a lot to discuss," she said, before giving him a wink and departing the great hall with the baby.

Radamuck laughed, grabbed another flagon and joined his people, who were drinking heavily. Soon, the king's crown tipped from his head and he downed mug after mug of the drink and eating just as heartily.

***

As the skies darkened outside Lowbridge, torches were set alight next to the city's battlements. The watch had just been changed, and the tired dwarves who had been on watch were eager to hit their beds—or to join the celebration that had been going on for some time in the great hall.

With the sun's brightness extinguished, the watch would be hampered by the lack of light—unless an attacking army brought torches of their own. The rain was no threat to any torches as the wind shifted and sent the clouds to the east of Lowbridge proper.

However, it would be easy for one man, torchless, to slip through the watch's blindness and enter the city, full of armed dwarves, and cause unthinkable malice.

On this night, one man and one man alone, would do this.

The spy Frampton had made his way to Lowbridge, making a stop in Briskey Bucktooth to the northwest. There he purchased a crossbow from an underground merchant, as well as a small cache of darts. He needed these items to make his initial penetration of the dwarves' outer defenses.

As quick as a hawk, Frampton abandoned his camp, located out of the sights of Lowbridge's watch. Not bothering to extinguish his campfire, he donned his magical cloak and slipped into the trees. When he reappeared minutes later, he found himself staring directly into the stone face of Lowbridge.

With the cover of darkness as his ally, Frampton slid through the brambles and bushes near the northwest corner of the mountain, slinking along the ramparts of the dwarven city. Inching his way with his back against the wall, he kept a look for armed dwarves marching the perimeter.

Luckily for the spy, he saw none, and he made no noise to attract any dwarves to his location. Frampton looked up at the battlements nearest the gate, saw three dwarves looking here and there for attackers that would never come, and smiled to himself. They hadn't seen him yet. That was something he had counted on, for he needed the element of surprise for his next task.

He removed a sleeping dart, one of the ones he purchased in Briskey Bucktooth, loaded it into the crossbow, and took aim at the nearest dwarf's neck. With an eye closed and another fixed through the targeting scope, Frampton squeezed the trigger and with a "woosh," the bolt sped upward, gaining speed until it collided just to the left of the dwarf's jugular vein.

Startled by the dart's pinch, the dwarf's hand came up to feel the dart poking out and when he felt it, his eyes rolled into the back of his head. It only took a few seconds for the potion to take hold, and soon the dwarf collapsed under his own weight, falling to the floor of the seven-foot wide battlement.

The two dwarves next to the punctured one rushed over to help, checking on him as he snored loudly before they called for others from other battlements to help. As other dwarves came running from inside the city, other members of the watch scanned the area surrounding the mountain for any sign of the mysterious attacker.

But they wouldn't find Frampton. He would prove to be too hard to catch or to detect.

With their attention diverted, the slippery spy, all in black, stole the advantage: he quickly sprang into action, stepping over stones and sneaking onto a causeway.

Practically running up the small road, Frampton reached an unguarded entrance. He walked along one empty passageway before he came to another, equally empty stone walled corridor. Taking a guess, Frampton decided to go toward his right and, thinking that the city would be toward the center of the mountain, he would then make the earliest left-hand turn possible. He walked stealthily, careful not to make a sound with his footfalls on the stone floor, as they would echo far into the dwarven city.

Frampton didn't believe he hadn't seen anyone to prevent him from continuing his trek inward; he found it peculiar there were no patrols guarding the hallways. But as he thought those words, his finely-tuned ears heard the sounds of voices coming from up ahead. And they were gruff voices, too. The sounds echoed off the corridor walls, ricocheting and bouncing until they met Frampton's ears.

There were dwarves ahead, and they would run directly into him if he didn't move.

So much for the lack of patrols, Frampton thought.

Without panicking, Frampton slid into a small crevice along the left-hand side of the corridor, one to shield him greater than any on the right. He squeezed his tall frame into the space and got himself far into it, without getting stuck. He also kept his gleaming sword, belted to his waist, from clanging around the hidden chamber.

And as he had finally got situated, the echoing footsteps grew louder and the voices clearer, until they were practically on top of him. He partially removed his sword from its sheath, in case he needed to draw it should the dwarf patrol see him.

"A poisoned arrow got the drop on the watch, that's what I heard."

"Means trouble is ahead for us, mark my words! There's an army attacking us any day now, with a flood of monstrous creatures ready to bite and claw us!"

"Nah, Briskey Bucktooth hasn't the gumption to attack us! And the only 'monstrous creatures' they have are fire gnomes! It is probably something or someone small and insignificant. We'll find it and beat it down for trying to incite the dwarves—and for trying to steal the dwarves' new treasure!"

Frampton ears perked up at this last comment, but still gnashed his teeth together, for he didn't like being called small and insignificant, especially from a being he towered over. He peeked his head out from the gape in the wall and narrowed his eyes as he watched the dwarves' shadows sneak around the corner, until the voices and footsteps and clanking armor were only fading memories. He re-sheathed the steel blade, its glittering light turned off as it snapped back into the scabbard.

Easing his way out of the crevice, Frampton eyed the dwarves' retreat one more time before he rushed off in the direction the dwarves came.

He hoped that would be the only dwarf patrol he would see, for he knew that his mission would succeed far greater with far fewer delays. He wanted to get the chalice and get out of the city before anyone, especially the human with the dwarves in the Forest of Purge, discovered he was even there.

Chapter 5

Deep in thought about his wife and his faraway home, Grumpet T. Paddymeyer blinked himself back to reality by a shadow passing in front of his door. Immediately, he knew it was not the shadow of a dwarf or the tiny shadow of Yanos Kingsfoil. Setting his flagon of mead aside and grabbing *Fladrul*, his mighty sword, which lay in his lap as he polished it, Grumpet followed the unidentified intruder down the corridor.

He saw shadows duck around a corner and immediately quickened his pace. He rounded the corner and thought he saw a human's foot, but it disappeared just as Yanos came out of a side tunnel near the corner. He was, as usual, eating what looked like his fifth meal of the day; obviously, Yanos ate Radamuck out of rock and cave.

But food was the farthest thing from Grumpet's mind at this point, for someone was in Lowbridge that had no business being here.

And it was up to Grumpet to find out who this person was, even though he had a pretty good idea who it was.

Bumping into the halfling, Grumpet looked down to see Yanos sprawled on the floor of the corridor, goat legs with meat hanging off the bone on top of his dinner coat. Yanos looked up, not in a mad way, but just to see who had unceremoniously dumped him onto the passageway.

Yanos wanted to say something about the rude interruption of his walk and post-meal snack, but Grumpet found his words first.

"Yanos, make haste and find Radamuck. Tell him we have an intruder in the city. Tell him he better check on the location of the chalice or it will be stolen from under our noses!" he said, and without picking the goat legs from the ground, Yanos hurried to find the king as fast as his hairy halfling feet carried him.

Grumpet watched the halfling run off before he dashed off after his quarry, which now had additional time to scamper away from him. With his height and fierce gait as an ally, Grumpet made up the time quickly, and before he knew it, he had the intruder within his sights.

The intruder was in a wider hallway, which looked like a small room with smaller passageways attached to it. There were no chairs or beds or tables in the hallway, just jagged stone walls and a dusty floor. The intruder simply stood there, as if waiting for someone to find him.

"Halt, intruder! Stop where you are!" Grumpet yelled, before ordering the man to turn and face him. "You have no where to run."

It was indeed the spy, Frampton, who was the intruder, but at that moment, Grumpet realized, Frampton was now much more than that. He had become a thief, for in his right hand was the Chalice of Obloeron. Frampton now wore a wicked grin on his face, distorting the mustache that lay on his upper lip. His grin looked more like a sneer of triumph than anything else, for it seemed the human had outwitted the dwarves and had done what he had said he would.

I will have the chalice by hook or by crook, the spy had said.

Obviously, thought Grumpet, he had to take it by crook. It was up to him to get it back.

"You hold property that does not belong to you," Grumpet said powerfully, "and you will hand it to me, now. You will then leave this land, and shall you return, I will personally make sure you are killed."

"But how will you do so if you are far away, Grumpet Paddymeyer? Yes, I know of your home in the north. You won't always be here to protect the dwarf, and Frampton would claim the chalice as his own if the dwarf dies!" Frampton replied, his left hand now holding the chalice and his right going for his sword. "If you want to take the chalice from me, you might as well fight me for it!"

Grumpet had no other alternative; he couldn't let this thief simply walk into Lowbridge and try to walk out of it with the magical item Radamuck had sought after for so long and so far away from home. He twirled *Flad-rul* through his fingers, the regal blade flaming as it circled. Holding it back at the right shoulder, Grumpet set off at a run toward the spy.

Securing the chalice inside his belt, which magically altered itself to handle the new addition, Frampton drew his own sword, a long sparkling steel blade with a bronze handle and a flattened pommel. He held it in both his hands, the sword out in front of him as he prepared for Grumpet's attack.

The attack came swiftly, as the powerful human from the northlands opened the duel with a hard chop at the spy's left flank, as if chopping down an aged tree, followed by a spin and another swipe at the right flank. Frampton parried these with ease, almost too easily, and Grumpet was shocked. He hadn't faced a worthy opponent since Dramin, and he had defeated him after a lengthy sword fight.

But he was more relaxed now and had time to rest after the long march, and thought he should easily dispatch this opponent.

With a sneer, Frampton pulled his sword back and thrust it forward, attempting to stick the blade into Grumpet's gut. Grumpet avoided the cut, getting his sword over in time to block the spy's attempt. He then tried to scalp Frampton with an uppercut toward the right side of the spy's head, but he ducked quickly and only felt a breeze fly over his head.

Frampton then spotted an opening near his opponent's legs but didn't react in time, as Grumpet had spun in his miss, coming around and, with a thunderous parry that echoed throughout the room, stopped the silver blade as Frampton tried to take out his knees.

Back and forth the two men traded blows, extending their swords to their opponent, hoping the other would make the wrong move, allowing them to strike the killing blow. With Grumpet's size, he held a great advantage over the smaller fighter: he pushed that advantage on Frampton heavily, pushing the spy into a darkened hallway. As swords clashed off the walls as much as they clashed against each other, sparks flew at the combatants. Grumpet's muscles flexed and corded with each stroke, the burly warrior spending much more precious energy against the smaller and faster swordsman.

As the fight continued, Grumpet tired, but he reversed the thrust of Frampton's blade with ease. With a sneer that sensed an imminent victory, Frampton had aimed a crossing slice that Grumpet had barely blocked, but his mouth opened in awe as his opponent turned his wrists around and knocked Frampton's blade and his body around.

Grumpet backed him to an even smaller corridor, one he surely wouldn't be able to fit in to continue the fight. As he hacked madly at the spy and not scoring a hit with his ripostes, Frampton ducked and rolled under a heavy overhead chop laid out by the warrior, before he got back to his feet and quickly rushed toward the opening. With his size, he slid into the opening easily.

Grumpet cursed his muscles as he moved slowly through the gaping hole.

***

Frampton smiled at Grumpet's obvious discomfort and then turned to find a means for his escape. He saw two ropes tied to a railing nearby, as he came up on the causeway that overlooked Lowbridge's mining operation. With another look back, he saw the human attempting to squeeze through, and decided his welcome in Lowbridge had quickly grown colder and colder. He walked toward the ledge and was nearly there, when two dwarves on patrol walked around the corner nearest the ropes and spotted the spy walking their way.

"Hey, you're not Grump—" the first dwarf began to say, but never got the last syllable out as Frampton had given the dwarf a mighty backhand with his sword, cleaving out the dwarf's voice box, letting him fall to his knees as blood rushed out of the wound.

As the dwarf pawed at the open wound and trying to gasp for words, the other dwarf reached for his axe. He fumbled with it and had it nearly out of its holster, when Frampton gave the dwarf a roundhouse kick with his right foot and had knocked the dwarf into a daze and backward several feet, making the dwarf collapse against the wall, his axe falling out of his hand and to the floor.

Quickly untying one of the ropes, he tied it around his waist and looked around to see if anyone impeded his progress. He saw that Grumpet's upper body was now out of the crevice, his hair falling all over his face, bathed in sweat. And then he turned back toward the corridor where the other dwarves came out, and saw the halfing lead a black bearded dwarf to the scene.

Smiling, Frampton drew his sword yet again and severed the other rope. And as the dwarf issued a horrid scream as he saw the chalice on the spy's belt, Frampton pushed off to ledge and soared across the chasm, landing clearly on the other side.

Looking back to where he just came, he saw the dwarf and the halfling standing against the rail, looking to see where the spy had gone. He then saw Grumpet amble over to the railing, his arms bloodied from squeezing through that opening, *Fladrul* held limply in his hands at his side. Frampton gave a flourish and a bow, tipping his fingers to his eyebrow in a mock salute. He then took his sword and, with a powerful swipe, sliced the rope.

And removing the chalice from his belt, Frampton disappeared from sight, sliding into a passageway that he hoped would take him to the outer reaches of Lowbridge to where his cloak lay. The last thing he heard was the dwarf king screaming, "Find him! Don't let him get away with me chalice!" before he hurried off at a trot.

Like the dwarves on the battlements outside Lowbridge, the dwarves inside Lowbridge would not find Frampton.

He was as good as home free.

***

Aidan Rosar sat at the top of the mountain, staring out toward the rising sun, oblivious to the goings on inside his home.

He was oblivious to everything, except the feelings in his own heart.

Aidan had just left Prestillia, his lady love, an hour ago to reflect on their conversation from earlier in the evening. He expressed his full love for her, and she for him. They even talked of the future, where they would be together forever and raise little dwarflings.

As he sat toward the east, he felt the love pouring forth from him. He wanted to ask for her hand in marriage, but knew that at any time he would have to depart at either his uncle's or his cousin's behest as part of the Lowbridge army.

And doing so would be painful for both of them, even though she reassured him she know how to deal with it: she had dealt with it before, and she stayed true to him.

Thinking of Prestillia's words made him smile. She was a loving dwarf, that much was true, but to stay alone for weeks and sometimes months at a time while her husband might find his death in a war? He struggled to wonder how his aunt did it all these years.

Aidan had avoided a discussion about this with his uncle—he had known he would have to talk with Radamuck about this situation at some time, ever since Kirkrik Dannell spoke to him at the chateau—but the dwarf couldn't postpone it any longer. He stood up and stretched, turning right and left to relieve the tension that built up in his muscles as he sat.

But as he turned left, toward the north, he thought he glimpsed a man running from the city, cloak billowing from behind him, in an apparent escape attempt. He hadn't heard the gongs of war go off, and just by the way the man acted, he felt certain this figure did not resemble a friendly to the dwarves.

Whatever it was, his uncle would need him in the city. He turned and made for the topside entrance to Lowbridge. Once he got inside, he heard rumblings of what had happened.

Worried, Aidan set off to find Radamuck.

***

Radamuck was not happy.

Simply put, Radamuck was furious.

"How in all the realms did that stinkin' highwayman get into me city!" Radamuck roared to those around him as he paced the floor where he, Yanos, and Grumpet had last seen Frampton, before the spy's exit. Spittle flew from the dwarf king's mouth as he railed.

"Me lord, we think he came in through a causeway and an unblocked gate into the city. He had to have set the dart to Rinnodick, the dwarf on the watch, and slipped in unawares. If it hadn't been for Master Paddymeyer, we would never have known about the theft—" Fib Niosh began, but bit back the rest of his thought as Radamuck glared at him, his coal black eyes burning with a new intensity.

Radamuck started pacing again when he stopped cold in front of the steward.

"Where's me family? Where's me wife and son? Make sure they are safe and bring them to me! Fetch me nephew as well!" Radamuck ordered, and two dwarves went in opposite directions to fulfill their king's wishes.

He was upset with himself now, Radamuck was, for not making sure his family was safe rather than worry about a golden cup. While the chalice had been nowhere near the king's family prior to its cupnapping, he still wanted to be sure they were safe before he continued his ranting and raving about what had happened.

But first, he had to have a word with Grumpet. Stopping in front of the warrior, who bandaged his wounds himself—the clerics were elsewhere, trying to save the dwarf who took Frampton's sword to the throat, tending to the dwarf who was kicked in the face, and the one who still slept off the effects of the dart—Radamuck placed his hand open Grumpet's left shoulder and looked him in the eye.

"Grumpet, I don't know what I'd've done if yeh didn't try to stop him. I don't blame yeh at all for what happened. Yeh were tryin' to save me treasure, and I can't thank yeh enough for that," Radamuck said, no hint of gruffness in his voice.

But Grumpet was just as angry as the king was.

"He still got away, didn't he? He has the chalice now. All that travelling you did to find it, Radamuck, all for naught now. It is gone in less time than it took Arrol to conjure Sapphire," Grumpet said, his shoulder aching from grazing it against the stone. "Without a doubt it was the highwayman we saw in the Forest. He threatened to take the chalice from you then, either by hook or by crook. It seems as if he has succeeded."

“We have no other choice but to send out a search party into our realm. If we can recapture the chalice, then a search party is the only way to do it,” Yanos Kingsfoil said, the littlest voice that carried a great deal of weight with Radamuck.

However, both Radamuck and Grumpet dismissed this notion at once.

“The spy is a master of deception and illusion. He got away from us in the forest, simply by waving his cloak and disappearing,” Grumpet said.

“If the spy doesn’t want us to find him, Yanos, he won’t be found,” Radamuck followed, patting his little friend on the shoulder and thanking him for his input.

Just then the dwarf with auburn hair returned, this time with Lady Rosar in tow.

“Yer wife, Yer Majesty,” he said, and stepped out of the way just in time as Radamuck nearly barreled him over to grab his wife in an embrace.

“Thank the gods yeh’re safe. Is Radasack safe? Is he hurt?” Radamuck asked his wife.

“Yes dear, Radasack is fine. Why dear, what happened?” she said, not noticing the blood on the floor where she entered the hall.

“The chalice has been stolen, me love,” Radamuck said, and felt surge of emotion as his wife raised her hand to her bearded mouth in shock.

“What? How? How can anyone simply walk into Lowbridge?” Lady Rosar said incredulously.

“That’s what we’re tryin’ to figure out. Calm down and we’ll figure out how he got in. Now, where is Radasack?” he asked.

“He is with my handmaidens, and as you know, my dear, they are well-trained in self-defense. Nothing is going to happen to Radasack while they have him in their care.”

A great weight lifted from his chest as he thanked the gods for providing his wife with such protectors.

“Okay, that’s good. Before I check on ‘im, I need to go see me injured dwarves. Ruddy highwayman,” Radamuck spat with disgust, but then Aidan walked in to find them all there.

“Radamuck, what happened? I heard there was an attack on the city,” he began, but stopped as Radamuck held up his hand.

“It wasn’t an attack on the city, me boy. It was a personal attack against me. The stinkin’ highwayman from the forest was here; he stole the chalice from right under me nose. Grumpet found him and fought him, but the passageways of Lowbridge betrayed its own folk for the first time in memory; the passage the spy slipped away from Grumpet was small enough for him to escape.

“But the next time he goes up against Grumpet, I know he won’t have that much luck,” Radamuck added. “We need to recover from this, but not think that somethin’ has not happened. A treasure that belongs here isn’t. We must be ever vigilant, and make sure no one that isn’t supposed to be in Lowbridge is here,” Radamuck said, turning to Fib Niosh. “I decree that the loss of the chalice is the fault of no one in Lowbridge. However,” he said, clearing his throat, “the tunnels and passageways must now be watched ever-more, in case the spy returns to cause more mischief. It will be the duty of all dwarves in Lowbridge to be on the alert for anythin’ out of place. Anythin’ that is must be reported to the Home Defense or the Guard of the King. I say it; it shall be law.”

With a bow, Fib Niosh departed with the new decree in his head. He would write it on parchment several times and post it in the great hall and in the mining areas. Every dwarf would know about Radamuck’s newest decree.

“Now that is done, I must go and visit with me dwarves and see that they are comfortable. I know one will; he’ll be out like a torch. G’night to yeh all,” Radamuck said, before he, Lady Rosar, Aidan and Yanos all departed to check on the dwarves.

Grumpet, however, stayed right where he was long into the night, sitting in the scene of what he considered a resounding defeat.

***

The spectral form of Victor Dramin smiled for the first time in ages. He couldn't believe what served for his eyes.

There was a way to defeat Grumpet T. Paddymeyer, and he looked straight at it.

With intent eyes, the dead wizard had watched the intense sword fight between Paddymeyer and Frampton, the spy, through the orb. He saw the way Frampton ducked a killing blow by the one who had killed the wizard, and was impressed. And his escape was one to be remembered.

As his newest minions milled around the wizard's new camp deep in the warmth of Stolidall Caverns, Dramin paced the room he took as his own, a room just outside the hall proper. On a makeshift stone table was the orb, still showing the defeat of Paddymeyer. Even through the mists the orb held, Frampton evaded the strong human with quick parries, lightning-smooth thrusts, and a sneer from a man totally confident in his abilities.

Dramin looked at it again and smiled even wider, for now he knew exactly what he had to do to defeat Paddymeyer, and to defeat him soundly: he needed to steal the spy's body. He marveled at his intuitive ways, of how he single-handedly reclaimed the Chalice of Obloeron before going toe-to-toe with him in a fight.

He quickly thought back to the teachings of Danolf Jenson, who had taught him everything he knew before the younger wizard murdered him in cold blood. He immediately thought of a spell which would allow Dramin the ability to inhabit Frampton's body, allowing them to mesh their souls to work as one unit. They looked of similar body structure; the hair the same color. They might have been brothers in another life.

But Dramin wasn't simply going to let the human live in a body he wanted. No, he would test him first to see if he was worthy of sharing a body with the great wizard.

And if he were worthy, Dramin thought, *then it would be the greatest victory I could ever achieve: combining my wizarding skills along with the cunning and swordplay of the spy, which would lead to the defeat—and the demise—of Grumpet T. Paddymeyer*.

Long had he waited for this, to even think about the death of the human who had caused his own. It was entirely possible to destroy Paddymeyer now, to force him to beg for his life, to put a sword to his neck, to let that sword slice through flesh and bone.

To take the life that took his.

Chapter 6

After thinking about the situation overnight, Radamuck awoke the next morning and reconsidered. As his first order of the day, he had Caz Axewielder take a group of rugged dwarves out into the woods just to the north of Lowbridge to search for Frampton and the chalice. He desperately wanted that chalice back to do what he had planned. Melted down, the Chalice of Obloeron was less dangerous to the entire realms—not to mention the people of Lowbridge—then allowing it to exist again.

And Radamuck wanted to be the one to melt it down, for he would entrust no one else—save Aidan, Yanos, or Grumpet—to do this important task.

But the mere fact the highwayman had stolen it right under his own nose drove Radamuck further: he said that the dwarf who brought him Frampton's head along with the chalice would receive more than just the king's gratitude.

With a nod, Caz accepted his orders. As the dwarf kingdom's new warmonger, Caz took the lead in this operation, and led the group of nine additional dwarves out the center gate and into the northwestern woods.

It was not as dark in these woods as it was in the Forest of Purge; rays of sunshine trickled through the boughs and branches, and deciduous leaves of all shapes, sizes, and colors littered the ground. They left no stone unturned, checking everywhere for the spy or a sign of the golden chalice.

After nearly two hours the dwarves had found no sign of the spy—until they discovered the campsite the spy had used. There was no sign of the spy or the chalice. Frampton had built a meager shelter from fallen boughs, and a small plume of smoke still sprouted from the fire.

"It's still hot," Caz said, his hand not six inches from the base of the grayish kindling. He saw additional pieces of wood nearby to keep the fire going, so Caz presumed the spy would return.

Stepping on the fire with his leathery boot, Caz stomped out the still-glowing embers before he had the dwarves smash the lean-to shelter.

Then he heard the click.

Eyes open in horror, he tried to tell his dwarves to move as fast as he could in any direction, but he was too late, for the dart stuck into the leg of a dwarf closest to him. The dwarf toppled over and immediately started snoring.

With axe in hand, Caz Axewielder started looking around, hoping to see a wave of a cloak to tell him the highwayman's location. Seeing no one, he scanned the branches immediately above him, for he figured the sneak attack had to come from above. His eyes darting this way and that, all he saw were branches, lots of them, and no clear place from which the spy could have attacked, unless he were incredibly high up.

Grumbling, Caz had no other choice right now: he needed to get back to Lowbridge and report his discoveries to Radamuck.

"We're heading back to the city. You four, grab one of his limbs," Caz said, indicating the sleeping dwarf. "He needs curatives, and a bed of straw."

Guffaws and dwarfly chuckles echoed throughout the woods as the four dwarves picked up their comrade; another took his axe for him.

"I think he had a little too much to eat at the celebration last night, this one did. He's too heavy 'round the middle."

"One good poof will lighten the load, it will," another said, pointing to his dwarven backside, causing the dwarves to howl louder.

Caz thought that despite not finding the chalice or the spy, the dwarf company was in high spirits. After all, they found his camp and destroyed it, and Caz would know where he found it should Radamuck want to see the campsite for himself.

He joined in the laughter as the dwarves carried their sleeping friend, the dart still protruding from the back of the dwarf's knee, to the city.

***

Frampton waited until the dwarves had departed. When he no longer heard their gruff voices over the steady hum of the breeze, he leapt to the forest floor from the highest branches, his cloak billowing behind him. He landed cat-like, with his sword arm ready to grab its weapon, if necessary.

And as he saw, he was quite alone. The dwarves were miles away by now.

Frampton smiled to himself, for he had outwitted the dwarves yet again.

He walked over to his former campsite and saw how the dwarves brutally destroyed his lean-to. He laughed softly, clucking his teeth as he saw the broken branches.

Oh well, he thought, *there is more firewood for my new campsite.*

Earlier that day, he had moved all of his belongings—except for the chalice; that stayed on his person at all times, as well as his steel sword—to a new campsite on the northern edge of the woods. With his new location, which wasn't found by the dwarves, he now had a clear view of Briskey Bucktooth, the larger neighbor to Lowbridge. He knew once word got out that Radamuck Rosar, the dwarf king to the south, had captured the Chalice of Obloeron, thieves from Briskey Bucktooth would try to steal the chalice from the dwarf, just like Frampton had already done.

That would mean the city's major guild houses would be empty. With the chalice, Frampton would walk into the city unnoticed, stroll right into the largest guild in Briskey Bucktooth, and offer his services to the leader, Blen Duffel. Should he be denied, he would merely show him the chalice, await the leader's reaction, and, when the time came, kill him out of sheer delight. With the chalice, he would easily take over the syndicate and rule the city with an iron fist.

And in Briskey Bucktooth, being the leader of a major guild meant being the king of the land around you. The Chalice of Obloeron would see to it that Frampton headed up the largest of the organizations Briskey Bucktooth held.

And no one in their right mind, he knew, wanted to challenge the leader of Briskey Bucktooth's number one guild house.

***

Caz Axewielder relayed his report to Radamuck minutes after returning to Lowbridge with the sleeping dwarf, and, as expected, the king wasn't too happy. However, he wasn't as upset as last night.

Thanking his warmonger for the report, Radamuck watched as Caz bowed and left the king's chamber, leaving him alone to his already nagging thoughts.

The situation has become increasingly dire, he thought. He already had three dwarves laying in the clerical, and Caz Axewielder brought them another. Two of them suffered from sleeping potions, which took time to get out of their systems. Another's nose was broken, but since he had broken his nose before this, it appeared normal now.

And then there was the dwarf who may not speak again, although as Radamuck thought, *a voiceless dwarf isn't always a bad thing, especially when the dwarf was as talkative as that one*.

The spy will pay for doing this much damage without steppin' one foot toward the king, Radamuck thought as he paced his chamber. The spy's attack was personal, but the king knew one other thing: The spy was a coward. He was cowardly because he had attacked the kingdom, but he hadn't faced the king himself. He had faced Grumpet and narrowly escaped with his life and the chalice.

Radamuck knew that if he faced the spy, his double-bladed axe would have been so deeply embedded in the spy's nervous system, he would twitch uncontrollably hours after his death. He smiled at the gruesome thought, knowing that if it came to pass, he would have the spy at his mercy, begging for his life.

Sighing, the king left his chamber and walked down the corridor to the room where Radasack slept. The baby had a room close to where he and Lady Rosar retired every evening, where the proud parents kept a watch over the sleeping child at night.

So far, even though the spy's antics both in the city and in the wood had spoiled his first two days back, he would peek in on Radasack to find the baby cooing, happy to see his father. The sight of the child automatically perked him right up.

When the handmaiden saw the king, she rose and bowed to him before departing, leaving him alone with Radasack.

Lying on his bed of straw all day, Radasack knew nothing of his father's troubles. Radamuck was glad for this, for someone so young should be learning how to grow his beard and not worry about wars and battles, even though Radasack wouldn't grow his for another fifteen years.

Smiling at his own thought, he looked into the crib set up for Radasack. The baby cooed and laughed a babyish giggle when his father's eyes popped into view, and immediately reached up for the king's long, black heard.

Chuckling to himself, Radamuck reached into the crib and picked up his son, resting him in the crook of his arm with Radasack's head peeking over his father's left shoulder.

"Yeh're so lucky yeh're young, Radasack. Maybe if yeh were older, yeh'd've caught this spy fer yer papa and this mess'd be over with," Radamuck said as Radasack drooled, his hands in his mouth. "But then again, maybe I should send yeh out to those woods and have yeh drool on him."

Radasack giggled happily.

"Oh, yeh like that idea, don't yeh? Well, it's easy fer me to have yeh go out there, but yeh still have to be taught how to fight like a Rosar should!" Radamuck said, looking into his son's eyes. "No one, and I mean no one, gets away from a Rosar. Believe it, no one will get away from yeh, once yeh've fixed them with a stare!

"But yeh've still got a lot of time before yeh can do that and cause yer men to walk the straight and narrow. It wasn't always like that fer me," Radamuck continued his tale, and as he couldn't yet speak, Radasack listened to his papa's lesson intently. "Back in the old days, when yer grandpapa was still alive, gods bless his soul, I was about fifty years younger than I am now, and I was just startin' to come into me own. He sent me and about a thousand dwarves to the southlands to fight in the Great Imperial Wars alongside the great Krampel Paddymeyer and legions of men. Radasack, yeh should've seen the stare that ol' Krampel fired on the High Imperial Inquisitor, Cairn Ford. It was almost as if Krampel was eggin' the man into a fight, a fight that would decide the war and the fate of the southlands. Ford took the bait, tried to stare down Krampel, and lost that fight hands down. But the battle was long and hard fought, Cairn Ford gave it everythin' he had, but he couldn't defeat that man. Krampel was such a great leader; I miss him sometimes, and I tell yeh, me son, he taught me a lot."

"I sure believe that," said a voice, and as Radamuck looked to his son, his son looked behind him to the figure who had just entered the room.

Radamuck turned and saw Grumpet standing there. He bowed to the king, before walking forward and looking into the baby's eyes.

"Jessica is going to want one of these before long," Grumpet said, referring to Radasack. "And I can't blame her. She's been longing for a family of our own for quite awhile, since we were betrothed to one another, before my grandfather passed.

"Hearing you talk to him about my grandfather's exploits made me think of that for some reason."

Radamuck watched as Grumpet sat down. He saw something troubling in his eyes. He put Radasack back into the crib and had to pry the baby's fingers from his beard. When Radasack didn't cry, he stepped away from the crib and sighed a huge breath of relief. Pulling up a chair, Radamuck sat down in front of Grumpet, knowing it was time for the talk he knew he would have to have with this man before long.

And he also remembered that he needed to talk to Aidan, as well.

"I bet yeh're wonderin' 'bout what I said in front of me people 'bout yeh," Radamuck said to Grumpet. "'Bout yeh being the heir of yer grandfather."

The human captain nodded.

"I told yeh when I first met yeh that yer grandfather was an incredible swordsman and that he defeated Cairn Ford in the Great Imperial Wars. Hurt 'imself doin' it, too. What I didn't tell yeh was that yer grandfather was named the new Inquisitor following Ford's defeat, yet he turned them down for he wanted to return to Kayiko to be with his family, yer great grandmother and yer father especially, for he was to get

Flad-rul when yer grandfather died. But, as yeh know, yer father died first, and yeh got *Flad-rul* a little earlier than Krampel hoped.

"But when yer grandfather turned down the title of Inquisitor, the folk of the southlands refused to name another successor, for they believed Krampel was the only one fit to lead them. They swore that no man will officially lead them unless it were Krampel Paddymeyer or his rightful heir, he who wields the Sword of the South. And that me friend, is yeh," Radamuck said.

Grumpet stared, open-mouthed and wide-eyed. Radamuck watched him as the lad finally learned of his destiny, a destiny that would change his life if he chose to go through with it. The dwarf knew he had never known of the destiny Krampel Paddymeyer had handed to him the day he died.

But now he knew.

"I know this is a lot of information at once, Grumpet, but one of these days, yeh'll have to take yer grandfather's place in the southlands as the Inquisitor. I know yeh have a good heart and that yeh'll be able to rule like yer grandfather would have; yeh wouldn't be a tyrant like Ford. Of course, yeh could return to Kayiko and abandon yeh destiny. The path is in front of yeh," Radamuck said.

"You're right," Grumpet said, standing slowly, "it is my destiny. I know now why my grandfather told me to wield *Flad-rul* with honor, for he inevitably wanted me to do what he didn't."

Radamuck looked up at his friend and smiled, for he knew Grumpet would eventually do the right thing if not for himself, but for his grandfather's memory.

That is what separated a Paddymeyer from the rest, Radamuck thought.

As he thought these things, he noticed Grumpet had gone to Radasack's crib and picked up the baby dwarf. He smiled as Radasack played with Grumpet's beardless face and how the man went from burly warrior to a soft-hearted man in a matter of seconds. Grumpet smiled and made faces at the baby, making the dwarf princeling laugh merrily.

Along with being a great Inquisitor, Radamuck thought, Grumpet T. Paddymeyer would make a pretty fine father.

But he would have to make sure he got back to Jessica in one piece, or she would make sure he was turned into a goblin's spawn.

***

After visiting the dwarves in the clerical—the clerics had said all four were progressing and had even found a spell that would save the voice of the dwarf Frampton sliced—Radamuck held a council with his high advisors. Included in the meeting were Grumpet, Aidan and Yanos, all there at Radamuck's request.

He wanted to hear their thoughts on what to do about the chalice.

"As you explain it, Yer Highness," Fib Niosh said authoritatively, "the spy Frampton is goin' to attack Lowbridge to end the dwarf civilization and steal the chalice. Well, he has already stolen the chalice; why should he bother to end the civilization of the dwarves?"

"Probably to scare Radamuck into keeping away from him," Grumpet pointed out. "I have heard the tales; those who want the chalice will turn to idle threats and empty promises of war and destruction to the chalice holder's homeland if they do not acquiesce to their wishes."

"Then it is all for naught; we do not have the chalice any longer, and, if I may be so bold in saying, Yer Highness, yeh haven't decided to send out any more patrols after the spy to retrieve it, correct?" queried Fib.

Turning his head toward the steward, Radamuck answer, "That is correct. We've nothin' to gain by sendin' me dwarves into harm's way, against an enemy that doesn't want to be found. It was me mistake and me pride that got in the way of me judgment.

"However, I want it to be known that if the time comes where the spy reveals himself, with or without an army at his behest, the dwarves of Lowbridge will be ready to fight, to die, and to cause as much damage to the enemy as I know they can," Radamuck said gruffly.

The council nodded.

"Yeh have already ordered the army to double their patrols, Yer Highness. Should we be preparin' for imminent war?" Fib asked.

Radamuck thought about this question for a while. To say yes would signal to his council he had grown worried about a potential threat. To say no would be to say he had grown lackadaisical in his thinking, misleading the dwarves under his rule and giving them a false sense of security.

But most of all, he had grown worried an invasion would hurt Lowbridge in more than just his own hard pride. Radamuck had innocent lives at stake, especially the innocent life of his son, not to mention the women and other dwarflings who did not fight in the army.

After thinking, Radamuck gave his answer to the council.

"Aye. We don't know when the enemy is comin', we don't know how many there will be. But as always, the dwarves of Lowbridge will be ready to fight for our city and our people. Let them come and let them feel the wrath of Dausonne! Let them come and taste the bite of our axes, or our swords! Let them come and see that it takes more than guts to attack Lowbridge! Let them come," Radamuck said, before walking toward the exit of his chamber. The members of the council who were seated immediately came to their feet as he passed.

But when he got to the exit, Radamuck stopped and turned back to those in the room. Looking at each of them with his hardened stare, he exclaimed, "Prepare for battle!"

Then he turned and hurried out of the room to the murmurs of ascent.

Grumpet, Aidan, and Yanos all followed Radamuck out of the room, Yanos running to keep up with the other three. Radamuck did not speak, his eyes forward, intense and focused.

He led them to his own sleeping chamber, where Radasack slept.

"I have to contact Kirkrik Dannell. I think I now know what he meant when he said we'll be facin' realm-altering events in the near future. And this blasted amulet has been burnin' me pocket for the last half an hour!" he said with a scream, taking the red hot crystal amulet out of his pocket, blistering his hands.

His scream woke Radasack, who immediately started crying. Yanos brought him a silver carved rattle and shook it for him. Radasack stopped crying immediately.

Tossing the amulet back and forth between his hands, Radamuck set the bauble to a stand. Using his fingernail to open the amulet, he got it open and jumped back in fright.

Instead of the oval face of Kirkrik Dannell, staring back at him were two bulbous eyes, and Radamuck wondered if the amulet had fallen into the wrong hands. But then he realized that the amulet had not fallen into the wrong hands, and nothing bad had happened to his wizard friend.

The amulet happened to fall into a pair of flippers, and not the pair of flippers Radamuck was too keen to see right now.

"Oh, it's you, beard boy. About time you answered our call; we were beginning to wonder if you drowned in your own ale. You know, I was just telling Kirkrik a day ago that you drink too —" Edison said, before Radamuck interrupted exasperatingly.

"Edison, put Kirkrik on, this is important," Radamuck said.

"Oh, it's important to you now, but not important to you for the past half an hour. Well, for your information, I'm holding Kirkrik hostage. If you want him released, you'll have to pay me ten sacks of gold and twenty sacks of jewels. Oh yeah, the raven wants a sack of gold for telling Kirkrik you were on the way—" Edison continued, but Radamuck's yell interrupted the bullfrog yet again.

"Just put the wizard on, yeh confounded reptile!" Radamuck bellowed, again waking Radasack. Yanos shook the rattle again while looking at the bullfrog in the amulet.

Edison sighed.

"Oh, all right. I can never have any fun with you, can I, beard boy? Kirkrik will be right with you, he's in the other room," he said, before he filled his froggy lungs full of air and screamed, "Kirkrik! The bearded wonder on the amulet for you! And I can't say I'm happy to hear from him."

Edison's eyes disappeared and soon the oval face of Kirkrik Dannell came into view. He was wearing an oversized sock on his head; it looked like he had been asleep.

"Did I wake yeh, Kirkrik?" Radamuck asked when he saw what the wizard was wearing.

"No, you didn't. I had waited and waited and waited for you to answer my call, but the magical answering device didn't pick up. I'm thinking you didn't set it up properly?" Kirkrik said, and, when he saw the look of utter confusion on the dwarf's face, he let the matter drop. "But anyway, I have news for you, Radamuck. I've learned of a plot that will affect you, Grumpet, and every living soul in Lowbridge, for that matter. I had known something was brewing when you were in my chateau, however I was unprepared to give it to you until I knew it was fact," Kirkrik continued.

"Very well, very well, what should I be awaitin'? I have the dwarves preparin' for a war, but we don't know when it will be comin'," Radamuck said.

"I don't know either, and yes, that disturbs me. You would have thought they would have gone over that part of the plan and let me in on their thoughts, but they haven't gone over any of those kinds of specifics and I'm really mad about that! The person is calling all evil to the Stolidall Caverns so they can launch an assault upon Lowbridge that will be remembered for all eternity, for they plan to attack the remainder of the realms when they defeat you," Kirkrik said, the hat flopping into his face. His eyes went from Radamuck to the hat, to Radamuck and back to the hat again, before he finally grabbed the tail of the sock and flipped it over his shoulder.

"Yeh said he's callin' all evil to him in the Stolidall Caverns? We were there before we met yeh! We're lucky we cleaned out that cache of weapons or else they'd use them against us!" Radamuck said, awed at Aidan and Arrol's ingenuity and insight.

Again he thanked the gods for the elves' involvement in that escapade.

But the thought of Arrol not being with them at that moment panged the heartstrings of the dwarf king even more than it did when he departed outside the forest.

"What type of evil are we talkin' 'bout, Kirkrik?" Radamuck asked.

The wizard looked into the dwarf's eyes.

"The most destructive evil you can think of, my friend. This person wants to cause Lowbridge and its people as much pain and suffering as you have caused him," Kirkrik said.

The look on Radamuck's face let Kirkrik know—as well as the others in the room know—that he had absolutely no idea what Kirkrik was talking about. Any group that Radamuck and the army caused suffering ended up dead. When it came to evil and wrongdoers, they made it a point to eliminate it. There wasn't a chance that any of Radamuck's opponents could do him harm any more. They weren't among the living. His axe usually made sure of it.

Radamuck clearly thought that Kirkrik had lost his mind and that the silly old mage was clearly wrong about this.

But then again, Kirkrik Dannell was hardly ever wrong.

"Who is it, Kirkrik? Who is it that wants to cause me and me dwarves pain?"

Kirkrik looked at Radamuck first, then Aidan, and then Yanos. His intense stare stayed on Yanos.

Yanos immediately blanched.

Then, without even having to think about it, Radamuck knew. That person had threatened Yanos' life once, sending shards of electricity and lightning from the observation point on Statuary Tower down toward the halfling. The electricity had coursed through his veins and shocked every inch of flesh that he still had nightmares about it.

"You mean...?!" Yanos whispered.

Kirkrik nodded. Tears ran down Yanos' usually pink face.

Radamuck felt his heart skip a solitary beat, for understanding did more than dawn on his mind; it practically parked itself there. He looked to his nephew; Aidan frowned.

Most of all, so did Grumpet, who had cut the person down at the neck, with a powerful cut of Flad-rul. He knew why Kirkrik didn't look at him when he gave Radamuck the clue;

Kirkrik had realized that Radamuck had talked to him earlier about his destiny as the Imperial Inquisitor.

By looking at Grumpet from the start, it would have signaled to Grumpet that Kirkrik insinuated the person wanted to come after him for his death. That would have put a great deal of pressure on him, especially after learning of Krampel Paddymeyer's legacy.

But everyone knew the person had every reason to come after Radamuck, too. He had claimed the chalice from him as his own, and it was only natural that the owner wanted his property back.

But he was dead. Grumpet killed him. There was no way he could come back.

Everyone in the room, including the wide eyes of Kirkrik Dannell, looked at Grumpet. Instead of catching their gazes, Radamuck noticed the lad looked into himself, as if asking his body if it had the strength to fight him once again. This was his fight, not Radamuck's, Aidan's, or Yanos', although the dwarf felt pretty sure Yanos would like nothing better than to have the chance to drive his sword through that person's heart.

Grumpet looked up into the faces of his four friends, and spoke the four words that confirmed for everyone that Grumpet knew what he faced.

"It's Dramin. He's back."

Hearts through the room sank. Even little Radasack felt the mood shift, and not even the rattle Yanos held would hold his crying in check.

"But, how can he be back?" Yanos said, looking to Kirkrik. "Grumpet killed him, he cut off his head."

"And if he wasn't dead then, surely the tower collapsin' after I took the chalice would have done him in," Radamuck added.

They looked to Kirkrik, who usually had all the answers.

"It seems as though Victor Dramin's soul left his body before Grumpet killed him. But when the tower collapsed, it tore the soul into smaller pieces, like pebbles. It took quite a while for his soul to come together and resemble a man. He currently does not have a 'body,' per se, but that could change," Kirkrik said.

"I'll have to inform our council that war is comin' soon," Radamuck said. "We'll need to prepare our dwarves quickly for what could be our last fight."

Kirkrik nodded, but then spoke again.

"I will make certain that it is not your last fight, Radamuck Rosar. I have already taken the initiative. I have contacted many different realms to come to your aid. Lord Baeron is sending many elves, including your friend Arrol Goldleaf, to help you fend off the attack of Dramin. I have contacted many other civilizations, many that have traded with Lowbridge in the past, and have also responded positively.

"Lowbridge has many long, lost friends, Radamuck Rosar. You are about to see just how many of them will return the favors of your predecessors," Kirkrik continued. "And I will, of course, aid you in your hour of need."

Radamuck seemed pleased, but there was still one thing he needed to tell Kirkrik.

"If this is a war over the chalice, Dramin should know I don't have it anymore. It was stolen two nights ago," he said.

"Yes, I know this. But Dramin doesn't care about the chalice, that I know of. It could be he comes across it before you do. However, should you defeat him, it should be your utmost priority to find the chalice and then destroy it," Kirkrik cautioned, before he turned his head and started to yell at Edison for getting into his sun-blocking cream.

Nodding at the wizard's words, Radamuck turned to his friends and ordered Aidan to tell the watch to keep their eyes peeled for both enemies and friendly folk, for both would be approaching soon. He told Yanos to go find Lady Rosar, before he told Grumpet to have the cooks start preparing meals for more warriors than Lowbridge has seen in ages, then to find a quiet spot and think about the upcoming battle.

Grumpet nodded, bowed to the king, and then set off to do his bidding.

Radamuck thought that at least one person on the side of good will be well rested prior to this fight.

Chapter 7

As the days passed, Frampton grew increasingly overconfident that the dwarves would not find him.

But with that overconfidence, all alone in the woods, came the jitters.

He felt as if something watched him, but he wasn't sure by what. It might have been a dwarf or a being unseen, but whatever it was gave him the creeps. He jumped at small noises and started keeping the chalice closer to him. His sword spent more time out of its sheath than in it, as he drew it to fend off a surprise attack that never came.

Frampton know that his mind had slowly grown unhinged by this, but he tried to pull himself together. After all, he needed to be calm—losing his nerve was not an option.

Four days after stealing the chalice from Radamuck, Frampton sat alone on a rock in a clearing, staring at the chalice. After running from the dwarves and what appeared to be his own shadow, Frampton finally had the time to just look at it, to marvel in its beauty. His eyes passed over the jewel-laden brim, which sparkled and hypnotized the spy. His hands caressed the cup lovingly, his fingerprints remembering every curve.

Then he heard twigs snap, and his fascination for the object abruptly ended.

Without thinking, Frampton put the chalice down and looked around for the sign of an oncoming predator. His eyes darted around, peering through the trees surrounding the small clearing, but he didn't find the twig-snapper.

But then the twigs snapped again, and, by the sound of it, much closer than he originally realized. He drew his sword quickly as he turned around, as he had heard the twigs break to the left and behind him.

No one—not even a bird—was there.

Still, that nagging sense of insecurity ate at him. He didn't mind being the most sought-after man now that he had the chalice, but he preferred to do battle with visible enemies, not unseen ones.

As his expression went from fierce to curious at the sign of no one there, he relaxed his guard, dropping his hands down, lowering his sword down to his knee.

Then, without warning, he felt the hands on his neck. Invisible fingers tightened around his throat, threatening to choke him to death. Dropping his sword to the ground, his own hands grabbed at the unseen vise around his neck, trying to pry them away from it, attempting to open up his air passages.

After a few seconds of this, Frampton knew he had failed. He had failed to keep himself out of danger and knew this failure would be the death of him. He started punching at the invisible arms, trying desperately to find a way to stop the assault, even as his vision grew fuzzy.

But then, the invisible hands picked him up and carried fast to a tree, his back nearly breaking under the pressure as soon as he met the wide trunk. He felt sure he now bled from the back of the head; it might have been sweat from his own fear, though, as he felt trickles of something liquid running down the back of his neck. The pressure then increased to the near popping of his brain stem, until he heard words he thought would save him from further harm.

"Let him go."

The voice sounded hollow, as if it had been badly tuned and wasn't perfectly clear. But the invisible hand relaxed its grip, however not letting go completely.

"I said let him go!"

The voice became deeper and more serious this time, and, as soon as the order came again, Frampton felt the constricting hand release its invisible talons from his throat. He immediately rubbed his neck, all while inhaling what seemed like gallons of oxygen. He coughed several times as the tears ran down his face.

"Sometimes trolls do not make for good enforcers. They seem to think destruction is the best way to do things, even though their leader told them death is not an option here. My apologies for its behavior," the disembodied voice said with a slight twinge of sarcasm.

Swallowing more air, Frampton looked all around for the disembodied voice, as well as the troll which had mysteriously grabbed him from nowhere and flung him unceremoniously into the tree trunk. He then heard a grunt from his right, and immediately knew the troll was still nearby.

"Where are you? Who are you?" Frampton asked, a bit of fear showing behind the usually calm demeanor.

"You shouldn't have the Chalice of Obloeron out where anyone can see it," the voice said, as if coming from the wind. It had clearly ignored the spy's questions. "Having a powerful magical object like that out in clear sight can attract such dangerous beings to your presence. They could even kill you for it." Then, in an undertone to the spy, the voice said, "You should put it away before more than just trolls come along."

The spy again looked nervously around, trying to find not only the trolls and the strange voice, but he also looked for additional attackers. Seeing none, he heeded the voice's request and walked, albeit gingerly, back to where the chalice lay.

He was not three steps from the tree when he felt his balance falter; the invisible troll had stuck its foot out and had tripped Frampton. The spy's chin hit the ground hard and seconds later, tasted copper.

As Frampton hit the ground, the voice became enraged.

"I told you to leave him alone! He is essential to our plans, and he is not to be touched again by any of you!" the voice said, malice pouring forth from its unseen mouth.

At those words, Frampton froze. Alarm bells went off in his mind. Partially because he had been tripped up by an unseen troll, but now knew more invisible beasts stood in the clearing, if he believed the invisible voice.

Despite that, Frampton felt terribly alone, more alone than he had these past few days, when it was just him and the chalice and a plan to stay alive.

It felt like he had none of those things now.

"I asked you to please put the chalice away, my friend," the voice spoke softly and soothingly. "As soon as it is out of sight, I will reveal myself to you, as well as a plan that I think; no, I know you will like the plan. I guarantee it."

Frampton got back to his feet gingerly. Blood now streamed from a busted lip, which he tried to dab with his black cloak.

He walked slowly with his eyes moving all around, hoping to see the identity of the observers.

They never appeared, and Frampton picked the chalice up from the twig-littered clearing floor. He then secured it under his belt so it wouldn't leave him.

Then the voice spoke again.

"Good, very good. Now behold me, but mind your eyes!" it said, and as Frampton turned to where he heard the voice, he saw a shimmering light appear to his right.

It was bright, which prompted Frampton to shield his eyes from the glare. The light elongated and stretched, until it resembled the body of a human. The light then dissipated, and, where a human should have been, there was only a misty figure.

All around the clearing, trolls and orcs also materialized from out of thin air. They looked murderous; the trolls had huge clubs in their hands, while the orcs looked at the spy with loathing. The misty being smiled, although it looked to the spy that he scowled. Frampton stood with his mouth slightly open as he narrowed his eyes.

"Who are you? You have yet to answer that question," Frampton demanded, looking at the misty figure in front of him.

The figure gave a laugh, a laugh that seemed to have come from its ghostly feet.

"I think the question you should ask, my friend, is not 'Who are you?' I think it would be appropriate to ask, 'What were you?'" the voice said, with a slight sneer as it paced the clearing.

That question set Frampton on his heels.

Am I looking at a ghost? he thought.

"Very well then, what were you?" he asked cautiously.

The ghostly image turned to regard him.

"I was once a man. A wizard, actually, and I was to be the greatest wizard in the world. But I was killed not too long ago by the human you faced after stealing the chalice," it said, pointing at the spy's waist. Frampton's left hand automatically went to his waist to touch the chalice through his cloak. "The dwarves destroyed my home by removing the chalice from its base; none of them died in the attempt, and I want retribution for that. I want to make them all suffer for causing the destruction of my home and for thinking of challenging me.

"And you, my friend, will help me in my cause," it said, looking directly into the spy's eyes.

Frampton blanched under the stare the dead wizard gave him.

"H-How w-w-will I help you?" the spy stammered.

"Very simply," the wizard said, as if the reason were clear as crystal and he was the only one who saw it. "Your battle with the Sword of the South proved to me you have the power to defeat Grumpet T. Paddymeyer in swordplay. It was he who defeated me by cutting off my head; I want you to cut off more than his head as payback."

Frampton heard the words and yet he couldn't believe them. The wizard wanted him to kill the human, but there was a chance that he would be killed, as well.

But there was also a fact that the spy hadn't taken into consideration before: he did battle against the Sword of the South—and had barely escaped with his life. If he could somehow get the sword into his possession...

"I fought the Sword of the South?! And survived?" Frampton said in disbelief.

The wizard came closer.

"Yes, you did, my dear friend. And I'm sure you know what happened fifty years ago surrounding that sword," it whispered.

Frampton did know; he knew that sword had a great impact in the southlands' history and that the wielder of it back then had been offered the Inquisitorship for defeating Cairn Ford. Frampton knew the wielder had declined the title, and the southlanders had refused to name another.

If I were to capture that sword, I could walk right into the southlands and rule it without question. Who needs Briskey Bucktooth when I have the entirety of the southlands? Frampton smiled.

He then looked at the wizard and saw him smiling, too. It occurred to Frampton that it was extremely possible that the wizard had the ability to read his thoughts.

I will have to tread carefully around this mage, Frampton thought, for he realized the wizard has already attempted to control him through his mind. *And*, Frampton thought, *had someone lesser than the wizard attempted to control my thoughts, they would find death quick.*

But it was the thought of great power that prompted Frampton to ask, "If I help you defeat him and I capture the sword, what do I get out of all this?"

The wizard looked back at the spy and gave him a devilish smile.

"Well, I think you and I will be attached for quite some time. You will get a bit of my power and possession of the sword. I think that is reward enough for anyone."

Frampton looked upon the spectral form of Victor Dramin and saw him still smiling. Just from that smile, Frampton knew he was in too deep before he had even started.

***

Battle preparations went on throughout the cavernous city.

Dwarves mined precious silver for shields and for mail, while clerics made sure that they had plenty of curative remedies for whatever came their way.

Radamuck gave orders to Fib Niosh to make sure every contingency was available, and while the steward carried out those orders, Radamuck made sure to spend every possible waking moment with Lady Rosar and Radasack.

When he wasn't working, Aidan spent quality time was Prestillia, and when he wasn't working, Yanos spent quality time stuffing his halfling belly with twice the amount of food and mead the dwarves ate and drank.

As some prepared for battle in their own ways, Grumpet T. Paddymeyer got his mind focused in his own special way. He found a small isolated chamber, free of dwarven clutter and debris. This would be a perfect place to spend his free time.

Grumpet was alone, with Flad-rul out of the scabbard and weaving it back and forth. He concentrated on his fighting skills, which he felt needed a little brush-up. He never wanted to be off his guard like he was against Frampton, even though Radamuck had told him it wasn't his fault.

Still upset at himself over that incident, Grumpet heard nothing of Radamuck's reassurances echoing through his mind.

Flad-rul sang and blazed a trail of flame as Grumpet made feints, jabs, and slices through the air. Holding the powerful sword in both hands, the knuckles had nearly turned white in his tanned hands as he gripped it. For many hours he practiced, swinging the sword with all his might against an invisible opponent. He sparred with empty air over and over again, anticipating moves a real opponent would make. Grumpet turned his wrists to the right to block what would have been an attack at the legs, but knew that *Flad-rul* and its four-and-a-half foot long blade would stop that threat.

He twirled the blade in his hands before circling it above his head, then coming across his body to the left. Grumpet made soft grunting noises as he made his moves, his eyes following his sword and making the noises as it stopped, imagining the clash of the steel against steel.

He had his face set as he concentrated on his style of fighting, but occasionally the warrior's concentration slipped. He thought of past duels. Of how he let Daniel Soutanic's taunts provoke him into fighting against him. Of how he had fought Victor Dramin on several levels of Statuary Tower, parrying and riposting the wizard's excellent moves.

Of how he had let Frampton escape through a small breach in the wall when he clearly had the spy beat!

Grumpet gnashed his teeth at the thought, his brow furrowed, his eyes alight with fire. He swung harder and faster, not over-swinging, but swinging just enough to put his invisible opponent on its heels.

He then calmed down, remembering to keep his frustration with that battle out of his mind. As Krampel Paddymeyer had taught him long ago, fighting with a clear head and with his emotions in check is the sign of a great warrior; however, one that fights with his emotions running wild and uncontrollable can cause unintentional pain to those close to him.

Grumpet shrugged his shoulders, shaking off the thoughts of the spy's cowardice. He began his sparring again, slashing and cutting at the air vigorously and slowly, just like Jessica had in the smithies back in Kayiko. She had found that special sword while working with Grumpet in the smithies, had taken it and kept it hidden until just prior to the Battle of Kayiko. She had taken the initiative and sharpened her own sword and was busy cutting at the air when Yanos Kingsfoil had interrupted her spar-with-nothing session, parrying a down-and-reverse thrust from her sword.

She had pleaded with Yanos not to tell Grumpet that she had done this, but Grumpet already knew; he said he was proud of her. Radamuck, at Grumpet's request, had put Jessica in charge of the township while the men and dwarves fought against the evil wizard's orcs and trolls.

Grumpet smiled at the memory, which seemed so long ago to him.

He didn't hear the soft footsteps approach him from behind, as he concentrated on his form. He sliced horizontally from right to left, before he turned his wrists and made a one-handed swipe down to his right.

The blade connected hard with steel, causing the chamber around him to echo with the sound.

Grumpet smiled to himself, knowing he had just done the same thing Jessica did when she practiced in the smithies.

"You know, Yanos," Grumpet said without looking back, "Jessica was right way back when. You do have a nasty habit up popping up unexpectedly. Why did you have to interrupt me while I'm practicing?"

He got no answer. Grumpet then turned to look where his sword collided with the other. Yanos Kingsfoil was not standing there, but someone else was.

And although Grumpet only needed to look at the sword to tell who stood there, he had to give the soldier a once over.

Where Yanos' face should have been were a pair of knees, and not the wide, bony knees of a man. They were smaller, and as Grumpet's eyes lingered upward, he was stunned to find the knees attached to a pair of supple thighs. The thighs were partially covered by the same type of corset Grumpet wore, and the person also wore a coat of chain mail. On the person's head were silky blonde tresses that cascaded down past the person's shoulders, and had the calmest blue eyes Grumpet had ever seen.

They were eyes Grumpet only remembered in a dream, and it felt as if his every dream had just come true all at once.

He couldn't believe it. He was stunned.

And she looked stunning.

Jessica Paddymeyer stood in front of him, parrying his sword with her own gleaming blade, a smile decorating her delicate, porcelain features.

Chapter 8

Grumpet didn't feel himself rise from the crouch he was in. He didn't feel his hand let go of *Flad-rul*, and didn't hear it clang off the stone floor.

He only concentrated on her eyes.

Grumpet's face had broken into a grin, and the look on her face matched it.

Jessica spread her arms as wide, dropping her own sword to the floor as Grumpet's body reached her. He grabbed her and pulled her close to him, his massive arms wrapping around her tiny frame twice.

Jessica's arms, small as they were, wrapped around Grumpet's thick neck. He picked her up and spun around, felt her body squeezed tightly by his bear hug.

As they held each other, both cried soft tears that splashed off each other's cheeks and onto the other's shoulders. They were happy tears; Jessica's for finally seeing Grumpet again, Grumpet's for being surprised as he was.

Finally, the pair released each other from their embrace, but their faces came closer as they kissed passionately. Their lips came together in a collision that warmed them and expressed every feeling in their being for the other. And when they broke away, the smiles on their faces told the other that is wasn't a dream; they were finally together again.

Grumpet's smile turned to an astonished look.

"How? When! How did you get here, my love?" Grumpet stammered incredulously.

Jessica, who had been a reserved woman back in Kayiko, giggled lightly at her love's questions. It wasn't something she would have done back home, and somehow this new attitude of hers attracted Grumpet to her even more.

"Well, we were requested to come here. The Defensive Brigade, I mean. A wizard came to speak with Madal and we came as fast as we could. The wizard provided us with Pegasi to make our trip easier," Jessica said.

"We're here to help the dwarves after they helped us," Madal Johannson added, as he walked up behind her.

Grumpet's smile became wider at the sight of his friend. He immediately embraced and clapped the man on the back in welcome.

"That's great! I'm sure Radamuck will appreciate the reinforcements," he said to Madal, but his attention returned to Jessica's lovely face.

"You're going to fight?" Grumpet asked her.

Jessica simply nodded.

"Yes, my love. I feel healthier than I ever did, and, even though the wizard is dead, I want to inflict some punishment on evil creatures in his stead," she said.

Grumpet's face suddenly became grave; they hadn't known the wizard had returned.

"The wizard has returned, Jessica," he said.

After a minute in which both Jessica and Madal looked at Grumpet with startled looks, it was Madal who spoke first.

"Are you sure? You said you killed him."

"Yes, I said that. But his spirit lingered over his remains and has returned. We do not yet know if he has reclaimed a body, but this we do know: he will be as dangerous as he was then, if not more dangerous. Jessica, are you sure you want to fight?" Grumpet asked.

It wasn't a question he would have asked a few months ago, but Jessica had proven herself to Grumpet in ways he couldn't believe. She had taken the initiative to sharpen her own blade and had led the people of Kayiko while the Battle of Kayiko was ongoing. She had even saved Yanos Kingsfoil from death at the hands of orcs, even when it put her own life in jeopardy. Yanos ended up saving her, but that didn't stop her from picking up a sword again.

"There is no question about it, I want to fight. After all, my love, I'm a lieutenant now. I have to set a good example for the rest of the army, right?" Jessica said, and laughed as Grumpet's mouth opened slightly at her announcement.

"I made her a lieutenant a few days after you departed, my friend," Madal explained, but Grumpet waved him off, a way of saying an explanation was unnecessary.

"That's wonderful," Grumpet said, looking at his love with admiration in his eyes.

"I'm pretty amazed myself," she said. "When the wizard had talked to Madal and told him it was the dwarves who needed help, I immediately volunteered to join the fight because I knew that was where you would be."

Grumpet smiled again, even wider this time, and Jessica's smile echoed his. The moved in to kiss again, and she had to take in air as Grumpet's kiss completely took the breath away from her.

When the pair broke apart, Grumpet said, "Come on. We have to find Radamuck and tell him the good news."

He picked up *Flad-rul* and sheathed it, before picking up Jessica's sword and handing it to her, handle-first. She accepted it and, with a right-handed twirl and a flourish that impressed her husband, Jessica put her sword in the scabbard with a snap.

Grumpet whistled, admiring his wife's ability with the blade. She had watched him fight and show off many times; he was pleased she could mimic his moves easily.

"After you both," Jessica said, stepping aside to allow this to pass.

But Grumpet grabbed her by the arm and shook his head. At her confused look, he said, "Together."

Jessica smiled, then stepped between the two men. The three friends then exited the chamber and walked down the corridor, looking for the dwarf king.

They found him a short while later, conversing with Fib Niosh and some of his other commanders. They were wondering what reinforcements would aid the dwarves when Radamuck saw Madal.

The dwarf howled with delight as the human entered. He rushed over to his friend and greeted him with a dwarven hug. Radamuck then turned to Jessica and bowed to her, before giving her a hug, as well.

"I knew yeh'd come to help us, I did," Radamuck said. "I'm sure it was Kirkrik Dannell who told yeh to come to our aid?"

"Yes, Radamuck. The wizard spoke to us days ago, he provided us transport, and we got here as quick as we could. But we brought more than just our army," Madal said to Radamuck, before turning to Grumpet. "Daniel Soutanic has returned to Kayiko," he said, and immediately Grumpet's face became set. "He has taken over control of the township; he murdered other councilors and brought an army of his own. Trolls, mostly. He refused to allow us to help the dwarves after Radamuck had gone over his head countless times. So we rounded up a great deal of the elderly, the infirm and our women and children," Madal continued, "and just left."

Grumpet couldn't help but notice the sly smile that crept over his friend's face as he said this.

"Aye, Soutanic was goin' to come back; we knew this," Radamuck said, his hands on his hips. "The people of Kayiko are welcome to stay in Lowbridge in perpetuity or until yeh decide to return to yer home to supplant Soutanic. Although, I may be biased me friends, but Lowbridge is a much prettier country; much warmer, too. I'm sure me councilors will find beddin' and food for the villagers after their long journey."

Madal bowed to the king and, after an unspoken order, was led out of the room by Fib Niosh. It would be Fib's job to get sleeping arrangements made for Kayiko's townspeople.

"It looks as if yer Defensive Brigade is the first to answer Kirkrik's summons," Radamuck said. While he looked happy about that, Grumpet noticed an unseen dread creeping through the dwarf's face.

"I'm sure more will come. Any word from him since he last spoke to you?" Grumpet asked, but Radamuck shook his head.

"Nay, I'm sure he's tryin' to convince people to come here. I'm thankin' the gods for bringin' him to the dwarves; he's doing all he can to help us. I'm hoping that Lord Baeron sends a battalion of elves; we could definitely use expert marksmen in this battle," Radamuck continued, before remembering his manners. "Yeh should go and spend time with yer wife, Grumpet. And I should go spend time with me wife and me child."

Grumpet bowed to the king, who left Grumpet and Jessica alone.

"So my love," Grumpet asked, turning to his wife. "We're finally alone. How should we spend this time together?"

Jessica looked at her husband and said, “Well darling, we never did consummate our marriage. Maybe we should find the time to do just that.”

Grumpet noticed the torches glittering in her eyes as she said this, not to mention the devilish smile that she wore.

“I have waited for this for many months, my love. Let’s do this properly,” he said, sweeping her into his arms and rushing for his sleeping chamber.

He hoped they would not be disturbed for many, many hours.

***

The new alliance of Victor Dramin and Frampton retreated from the woods to Stolidall Caverns; to speed up the departure, a troll had picked Frampton up, slung the spy over his shoulder, and rushed off. When they had arrived, Frampton was cold and hungry; Dramin had a troll fetch him warm mutton from the flames.

It was in the caverns that Frampton, after eating, discovered the size of Dramin’s army. Already, many different tribes of orc, gnome, and troll had gathered, but the spy saw many of these made new warriors through a spell Dramin had perfected over the months.

The wizard smiled. Things were going perfectly to plan.

“It is called blood sharing,” Dramin explained. “My master taught it to me. A useful spell that takes a creature’s blood to create an identical warrior to itself. I use magic and spells, chanting over the blood as it takes form into the warrior. If you’ve studied your history, you’ll realize this is the same methodology that Cairn Ford used in the Great Imperial Wars. This army will be larger than the one I had attack Kayiko, and significantly stronger than the one that defended my home from the dwarves.”

Dramin sneered and told Frampton about the battle.

“The orcs had fallen hard,” he said, “followed by the trolls. When the elves arrived, I had to find a way to combat them. I conjured the elementals via powerful magic—but they were not powerful enough to stop the enemy.

"And then Paddymeyer came. The human had the speed and the size to defeat me."

Frampton caught a twitch in the wizard's ghostly face. He saw, quite clearly, Dramin's perceived anger over his supposed superiority. He was a wizard, after all, and wizards were blessed with infinite knowledge and power.

But as the spy listened, he learned the wizard still couldn't defeat Paddymeyer at hand-to-hand combat, even though he kept up with the whirling blade his opponent had used.

The blade he used to separate the wizard's head from the rest of his body.

Dramin reached up and felt his neck, right at the spots where Grumpet had severed his neck.

"This army will do my will well. They will overwhelm the dwarves by sheer numbers alone, slaughtering them and leaving no being alive," Dramin said. Frampton saw a sneer crossing the wizard's ghostly face.

Dramin looked to him, and Frampton saw triumph and a lack of pity in his misty eyes.

"Look at all of this, my friend," the wizard said with a wave of his hand. "The army continues to grow in number. They will be armed in time, and they possess the killer instinct embedded in each of their psyches—they could use their hands and could do enough damage with them than with a sword. They know no other way; they destroy things because it is in their nature to do so. And they will do that to the dwarves. I have foreseen it."

Frampton walked closer to the wizard and peered down at the cavern full of deadly creatures. "Yes, but we should be moving faster. The longer we wait, the more time the dwarves will have to mobilize their defenses. They have already been breached once, and I can assure you they will not be so incautious when the next time comes."

Without turning to the spy, Dramin answered him quite casually.

"Yes, I know. It is what I want. I want the dwarves to mobilize. I want them to call for aid. I want them to feel threatened. I have as much time as I want to, my friend. You see, I am dead, which means I have an eternity to attack the rabble-rousing dwarves if and when I so choose.

"If there is one thing I have learned in the few short months I have been dead is that patience is the realms' greatest virtue," Dramin continued. "It is something that should be used to one's advantage. Now, while you showed little patience after the dwarves and Paddymeyer had decimated your band of men by stealing the chalice, you in fact set events into motion that will lead to their impatience, and ultimately their demise."

Frampton blinked curiously, as if he didn't understand his reasoning.

But then it dawned on him.

"So if they are waiting for us to come, that means they will grow impatient. They will want to get the war started," he said.

Dramin gave the spy a wispy smile.

"Correct. Dwarves like a good scrap, and when they are threatened, they want the fight to come to them as much as they want to bring it. Their impatience will grow and wane, and they will become complacent. That is when we shall attack. When they are least expecting it, we shall bring the full force of our army upon them."

"Still, I don't see why you do not help with the blood sharing process. You're a wizard, after all," Frampton said.

"I do not believe that I gave you permission to question my motives, my friend," Dramin said, turning and getting as close as he could to the spy without going through him. The spy immediately recoiled in fright. Dramin then eased the venom, and continued. "However, as you are my partner, I shall tell you my motives. I prefer this way because it is the only way I can do this—for now. Without flesh or fingers, physical magic of this type would be a strain on my already weakened form. Besides, where am I going to find a willing person to allow me to take over their soul?" Dramin smiled.

Frampton immediately felt fear, and he knew he hadn't hid this tell from his eyes—just before his sword flew out of its scabbard. The curved steel blade snapped out of its sheath and flew right through the corporeal form of the wizard.

With a cavern-rocking laugh, Dramin leaned forward and grasped the spy, forcing him to drop his sword to the ground, by the neck, before picking him up and placing him over the edge of the ledge. All he had to do was release his misty grip and the spy would plummet to his death.

Frampton's eyes bugged out as he felt only air beneath him. He tried not to look down, but as soon as he thought that he shouldn't look down, he did anyway. He felt sweat pouring down his face, and he stank as nervous pheromones flowed freely from his pores. He felt the invisible fingers of Victor Dramin constrict around his throat.

The wizard pulled him closer, with his toes grazing the edge of the ledge, and spoke soft words the spy had to strain his ears to hear.

"I am warning you now, my friend. You should watch your step and mind your attitude toward me, or you shall find yourself donating more than you will ever bargain for the war effort," Dramin sneered, before turning and hurling the spy into the stone wall behind him.

Chapter 9

Swords clashed in a chamber far from Lowbridge's central passage system. The combatants, a man and woman, two people who knew each other more intimately than any pair in the realms, matched each other's blows stroke for stroke.

But it was the woman who knew the man's fighting style rather than the other way around.

Grumpet and Jessica sparred hard, measuring each other's moves and exchanging them in harmony. Every so often, she came up with a move that stunned him, and she would retreat after making it, a smile on her face.

It was completely the opposite when he tried to fool her with a flurry of strikes and swipes. He went low with his sword and then upward, only to find her counter with a vicious parry. She then turned her sword over and tried to aim her blade for his side, but luckily for him, he got *Flad-rul* over just in the nick of time.

Then Jessica shocked Grumpet. Twirling the blade in a circle above her head, she chopped at his left side, bringing the blade down. When his sword blocked it, she twirled the sword once and brought it over to the man's right.

Using precision strikes, Grumpet intensified his attack, marking his wife's moves, trying to find a hole in her defense. Seeing none, he decided to make one.

Stepping back, he drew the sword that Aidan Rosar had loaned him for the fight with Victor Dramin. He smiled as he held both swords, *Flad-rul* in his right, the borrowed sword in the left.

"Oh, now you're getting tricky," laughed Jessica, as she saw how her husband would now to test her. She had the sword down, her defenses lowered.

"Oh yes, my love. Time to see if you can really handle that sword well. You're good at deflecting one sword. Let's see how you handle two!"

And Grumpet set on the offensive, noticing her flaw, yelling as he swiped *Flad-rul* first, coming in from the right. Even before she got her sword up to parry, he brought the other sword in from the left.

Jessica's sword was not quick enough to anticipate the strike; as she parried *Flad-rul*, she tried to get her own blade over in time to intercept Aidan's sword. But Grumpet's powerful swing was enough to knock the blade out of her hand, sending it clanging away on the stone floor.

"You are not anticipating. Think! I have two swords, and I will use them both! You had your sword at ease to start; it is unwise to have your defenses down, even in sparring. Be vigilant!" Grumpet admonished softly, as Jessica picked her sword off the ground.

"Okay, let's try it again," she said, holding her blade two-handed in front of her, her eyes on either side of the weapon, staring right into the warrior standing three paces away.

Swinging the blades low, Grumpet came up with the left-hand sword first, coming over in an arc that Jessica blocked easily, before she quickly brought her weapon over to the left to block *Flad-rul*.

Grumpet smiled inwardly, keeping his concentration on his wife's sword arm. His swipes and slices came quicker, making her work harder to deflect the blades that whirled in front of her, until finally she put every ounce of strength that she could muster and knocked Aidan's sword from Grumpet's grip.

Looking shocked, Grumpet recovered quickly and grasped *Flad-rul* in both hands. He cut faster and faster at his wife. She blocked everything, until she swung horizontally, knocking *Flad-rul* aside. She then threw a kick into his stomach, sending her husband reeling backward.

Grumpet dropped *Flad-rul* as he fell to the ground. He looked up at his wife, who walked over to him and placed the pointed tip of her sword right at his neck.

"Gosh, now I know how Soutanic felt," Grumpet said, before Jessica smiled and removed the sword's edge from her beloved's body. She extended her hand and pulled the burly warrior to his feet. "You must have learned some of those things from watching me over the years."

Jessica looked up into her husbands' eyes.

"Yes. Watching you fight, just in practice, has taught me a great deal. But I have also honed my own skills and added things to my repertoire that you could only imagine," she responded.

Grumpet gave a small guffaw at her words.

"Maybe the student will have to teach the teacher now," he said, earning a laugh from Jessica. "I am greatly impressed, my love, with your fighting skills. I promise I will continue to teach you how to fight, to make you an even better warrior."

Jessica smiled and, after sheathing her blade, grabbed him around the middle, pulling his body toward hers in a hug. He leaned down and kissed her.

As Grumpet picked up his sword from the ground, a faint horn blew from the outside of Lowbridge. Grumpet was surprised he could hear it from deep within the city. It perked his ears up as he searched for the source of the sound. Jessica looked at him, confused by his confusion.

Then it dawned on him. Grumpet had heard it not that long ago, and it brought a great swelling in his chest as he recognized its call. It was the Horn of the Elves, which had sounded several months ago during the Battle of Statuary Tower.

It only meant one thing: the Bastine elves had arrived in Lowbridge.

"We must hurry," Grumpet said to Jessica, grabbing his wife's hand and pulling her toward the exit. They rushed along the corridor, joining up with the main system of tunnels, winding their way through the massive, cavernous city.

Soon they found themselves overlooking the grassy plains outside Lowbridge, standing out on the battlement to the far right. There they saw the Pegasi of the elves dropping to the ground, landing with all four hooves. The elves were all dressed in full battle regalia, with quivers full of arrows.

It appeared to Grumpet that the elves appeared ready to do some serious fighting on behalf of the dwarves. The fields surrounding the capital city were full of the fair creatures; Grumpet couldn't count the number elves dismounting their Pegasi.

He looked down and saw Radamuck leading a contingent of dwarves down a center lane formed by the elves, all of whom had their helmets off and bowed at the knee toward the dwarf king, who walked out to meet an elf, Grumpet realized, was one he had only heard in tales from Arrol. Lord Baeron was there, as he flew to Lowbridge in a gilded chariot. Two powerful Pegasi led the chariot, both with gleaming white manes. Blue flames trailed it, its magic forcing the flames back for many axe lengths. It landed in the center lane, the Pegasi coming to rest right in front of Radamuck.

Grumpet saw the king look up to him and waved him down. He turned to Jessica.

"Radamuck wants me down there," he said.

"I shall wait for you, my love," Jessica said, leaning up to kiss his lips. Grumpet then headed for the main gate of the city to join the dwarf king with his guest.

When Grumpet got to where Radamuck and Baeron stood, the two friends embraced in greeting.

"Welcome to Lowbridge, Lord Baeron. I'm glad to see that Kirkrik Dannell's words reached yer ears," Radamuck said.

"They did," replied the elf lord, "and I immediately proposed to the elf council that we send aid. Arrol had only returned a few days before the summons reached us. He said you found the Chalice of Obloeron."

"Aye, I did. But it was taken the night we returned to Lowbridge. Some stinkin' spy found his way into me city, hurt me dwarves, and stole me chalice!" Radamuck said, "but we'll get the chalice back, me friend. That's a promise!"

"I assure you you will find it and reclaim it. But to more important matters," Baeron said. "Have we news of the enemy?"

Radamuck could only shake his head.

"Nay, the enemy hasn't showed its stinkin' head yet over me city. But when it does, my dwarves will be ready for 'em," Radamuck said.

"Yes, I have no doubt our combined forces will be ready," Baeron said, slightly correcting him. Radamuck heard him and nodded, but he was more concerned with the elf behind his old friend.

"Arrol!" he roared, and held his arms outstretched as the elf general walked to him, went to one knee and hugged the dwarf king. "Good to see yeh. I'm sorry to tell yeh that our quest ended up all fer naught."

"No Radamuck, it was not for naught, because we all shall re-claim the chalice for you. The evildoers will be punished, and the army that marches against Lowbridge will be defeated!"

Great cheers from the elves followed Arrol's words, as the blond-haired elf greeted Grumpet, Aidan and Yanos, the halfling jumping into his arms.

Radamuck then introduced Baeron to Fib Niosh and his councilors, before coming to a stop in front of Grumpet.

"So this is the great warrior whose wife I cured," Baeron said to Grumpet, stepping forward and grasping the man's hand. "I must relay to you that I am proud to meet the heir of the southlands. I fought with Radamuck and your grandfather during the final battle of the Great Imperial Wars. I was sorry to hear that he had passed on."

Grumpet nodded his thanks and bowed to the elf lord.

"Thank you, my lord. He passed quietly in our homeland, but handed me the sword that has awarded me a great destiny before he died. I must also give my thanks to you for healing Jessica from her illness, my lord. You have my gratitude and my service," Grumpet said, taking a knee.

But the elf lord waved the thought aside.

"No, my young friend. Your service is unnecessary; it was my pleasure to do that favor for one so beautiful and young. However, a tale or two of your grandfather's later life would suffice in exchange for my healing, and I could also tell you several tales of his exploits when he was young and full of life to match. Now I understand your wife is here? I would like to check upon her, if I may," Baeron said, and Grumpet thanked him again with a bow.

"She is inside the city, awaiting my return. We can go to her soon," Grumpet said. Baeron nodded.

Radamuck said, "My lord, we would have had a feast prepared for you and the elves, but due to the urgency of the war we have some food prepared for you."

Baeron waved off such an idea.

“I would be a poor guest, my friend, if I requested one be made. The priority of the elves is to make sure your city is properly made ready for the enemy’s attack. We have our elven bread; we will be content with that in lieu of a feast.

“However,” Baeron continued, “I wouldn’t say no to a mug of your finest mead, Radamuck.”

Radamuck laughed heartily.

***

Armies continued entering Lowbridge. Most days, an army or two, regardless of size, would come to the dwarf city to align themselves with Radamuck’s growing forces. And there were some days when no armies arrived, which did not please Radamuck much.

“How are we supposed to fight the wizard without a large enough army?” Radamuck asked anyone who would listen.

His rumblings were not necessary: with the Bastine elves among the dwarf and human forces, the combined strength of the army was greater than three thousand souls.

And he also forgot that Kirkrik Dannell had yet to arrive in Lowbridge. The wizard’s power was greater than any army, and Radamuck knew that he was just being silly.

***

Nearly a week after the elves arrived, an army of men came to Lowbridge after nightfall, resplendent in their battle armor, and every one of them astride horses. They all had shoulder-length blond hair under their full-faced helmets, and their faces were a light brown, as if the sun’s rays hardly penetrated their skin. Each carried a sword on their belts as well as a shield each. One carried a flag standard with him, bearing the mark of the lands they departed.

They were Imperialists, a group of warriors that roamed the southlands. Bereft of a true home, the Imperialists were the defenders of the lands that stretched the lower reaches of the realms.

Now, they had come to Lowbridge to help defend it.

Their leader, Semper Infidelius, was a young man who held his high stature with the nobility of kings, yet fought with the bravery of knights. However, it was his tongue that got him into great amounts of trouble over the years: Infidelius was arrogant and treated those he felt were lower than he like servants.

He led his horsemen through the throng of elves that had already camped outside the gates of the underground city and stopped outside the heavy silver entrance. Infidelius looked to the battlements and ordered the gates be opened.

"In the name of the southlands, open your gates and grant us houseroom!" he said.

The dwarves standing guard in the Homeland Defense platforms did not open the gates, but did look down upon the horsemen.

"Nay, strangers from afar, none may enter the city without the leave of Radamuck Rosar, Twenty-fourth King of Lowbridge, son of the late Ricanack the Wise. Prepare to receive the steward of the city. Hold *yer* tongue and stand back!" they said, and the horsemen edged their horses backward to allow the mighty gates to swing open.

When the gates were open far enough, Fib Niosh walked out to greet the men, followed by Grumpet.

With a huff, Semper Infidelius dismounted his steed and handed the reins of the horse to another man. He walked up to the dwarf and tried to push him out of the way.

"Excuse me, me lord, but yeh may not enter," Fib said, which caused Infidelius to stop and look down at the dwarf with contempt. "The king has not received yeh—"

"So then fetch him and have him admit us," Infidelius said haughtily. "We have traveled a long way and need bed space and food. Move quickly!"

But the steward stood his ground. Grumpet looked at the man with his eyes narrowed.

"His highness is sleeping, me lord. Yeh may find space to set up yer camp to the north side of the city, and I will have our chefs send out a good amount of provisions for yeh to replenish your strength with. I assure yeh, me lord, that King

Rosar will learn of yer arrival when he awakens," Fib countered.

The steward's words were then cut off as Infidelius drew his sword, a blade three inches wide at the hilt and four feet long, and pointed it at the dwarf's neck. Despite the pointed tip pricking his throat, Fib Niosh did not move.

"I will not be announced later than my arrival, and I should not have been met at the gate by the king's designee! I, Semper Infidelius, should have been greeted by the king himself! We are men, not elves or lower races, and deserve to be treated like the rulers we are!" he said arrogantly.

Some of the elves had heard the commotion and peeked their heads out of their tents. One had a sword drawn, just in case a fight broke out and needed to intervene.

"Our demands are to be met at once, dwarf!" Infidelius spat. "Or I will find a good reason to separate your head from the rest of your tiny, insignificant body!"

At those words, Grumpet flew into action. His right hand was a blur as he drew *Flad-rul*, snapping it out of its sheath with blazing speed. Fire trailed from the Sword of the South as it came up from the left, intercepting Infidelius's blade and knocking it from Fib Niosh's throat, a trail of flame behind it.

Several of the men on horseback muttered to each other as Grumpet's sword knocked Infidelius's weapon aside with ease. The men could not take their eyes off it.

Infidelius looked straight at it, too. His eyes went wide in shock as his sword was unceremoniously slapped aside by the human standing behind the dwarf. But then his arrogance returned, his anger rising by the second.

"Oh ho! Someone steps up for the dwarf, carrying a flaming sword, no less!" Infidelius said, looking at Grumpet with eyes like daggers. "You have taken a potential kill from me. I should take that kill out on your hide!"

Grumpet did not feel threatened by Infidelius, but used reasoning to try to disarm his opponent.

"If you claim to come to Lowbridge to defend the dwarves, then you'd be best to save your kills until the battle. There will be plenty of orc blood to spill then!" Grumpet said calmly, Flad-rul at the ready in case Infidelius decided to attack.

The southerner's eyes got even narrower at Grumpet's request. He cared not for what Grumpet had said.

"You will fight me now, or I will mark you as a coward!" he said, pulling his sword back to his shoulder, ready to do battle. Horses were then led away, getting them out of harm's way. There were more elves awake now, and the dwarves on the battlements sent word into the city of a battle brewing on the plains.

Grumpet had no intention of fighting him; he had already said he would rather the southerner put his sword away until the real battle begins.

But then the southerner spat in his direction, a load of saliva landing on Grumpet's cheek.

That made Grumpet have another thought, as he wiped the spit off his face.

He twirled the great sword in his hand and sprinted toward the man, letting his blade chop down from the right.

With flames bursting from it, *Flad-rul* came down hard, only to find it parried by the southerner. Grumpet reflexively twirled the sword, taking his left hand off the handle to twirl it and putting it back on just below the hilt as he came around to the left. The southerner blocked that advance, too. Grumpet sliced low and chopped high, locking his wrists as he swung his mighty blade. He pressed his advantage, keeping his feet moving as Infidelius backed away from Grumpet's strong attack.

Each warrior took chances, swinging their swords, looking for a chance to break through the other's defenses.

Infidelius nearly got an opening: as Grumpet's sword came in at his head, Infidelius ducked the blade and *Flad-rul* soared through the air where his opponent's head had been. Infidelius saw Grumpet's back wide open to attack, and made a perpendicular slice that would have put a long gash along Grumpet's lower trunk. But Grumpet's momentum from the over swing brought *Flad-rul* over and behind him, bisecting Infidelius's sword in the nick of time.

Infidelius cursed as his opening quickly closed up.

Grumpet smiled at his luck, but he knew he wouldn't get more breaks like that against this opponent. Infidelius was a good swordsman who handled the blade well. He anticipated Grumpet's moves and was able to counter them efficiently.

He dazzled the southerner with his skills, slicing at his legs before he feinted at the man's knees. He backed off and twirled the sword to the back, grabbed the handle with two hands and chopped hard toward Infidelius's head.

Infidelius parried, then offered a quick riposte that sent his sword screaming past Grumpet's ear. Grumpet dodged the attempt, but took his left hand off *Flad-rul*, brought his left arm down over Infidelius's arms and pinned them against his body. He quickly turned *Flad-rul* over and sent the pommel of the blade crashing into the man's skull.

Dazed, Infidelius broke away from Grumpet's grip and tried to re-orient himself. He had his sword up in an en guard position in front of him, and awaited Grumpet's next attack, despite the throbbing pain that shot out from his forehead.

A flurry of moves followed as the combatants fought, with Grumpet's size pressing the duo backward through the campsite of the elves. Each wielded their weapon with grace and deadly precision, as the pair exchanged moves like they were handshakes. Every time Grumpet cut low, Infidelius would cut high. And occasionally, their swords were forgotten, using their hands and arms: Grumpet's fists and muscular arms were considered weapons in their own right. A punch to the gut by Grumpet led to an elbow to the back of the head by Infidelius.

It went on in that vein for quite some time, until Grumpet slapped Infidelius to the ground with a mighty backhand to the face, the point of *Flad-rul* cutting the man's right cheek from jaw line to just below his eye.

Infidelius gave a howl of pain as he dropped his sword and pawed at the deep gash as blood poured from the wound. He fell to the ground, and several of the horsemen yanked their swords free and pointed them at Grumpet.

But they didn't count on the elves, who had their bows drawn with a nocked arrow ready to fly from each bows' strings.

Ignoring the horsemen, Grumpet picked up Infidelius's sword and pointed both blades at the man's neck. Infidelius lay on the ground, his right hand clutching his face, his left hand outstretched, looking for mercy at the hands of the burly warrior from the north.

Grumpet began to speak, and all was quiet as the words flowed from his mouth.

"You are beaten, Infidelius. You are beaten by your own arrogance and by the Sword of the South! The blade that defeated Cairn Ford and the wizard of the northlands has cut you deep, and you now have a choice—to repent for your aggrieved action, or add your head to those it has already cleaved! I am Grumpet T. Paddymeyer, leader of the Kayiko Defensive Brigade, destroyer of Dramin and heir to the Inquisitorship of the southlands! Challenging me to a duel was the most ignorant thing you could have done!" Grumpet continued, and felt the awe burn off the surrounding crowd as he spoke.

"What is all the ruckus outside me city?"

Radamuck appeared through the crowd, a dressing gown covering his body, while a stocking sleeping cap adorned his black-haired head. He looked clearly agitated at being awoken so late at night. Yanos Kingsfoil followed him, who looked like he had been awoken from a very deep slumber.

"Fib? What's goin' on here?" Radamuck asked the steward, who had watched the fight from afar.

The steward calmly told the king of Infidelius' rudeness and of how Grumpet had defended him.

Radamuck listened intently before walking up to Grumpet and the southerners.

"What's yer business in me lands, strangers?" he asked them.

"We've come to fight on your behalf, lord. However it seems our help is not needed, being so rudely denied entry into your fair city," one of the blond men said.

"Well I ruddy well think yeh wouldn't be let in! Me city is now under strict orders to be protected at night! None enter except on me command! And yeh'll take the camp yeh're given! Talkin' to me steward like that! Bah!" Radamuck said, before turning his eyes on Grumpet. "Grumpet, take the sword away," he said gruffly. Grumpet complied, albeit reluctantly.

Radamuck then walked up to the injured Infidelius.

"Yeh may be here to help us, southerner, but I don't take well to those who make demands of me stewards and representatives. Yeh can leave if yeh want. But if yeh stay, yeh'll be puttin' yer men under me command and the command of me designee when I'm sleepin'! And if yeh ever talk to me steward like that again, I'll make sure Grumpet finishes the job next time!" he said, before turning and walking away, his arms swinging madly.

***

Nonplussed, Infidelius looked hard at the king as he walked away, and decided to keep his promise to defend the dwarves, despite their so-called "hospitality." Two of his men helped him to his feet, then ordered them to go to the camp they were assigned. They all looked downtrodden, bewildered at how their captain had lost so easily.

As they walked toward the camp, a dwarven cleric, at Radamuck's orders, hurried up to intercept Infidelius and performed a spell that healed the man's cut; a white scar was left as the skin knit together.

When the cleric left, Infidelius found Grumpet still looking at him. He stared at Grumpet with utter loathing, promising to himself that he would have to finish the fight on his own terms at another time.

He didn't like being beaten, especially as bad as he had been defeated by the brown-haired northerner.

He would win, and he would claim the title he had so longed for.

Chapter 10

Ever since his spirit reformed itself back at Statuary Tower, Victor Dramin had longed for a body of his own. It was the most crucial part of the wizard's plan, and until he got one, extended bursts of magic was a luxury he couldn't afford to perform.

But he now had his body. He was ready to dominate.

In a decision spawning from Frampton's fruitless attack of Dramin in the caves of Stolidall Caverns, Dramin took over Frampton's body several days after that incident, leaving the spy's soul to wander freely through the realms. Dramin was happy; he had a suitable body to perform magic, he had a physical form, and he was essentially whole again.

But he was a combination of two beings, something Dramin did not count on.

When Dramin took over the body, a radical transformation took place.

Frampton's body ached as Dramin forced his soul into it, effectively forcing Frampton's soul out. Frampton's body morphed, taking on the appearance of two different people, meshed and mixed together.

Dramin, who was beardless, now had the goatee of the spy. Frampton's body, whose hair was short and clean cut, now had wild hair that shot out in many different directions. They now had mismatched eyes; the left was Dramin's cold, feral black, while the right was Frampton's light blue.

But for the spy, it was different altogether.

Frampton now knew how Dramin felt like, traveling all those days in a void. The only thing was that Frampton did not have the ability to control his movements like Dramin had; he didn't have magical powers. His motions were like Dramin's, jerky and over-exaggerated. Frampton's sense of hearing had increased by double, as the wind around him blew like a hurricane in his head, even though to Dramin it had been a light breeze.

Frampton now knew the evil nature of Victor Dramin. He knew the wizard would stop at nothing to achieve greater power.

Upset with himself at being so easily fooled, Frampton found a rock, a small stone, actually, and kicked at it. It didn't move.

Frampton's corporeal form moved instead.

The spy's movements caused his wispy form to over-balance itself, dropping it onto his backside. He picked himself up with great difficulty and, after holding his arms out to the side to give him balance, regained what little composure he had.

He did not like the position he was in; he decided to do something about it.

Now that Dramin had possession of the Chalice of Obloeron —he reclaimed it once he took over Frampton's body— Frampton wanted it back. The only problem was, he would have to wait until darkness fell to make an attempt at pilfering it. There were many trolls and orcs lingering near the chalice, and to steal it would take all the cunning he possessed.

When night finally came, the area surrounding the chalice appeared empty. The chamber it sat in was plain, with two large crevices along the sides of it. The chalice glittered in the torchlight, the jewels on the brim sparkling beautifully as the flames danced.

Frampton's ghostly form went around a corner and saw the chalice, where it sat on a flat rock in a small crevice. He stared at it, his milky white, featureless head fixed on it like it had been in the clearing before Dramin entered his life.

He then looked around the chamber, saw the darkened crevices and saw no one near him. He was alone, alone with the chalice. Frampton remembered the first time he was alone with the chalice. He remembered he captured it and then began to duel with Grumpet T. Paddymeyer, a duel that he nearly lost.

Frampton glided forward, his feet dragging along until he was right in front of the chalice. He dropped to his transparent knees and reached for it.

His hands passed right through it.

Puzzled, he reached for it again and again, each time his hands not touching its solid gold handles.

Or, he began to think, was it just as transparent as he was?

He heard loud footsteps behind him, and Frampton turned to find Victor Dramin standing behind him, in Frampton's own body, holding the real Chalice of Obloeron.

"Looking for this?" Dramin taunted, holding the chalice by one of its handles with his right hand's fifth finger.

Frampton looked at the chalice and wanted to dive for it. He tried to do just that, but his body seemed to just hover above the stone floor before becoming upright again.

He then looked back at where the chalice had been—it had disappeared. It had been a mirage.

"You see, my friend, I had to trick you. I knew you were going to make an attempt at stealing it. I simply created a copy of it with my mind," Dramin said with a sneer. "Having a body is so *useful*."

Frampton was beyond himself with rage.

"I want my body back! You promised I would be kept alive if I helped you defeat Paddymeyer!" he screamed, his voice hollow.

"And so I will keep you alive," Dramin responded. "With my powers fully returned to their proper state, before I was senselessly murdered, I now can control the minds of men—I just showed you that I could control yours in thinking that the chalice you grabbed for was real. You see, I will be able to control Paddymeyer's mind while you are defeating him with your sword.

"But give you back your body so soon after I have so cleanly stolen it from you? I think not," Dramin laughed before he turned and left the chamber.

Frampton yelled in agony, falling to his knees.

"I can beat Paddymeyer! I need my body to beat Paddymeyer! You promised, wizard! I can beat him in a duel, you know it!"

Dramin returned to the chamber a heart beat later.

"I will think about giving you a chance to get your body back. Perhaps you can learn to be co-operative with me, or at least until you realize that I am in charge of the way the army is created," Dramin said, reminding the spy of his doubting the wizard's reasoning. "You may be in charge of the army in battle, but first you have to learn to be dependent on others, namely me. You have learned and mastered how to survive on your own, but now you will need to learn and master how to survive outside of yourself, just like I had to when I was killed.

"Then, and only then, you may get your body back," Dramin continued, before he then walked away.

Deep in thought, Frampton remained where he was for several minutes before he followed after the wizard, not looking forward to being dependent on him.

***

As the next morning came, a sudden shaking coming from outside the dwarf stronghold roused Radamuck, Grumpet and the others from their straw-covered beds. It startled them, the rumbling knocking tiny Yanos onto the floor.

Radamuck left his sleeping chamber and entered the main system of corridors that led to the Great Hall. When he got there he found dwarves muttering and running about, excited about the "new visitor outside." Radamuck listened intently to the muttering, anxious to hear what it was about.

But then he thought to himself: he was the king. The king doesn't listen to rumors.

The king goes straight to the source.

Pushing past the dwarves converging in the tunnels, members of the Guard surrounded him and yelled, "Make way for the King!" as he walked. The going was quicker this way, and within minutes Yanos Kingsfoil, who looked like he was ready for a fight, joined him. He had his sword out and was already dressed in mail.

"Time for battle, Radamuck? Let me at them!" the halfling said.

Radamuck had to back out of the way as the halfling swung the sword; the dwarf had to jackknife backward to avoid the slice.

"Yeh're going to want to be careful with that sword, me friend. We don't know if it's enemy or friend, so please, put the sword away until I ask yeh to draw it," Radamuck said, slightly flustered.

With a shrug, Yanos slid the sword into the scabbard as Radamuck walked past. The halfling followed.

When Radamuck got the gates of the city, he found quite a crowd looking out toward the sight on the plains of Lowbridge. They pointed and gasped, holding their hand to their mouths and talking rapidly. They had never seen such a sight before in their lives, and they all wanted to make sure they got a good look.

Radamuck approached and the sea of dwarves parted for him. He stood at the gates to the city and stared out over his domain, looking for the source of the disturbance.

Then he smiled. It wasn't a disturbance, after all.

It was a welcomed intrusion.

Sitting on the grassy plains was a white house that stretched, to some of the dwarves' eyes, for miles in either direction. It reached for the sky with invisible hands, and the dwarves looked at it with wonderment.

All except for Radamuck. He knew what that house meant, and who was inside it.

He turned to Yanos.

"Me friend, fetch me wife and me son. They'll need to meet him," Radamuck said, and without a word, Yanos rushed off to get Lady Rosar and Radasack.

As Yanos scurried away, Radamuck kept staring out at the building which had created such a stir that morning. He looked upon the doorway and saw the upside down tree that he had seen the first time he came upon this dwelling. Even though the tree was strange, it was nothing compared to the kooky inhabitant of the house which now sat on Radamuck's front lawn.

He waited several minutes as the dwarves stared open-mouthed at Kirkrik Dannell's chateau. If the king knew his people, they would want to explore every nook and cranny of that house, something he felt sure would unnerve the wizard to no end.

He smiled as he fondly remembered the first trip into the chateau, of how Kirkrik's eyes has stood out on end when Aidan had touched the spear-shooting axe.

His eyes would stay out of their sockets permanently if this lot wreaked havoc inside, he thought.

Yanos returned to the king's side shortly thereafter, with Lady Rosar and the dwarven princeling hurrying in the halfling's wake. Radamuck saw his family and smiled; despite being woke up so early, his wife looked breathtakingly beautiful, while his son slept through the disturbance and didn't seem to realize he wasn't in his crib.

After thanking the halfling, Radamuck turned to his wife.

"Me love, I want yeh to meet the wizard who has helped me dwarves in our long trek to find the chalice. He has just arrived, and thank the gods he arrived now and not when the war had already started," Radamuck said, but as he finished, he wondered what would happen if the wizard—and, if Radamuck knew Kirkrik, that bullfrog was there, too—showed up in the middle of the battle.

Probably would squash half the enemy with his house, he thought, smiling to himself as the image of Kirkrik's chateau slammed on top of orcs and trolls.

His wife moved to his side and her eyes widened as she saw the house. Her gasp woke Radasack from his deep slumber, causing him to cry. The queen quickly took a small, burlap container of goat milk from her voluminous pocket and put it to Radasack's mouth. The baby stopped crying immediately as he sucked on the small bag.

Radamuck nodded to his wife and the trio walked forward, with Yanos behind them, toward Kirkrik's residence. The horns played a royal march as the king and queen walked, announcing their presence with a flourish.

Radamuck thought he had finally grown used to the pomp and circumstance of kingly life. When he was younger and not yet the king, he had difficulty standing and waiting in a receiving line with his father as they greeted important visitors to Lowbridge. He would have rather been exploring the myriad of caverns in Lowbridge with his best friend, Fallon O'Shera.

But now he was used to it and knew it was expected of him as the king of the dwarves. His father Ricanack had told him, "Son, 'tis yer duty to uphold the long traditions of yer sires, because if yeh don't, I'm gonna come back from the dead and haunt yeh 'till yeh get the durned thing right!"

Being threatened by his behemoth of a father wasn't something Radamuck liked, so he decided at the beginning of his monarchy to continue the traditions set forth long ago, even though he would have rather done away with them from the outset. Such flourishes and processions were a part of the job, he reasoned, and even though Radamuck would rather carry his axe, carrying his crown was something he knew he had to do.

Generally, he would have held his wife's right hand in his left as they walked, but since Lady Rosar carried Radasack, he placed his hand upon her shoulder blade.

The elves camping out in front of the dwarven city all left their tents and stood at attention as the dwarf king and queen marched past them; Radamuck nodded to those he recognized.

At the end of the line, Lord Baeron stood there, awaiting Radamuck, with Arrol behind him. Dressed in his best robes, the lord of the elves looked all of his three thousand years, with little gray hair flecking his head. He, too, wanted to meet the wizard who had summonsed him to aid the Lowbridge dwarves at such a crucial time.

Smiling at his friend, Radamuck stepped up onto the doorstep of his dear wizard friend. The door immediately opened.

Kirkrik Dannell stood there, and Radamuck almost didn't recognize him. If it wasn't for his white hair, he wouldn't have recognized him at all. His face was beet red and his long nose looked like a radish. His hair looked even whiter against the red skin. But his eyes remained as fiery as ever, even though he spent quite a bit of time in the sun recently. Radamuck silently hoped the wizard's brain wasn't cooked.

Kirkrik looked down at the dwarf kindly.

"I heard that, Radamuck," he said, giving a slight chuckle. "I've been experimenting with a new cream I've created. I call it 'Instant Sun,' though I think it's too instant for my liking. Works too well, I'm afraid. But that's not the reason why I came here." Kirkrik stepped forward to address both Radamuck and Baeron, but not before bowing to Lady Rosar and kissing her hand in greeting. "I have been meditating, both in the sun and out of it. I have discovered that the wizard Dramin has truly returned to being," the wizard said calmly.

"Dramin? The wizard our forces beat months ago?" Baeron said, disbelieving.

"Yes, my friend. He has returned. He has used ancient magic of taking over a body to regain use of his own magic. While he could do simple spells as a ghost, he now has his full powers restored. But that is not all: he has taken over the body of the spy who stole the Chalice of Obloeron from Radamuck. He now has reclaimed the chalice, as well, and he must be defeated in order to get it back," Kirkrik said, waving the leaders inside the home, along with Yanos and Arrol. Lady Rosar also brought the baby into the home, and sat him down on the floor in front of her as she sat next to her husband.

While the leaders spoke, Radasack crawled on the floor and managed to sneak away from his mother. The cooing baby seemingly enjoyed his freedom, crawling on Kirkrik's wonderful carpets. Unbeknownst to the child, the steady eyes of Edison the bullfrog kept an eye on him. The frog's eyes followed the dwarfling as he crawled, completely amused by the sight. The baby made his way to a pile of books the wizard had left off to the side. Concerned for the child, he tried to interrupt the leaders as they talked, but they weren't listening.

"Hey, beard boy—" Edison started, but his words went unheeded. Radamuck asked his wife to find Grumpet and Aidan and to have them come to Kirkrik's chateau. She departed.

"Ahem, pointy ears—" the frog said to Baeron, but the elf lord feigned deafness at Edison's rudeness.

Radasack then tried to pull himself up with the help of the book stack. It started to wobble and the baby's unsteady hands grabbed at them.

"Hey, Kirkrik, baby alert—" he said, but the wizard paid no attention to his beloved bullfrog.

Frustrated, Edison rolled his eyes and sighed before he reared back on his hind froggy legs and lurched forward forcefully, sending his elastic-like tongue soaring through the air like a bullet. It landed on the right side of Kirkrik's nose.

Seeing that he had hit his target, Edison pulled his tongue back toward him. Kirkrik's face turned as Edison's tongue retracted, and he finally saw what Radasack was up to.

The baby had pulled himself up, but at the moment Kirkrik looked his way, Radasack lost his balance and fell to the floor on his rump.

But as he fell, so did the books.

Kirkrik's eyes bulged as he quickly added one and one together. With a thrust of his hand, the heavy books froze in midair. With a wave, the books fell casually to the side, not touching the baby.

Radasack laughed a happy baby chuckle as the tomes fell harmlessly beside him. He clapped his pudgy hands together as if wanting to see more.

Kirkrik walked over and picked up Radasack, holding him in his arms. Radasack cooed, and the wizard smiled at him.

"He was lucky you were here Kirkrik, or he would have been learning how to read at a very young age," Edison said dryly.

Kirkrik threw the frog a look, and Edison turned away and whistled, all while twiddling what served for thumbs on his flippers.

***

Grumpet and Aidan entered the room, followed by Jessica and Madal Johannson. All were ready for a battle, their swords on their hips, their coats of mail polished and repaired.

They all shook hands with the wizard, and again Kirkrik bowed to Jessica, kissing her hand like he did with Lady Rosar.

Radamuck looked directly at Grumpet.

"Yeh were right, Grumpet. Dramin has returned, as yeh thought. We have to be extra prepared for whatever he brings," he said. "And he has the chalice now; we must be wary of his attack, for he will lead the army against Lowbridge. He has taken over the body of the spy yeh fought. I fear he will be even more dangerous than he was the first time we fought him."

"Why don't we begin a charge after him and catch him off guard instead of us being the ones off guard?" Grumpet asked. "We have a sizable force—between the dwarves, elves, and humans, we have enough to handle any army he brings!"

"We will do as the king of these lands command, young Grumpet," said Kirkrik Dannell. "He says we must be wary of the attack and we shall be extra vigilant when it comes to our guard. I will know of when the attack comes, and I will—"

Kirkrik stopped speaking and whatever red was in his face seemed to drain out of his skull quicker than water dribbling through hands. His eyes had grown glassy and unfocused, and his body began to sway back and forth, as if his life force had left him. The group looked at him as if waiting for him to finish his sentence.

But he had gone as rigid as a statue.

Radamuck stepped forward and waved his hand in front of the wizard's face to see if his eyes would blink. They didn't move. Radamuck then snapped his fingers, but again, no recognition.

Then like a snap, Edison's tongue flashed out of nowhere and hit Kirkrik behind the head. Edison pulled Kirkrik's head back so that the wizard fell backward into his armchair. The wizard's arms became draped over the arms of the chair, and his head lolled over the top of the chair.

"Kirkrik?" Radamuck asked, trying to see if the wizard could hear him.

Kirkrik's head slowly rose, the eyes more focused than they were.

"Yeh were sayin', Kirkrik?" Radamuck said.

"I was saying that I will know when he's coming," Kirkrik said, gasping. "And my friends, he's coming tonight!"

The words took several seconds for them to register with the assembled group, but it was in Radamuck's eyes that they registered first.

So it is finally coming, he thought. *A war I feared would come is on its way, and there is nothing I can do about it.*

The king found everyone's eyes on him as he looked up from his thoughts. The placated look on his face removed, he looked ever the leader of Lowbridge's army.

"Well, yeh heard the mage! Prepare for battle!"

He then went into commander mode, and started issuing his orders.

"Baeron, have yer forces moved to the top of the mountain. They can attack the enemy from above, as well as run the war machines we have built," he said, and the elf lord bowed to his friend. "Grumpet, have the armies of Kayiko and the southlands fitted for mail and shields if they haven't been already. I want none of yeh people killed for not being prepared.

"Yanos, have the women and children of me people that are too young to fight to seek refuge in the sacred chamber. Aidan," he said, turning to his nephew, only to find him looking at the floor with a solemn look on his face.

"Aidan? Are yeh okay?" he asked.

Aidan snapped out of his reverie and looked at his uncle.

"Yes uncle, I'm fine."

"Aidan, I will need yeh to alert the clerics and make sure they are ready to deal with injured. Then I want yeh to spend time with Prestillia. She will need yeh over the next few hours but be sure to report in with me afterward. I'll be advisin' me councilors 'bout this. Yeh all understand yer orders?" Radamuck said to all.

Everyone nodded.

"Alright then. We all have work to do. We will not let that wizard take us by surprise; we shall be ready to fight like an army should! No one brings war to Lowbridge and gets away with it!"

Everyone rushed out of the door, leaving Radamuck and Lady Rosar with Kirkrik.

"This will be a war that will change Lowbridge forever, me friend," Radamuck said.

"Yes, but you will defend it as you always have defended those in need; you have great forces behind you. And you have my power too, so don't forget that!" the wizard said. "Along with my sun cream, I've been cooking up a few spells that are sure doozies!"

Radamuck looked at Kirkrik with a keen eye. He knew of Kirkrik's behavior and knew it not of sane mind, but when Kirkrik spoke in a cool voice as he just had, Radamuck felt the power behind it.

He knew that if Kirkrik set loose a spell upon the wizard's army, then woe betide the enemy.

As Radamuck turned to leave, he remembered that Radasack still crawled around the floor of the wizard's chateau. He found him from near a window that overlooked the wizard's garden and picked him up.

Radamuck and his queen walked through the doors as Kirkrik said that he would see him soon, and the king had the prince held at his right shoulder as he walked back toward the city. The elves were packing their tents up and moving to the top of the dwarven city.

"I will make this world safe for yeh, me son," Radamuck said, looking into the child's eyes, "'cause if I don't do it now, yeh won't have a world to live in."

Chapter 11

As dusk fell upon the realm of Lowbridge, and with the women and children safely secure inside the deeper halls of the mountain city, the anticipation and anxiety levels of the defenders rose with every passing minute. By that point, the defenders' ranks had swelled to several thousand, coming from all over the realms to help the dwarves.

Standing in the battlements dressed in his full battle armor, Radamuck looked over the scene and smiled. His heart, swollen with pride by the peoples who had come to assist him and his people, raced along. He saw men with swords, dwarves with axes, elves with bows and arrows. Above him, dwarves tended to the war machines, the catapults to send balls of fiery pitch screaming through the air at the attacking army.

It was, Radamuck saw, the largest army of which he had ever commanded.

While looking out at the darkening sky, he thought of how everything had arrived to this point, including two previous battles with the wizard from the northlands. He lost many dwarves in those two battles, and knew he would lose more today. He would lose elves and humans, too. That was a fact of war.

But this one was on his doorstep, and as his father Ricanack had always stressed to him, war had never before come to Lowbridge. The knowledge a battle was now within hours of occurring had weighed his armor down until it cut into his broad shoulders. He took a deep breath and held it as he bowed his head.

Father, me king, he thought, *I'm sorry I let yeh down*.

If he had the ability to sense his father's presence from the Great Void Beyond, he hoped his forebears—all twenty-three prior kings—wouldn't look too harshly at him for what was about to happen.

He swallowed his fear and brought his head back up as soon as another dwarf joined him.

Radamuck found Fib Niosh standing next to him, the old friends giving each other a curt nod. The steward also wore battle armor, with a longer axe attached to his hip. His didn't have the regular curved blades dwarves used, either in a single or double-bladed form. His blade was smaller, but it was no less sharp than others. Its top was square with the handle, which was only two feet long, giving him slightly less torque than a handle of some other weapons. The blade curved back toward the handle by several centimenters, and Fib used that viciously sharp part to slice out throats.

Radamuck recalled how prodigious the dwarf was at that task, and felt was glad he was on their side.

"Fib, I'm very humbled by what the realms have sent us. Who knew that the dwarves would live to see such togetherness?" Radamuck said.

"Yer Highness, yeh have a very good friend in the wizard, and it was he who brought them here. I think yeh should ask him that question. As for the Imperialists, I do not believe they can be trusted, especially after what they tried to do to me. But thankfully Grumpet was there. I hate to think what would happen if he wasn't," Fib said, absent-mindedly feeling his neck.

Radamuck smiled for the briefest of moments; while he didn't like his people threatened, he liked them to have a little bit of adversity every once in a while, as it kept them on their toes. While he didn't show it, Fib's words stayed in the back of his mind: if it came down to it, he would have Grumpet carve a hole in the leader of the Imperialists if they were found untrustworthy.

He continued: "I have not foreseen the victors in our battle; this battle could take hours, or it could take days. Our strength shall hold out, though—it must hold out—and we must trust each and every person and being that is here in the name of peace and justice."

Just as he finished, the horns sounded from the very top of the mountain, drawing their attention toward the sky. Radamuck had only issued one order to the horn-blowers above: only blow the horns for when they caught first sight of the enemy army's approach.

His chest plate bounced for a few seconds before Radamuck remembered it was time for war. He turned and sent a younger dwarf runner to the top of the mountain to get a word from the watch. He wanted to know exactly from which direction the enemy came.

Several minutes later, the young dwarf reported in, meeting Radamuck in the entranceway. The whitesilver gates had yet to be closed.

"Me king, the watch says the orcs come from the direction of Briskey Bucktooth," the dwarf said.

"Thank yeh, lad," the king replied, patting him on the shoulder. "Now, head into the mines and be safe."

But the young dwarf stood stoically in front of him.

"I would like to stay and fight, me king. I owe it to me family."

Radamuck didn't want to send one so young to his death, but saw courage in the young dwarf's eyes. There was a bit of trepidation in his face; his flesh and golden beard trembled every so softly. The black-bearded dwarf that towered over him wondered if the trembling was due to the war, or from the presence that stood before him.

"What is yer name, me lad?" the king asked.

"Andrew Flibberstimmer," the dwarf responded.

"I wish not to accept yer service, young Andrew, but since yeh seem to do this of yer own will, I will not refuse it. Pick up yer weapon and join the others," Radamuck said, "in the rear guard."

Andrew Flibberstimmer appeared so happy that he rushed off to find his weapon, which turned out to be an axe with a single curved blade. Trotting away, he joined the ranks with wide eyes.

"Those eyes will see too much today," Radamuck said as they started walking outside.

"But it will make him a better warrior in the future," a voice coming from behind Radamuck and Fib answered.

Kirkrik Dannell walked up to the pair, nodding to Fib. The steward also nodded, then hurried away.

"The young dwarf will not die today, but he will get an eyeful of what dying is. It will prepare him for his future in your army. Radamuck, I have come to help you in any way I can. Where would you like me to be?" he said. But before the dwarf replied, Kirkrik turned and saw his beautiful chateau standing in the middle of the plains, right in the heart of the battleground. He clapped his hands and threw them forward. A wave of invisible energy poured forth, and within seconds, the large house shook and rose from its magical moorings. It sped toward the mountain as soon as it cleared the army.

When the rushing house drew to within twenty-five feet of the city, it started shrinking. Smaller and smaller it shrunk until it became the size of a small pebble. It shot into Kirkrik's right hand and rested there until the wizard put it into his pocket.

"I think I'll just stay out of the way during the battle. But," he said, "I will be able to inflict some punishment here and there as I see fit."

"Good. We haven't seen hide nor hair from Briskey Bucktooth yet, correct? Are they goin' to come help us?" Radamuck asked before Kirkrik had the chance to turn away.

A dark shadow passed over Kirkrik's eyes before the mage nodded.

"I spoke with an archmage in the most powerful guild, and he said he'd relay the message. But from what I got out of Tiks Rinyard, it would be difficult to get his master to organize an army. But who needs an army when you have me!"

Kirkrik winked and shrugged before setting off back inside the city. Alone, Radamuck frowned. He felt an ache growing in his heart, and it wasn't from a lack of air or anticipation of the looming war, either. The news Kirkrik had delivered was, from his point of view, surprising: He had counted on receiving aid from the guilds, even though he hadn't spoken of it to anyone; he had figured Kirkrik, using the powers of mind reading, had discovered Radamuck's unspoken desires and made the call through his orb. The economy of Briskey Bucktooth was practically intertwined with the success of Lowbridge's mines. It was a no brainer, at least in his mind, that they would come to the dwarves' aid.

Grimacing, Radamuck shook the thought from his head, for he needed a clear mind during this battle. He then turned away from the gates, heading toward the front lines to be with his men.

***

When he arrived at the front lines, he found Fib standing near Grumpet, Jessica, Aidan, and Arrol Goldleaf, who would lead the smaller contingent of elf forces on the ground—the remainder were on the top of the mountain with Lord Baeron.

Grumpet and Jessica bowed as the king approached and allowed him to pass. But Radamuck halted and spoke with the human captain he had grown to trust.

"This should be a very long fight, Grumpet. Are yeh rested enough to go the distance for us?" the king asked.

"Without a doubt, my friend. I am ready to go as far as I have to. And then, when I reach that breaking point, I will go over it. I do so to serve you, my friend, and to protect the lands surrounding us. I have been here briefly, but I already consider these lands a second home. I would die for this land, Radamuck, and you have my pledge that I will protect it to the best of my ability," Grumpet said.

Radamuck smiled and thanked his gods silently for Grumpet T. Paddymeyer.

"We have plenty of back-up. I'm hoping this war goes to our advantage; any war against that wizard has gone well. But I know he is angry, at yeh especially. He has the chalice now, and I'm sure he is still angry with me. But yeh better keep yeh're guard up, because that wizard will have yeh in his sights at all times," Radamuck cautioned.

"I wouldn't be surprised if he orders his minions to keep me alive for himself. They'll see Flad-rul and they'll know to stay away. But that won't stop me," Grumpet said. "I'll just go after them and bring their pitiful lives to an abrupt end."

Radamuck chuckled heartily.

"I wouldn't doubt that. Just be careful, and keep an eye on yer bride," he said.

Grumpet squeezed Jessica's hand harder, then brought it up to his lips. He kissed it while looking into his wife's eyes.

"My eyes will always be on her," Grumpet answered, keeping his eyes locked on hers.

Radamuck turned and began to address his troops.

"Me friends, we are at the crossroads. Our land is now under attack. It will begin soon, and I want yeh to know that I am already proud of yeh more than yeh know. It will be a remembered fight, for the wizard of the northlands has come back from the dead to wage war with the free peoples of the realms. I tell yeh that we must not let him win; we must not let him think he has the upper hand. Nay, it will be up to the front line of defense of Lowbridge to hold his forces back, and it will be up to us to make sure that we push them back. Our elven friends are at the summit of our fine city and will shoot arrows down upon the attackers. Our wizard friend, Kirkrik Dannell, will help us with his own brand of magic. And we have our great friend, Grumpet T. Paddymeyer, the heir of the southlands who wields the Sword of the South, who has already defeated the wizard once before. He is on our side, and we shall rejoice when this war is over!" Radamuck said, and the large contingent of dwarf warriors gave a great cheer for their king.

After speaking, Radamuck turned and got into line next to Aidan, Yanos, Grumpet and Jessica. They were ready, and all had their weapons drawn for what approached from over the bend.

The horns continued wailing and the wind picked up in strength and intensity. Soon, the enemy would be upon them.

And Lowbridge as they knew it would never be the same again.

Chapter 12

The army of evil marched over the embankment, trampling the grass left in its wake, halting at its crest. Nearly ten thousand strong, the front lines of the blood-shared orc army came to rest three hundred feet away from of the front lines of the dwarves.

Pushing his way to the front, Dramin, in the body of Frampton, wanted to see the dwarf king and his allies one last time before they died. He wanted to remember the look of fear on their faces as they saw what he had cooked up for them this time. The spirit of Frampton followed closely, for he had told Dramin that he wanted to see what the dwarves had for defenses, too: As he had already penetrated their defenses once, he wanted to see if he could do it again.

Their eyes widened—one pair human, another pair ghostly—when they reached the front. The pair looked across the expanse and saw many dwarves, as if the whole of Lowbridge had emptied and readied itself for this fight. They saw elves readied at the mountain's summit, all watching the approaching army. Humans were there, swords drawn and shields in hand, with some mounted on horseback.

And then they saw him.

They saw Paddymeyer, with *Flad-rul* drawn and held down low in his right hand. Both Dramin and Frampton wanted a piece of him, both for entirely different reasons. They stared at the burly human with looks of utter loathing, their combined heart rate speeding along, the blood thundering in their combined ear canals.

"It is time, my body-less friend," Dramin said, his eyes riveted on the tall brown-haired man. "It is time for my revenge. I want him now!"

He moved forward, but surprisingly, Frampton laid a ghostly hand on Dramin's shoulder, stopping him in place. Dramin actually felt it: He turned back with fire in his eyes and looked hard at the spy. But before he opened his mouth to speak or utter a defensive spell, Frampton shook his wispy head.

"Now is not the time. Let him expel as much energy as possible. Let our warriors combat him until he is weary, and then together we will destroy him," the spy said.

"I have fought him when he is weary; he is just as dangerous!" Dramin spat.

"And I fought him, as well. And I have defeated him."

"You got away by sheer luck!" Dramin's eyes had widened.

"But it is still a victory, my friend. Trust me in this. His weariness will be his weakness. If this war lasts long, and he continues to exert energy in fighting while we hang back and let him dismantle our forces, then it will be a victory for us when we have lots of energy left after killing him and the rest of the dwarves."

"Even at our full strength and he exhausted, he can still destroy both of us: remember, I hold your body. If he were to kill me a second time, your soul will hang in limbo for the remainder of eternity."

"Which is why it is best for us to hold back," Frampton said, not missing a beat. "You choose to fight with anger. It is not prudent to fight battles such as this when you are angered; it clouds the judgment. I suggest we hold back until the proper time."

"And when will the proper time be, spy?"

Frampton's ghostly form grinned, knowing he had control over the situation at once, knowing he had thought of a contingency the wizard hadn't.

"The orb will tell us," Frampton said with a nod toward Dramin's cloak, where he kept the mystical sphere.

Dramin thought about it and swallowed. He had nearly forgotten about it. Thoughts of domination had filled his mind, and he had forgotten to consult with its wisdom. He pulled the glass ball out and brought it toward their faces, just as the mists of time started swirling. The rapid revolutions continued until they saw a vision, one crystal clear vision, come to it and reflected in their eyes. Both stared hard at it, and each had a different reaction: Dramin's eyes bulged, his lips separating by mere millimeters.

Frampton simply smiled.

"That is when we will act, my friend. Until that time, we will allow the events to go as they will. This orb has never lied to you, am I correct?" the spy asked.

Dramin nodded, his eyes still wide from the scene the orb showed them.

"Then it is settled, Victor. We will do what the orb tells us to do," Frampton responded. Dramin finally looked at him, his face impassive. "And I mean everything the orb tells us to do."

The spy then pulled the wizard back through the crowd of orcs, his hand still grasping the orb, just as the black storm clouds approached.

It looked to be a rather wet war.

***

The alliance continued its steadfast vigil, awaiting the enemy to pounce. They stood in the valley between the hill and the city, conscious of the fact a storm blew in off the Enchanted Sea, and that behind the hill, there were even more warriors.

Grumpet saw what looked like the spy coming through the crowd, however changed he looked. But then he saw a ghostly form behind it looking exactly like the spy!

He looked at Radamuck to see if the king had any answers, but Radamuck looked just as confused as he was. Then Kirkrik made his way through the crowd.

"I'll be," the wizard said breathlessly. "Dramin has pushed the soul of the spy out of his own body! That is the most dangerous magic ever!" When he saw the continued confused looks on the faces of Grumpet and Radamuck, he explained his observation. "By pushing the soul of one out of its body, he is not only jeopardizing his own life, but the life of another. Dramin must not know—or care, for that matter—what he has done. He wanted a body so bad that he must have stopped at nothing to get the spy to agree to this."

"Or maybe he stole it without thought to the spy's life," Jessica said somewhat dryly.

"That is the more likely scenario, my dear," Kirkrik said, not picking up the sarcasm. "It wouldn't surprise me if there was a disagreement between them; I do recall hearing the spy conversing madly with himself a good time ago when at the caverns."

Jessica looked puzzled at Kirkrik's pronouncement, until Grumpet stepped in.

"Our dear wizard friend has the ability to read the thoughts of every single being in all the realms, my love," he said. "It is how he determined that the enemy would attack tonight."

"You're quite right, Grumpet," Kirkrik said with a smile. "Now look at them: they disagree at the course of attack. Dramin wants to fight you now, my friend, while the spy is using caution at the start."

He paused, with his ear pointed toward the enemy as if trying to hear their words.

And then he heard it. He heard the thoughts of Frampton as Dramin looked into the orb and saw the vision.

"Oh my," he said, surprised at what he heard. "This is indeed perilous! Grumpet, you must keep an eye on your wife! They mean to include her in a plot to anger you, to make you lose your cool in battle. They want to weaken you by capturing her!"

Jessica didn't look as shocked at this as she should have been, hearing about a plan to take her captive. Neither did Grumpet.

It was his worst dream coming true.

"I have thought about this for many weeks. I have dreamed that Jessica would be harmed by the wizard, kidnapped and tortured. Now that I hear our friend speak of this as if it is freshly thought, I am wary of letting my beloved fight in this war," Grumpet said, before turning to Jessica. "I do believe you should fall back, my love. Save yourself from their control."

But as convincing and caring as Grumpet was, Jessica wasn't having it.

"Grumpet, they will not get a hold of me, for if they come near me, they will feel the bite of my sword. And if I should miss, I know that yours will cut them down and make them rue the day they threatened us and our love. I refuse to fall back.

I am willing to stand by your side, to die if I have to. But they will never steal the love I have for you," she said.

Grumpet, stern-faced with doubt, nodded. Jessica then leaned up to her hero's lips and kissed him, standing on her tiptoes.

Radamuck stepped forward and laid his hand on Grumpet's elbow.

"Yeh should know yeh'd never get her to do as yeh say, me friend. She's as stubborn as a mule! And anyway, them wizard and highwayman won't get near her! Nothin's goin' to get near her, I've seen her fight yeh! She nearly had yeh beat, Grumpet. And thems got nothin' on yeh as a swordsman, me friend!"

That softened Grumpet's heart.

Jessica can handle herself, he thought. *I have trained her well.*

He took his wife's hand, brought it to his lips and kissed it.

"I'm sorry for doubting you, my love," he whispered, looking into her pale blue eyes.

"There's nothing to be sorry for. You are my protector; I expect it. I will watch your back just like I know you will watch mine. And I will be careful," she said, before kissing him again.

And as they kissed, the rain started to fall, tinkling off the armor of the dwarves and humans.

"Well," Kirkrik said with a laugh, "there's only one thing to do about this rain."

And then he raised his hands to the sky, spoke a few well-chosen words, and quickly sent a spell into the heavens. The spell went upward, and about fifty axe-lengths above the dwarves exploded.

But instead of shrapnel and other debris raining down upon them, a blue tint formed and congealed and spread in front, over and behind the dwarf army. The rain seemed to have stopped but as they looked up, they stil saw the drops falling and beading on top of the formation.

"I've just created a covering that will protect us from the rain! We will stay dry through the battle, unless we stray from the bubble. Rain stays out, but unfortunately, our enemies don't," the wizard said in his usually high-pitched voice.

Radamuck rolled his eyes at Kirkrik's pronouncement.

"Silly ol' mage," he said, before he turned to his troops. "Prepare for the first wave! They'll be comin' soon!"

Grumpet let go of Jessica's hand and twirled *Flad-rul* gently through his fingers, getting into his battle stance. Jessica likewise took her sword out and similarly swung it. She looked at him and gave him a wink.

And then, without further preamble, the enemy charged.

Three feet high and covered with spiny, brown mandibles in place of armor on their grayish bodies, the fire gnomes raced down the hillock with murder in their beady, red eyes. They had razor sharp teeth that formed a V-shape, interlocking together with their brothers in their deadly mouths. On their hands and feet, each had elongated fingernails and toenails, all of which had the ability to tear the flesh from an unprotected being. Brandishing miniaturized swords that were about the same size as the sword Yanos held in his tiny hand, the gnomes attacked with a yell that came out like a high-pitched squeak.

Created for killing and weakening the enemy, the fire gnomes were the first line of the evil wizard's deadly attack.

Grumpet looked to Radamuck and smiled. The human liked long fights, and as he saw the gnomes stream in and the orcs hang back, he had the feeling the battle would be long. Twirling Flad-rul one more time, he was ready for the fight to come.

But then Radamuck shocked him: the dwarf king ordered his troops to charge toward the fire gnomes. This was unlike Radamuck, as he usually held his troops back until the last possible instant to attack. Grumpet quickly recovered from his daze and sped into action, running after the first line of dwarves.

The two forces came closer and crashed together, the gnomes throwing themselves at the dwarves, while the dwarves hacked at the gnomes with their axes. Two dwarves fell quickly as the gnomes sunk their teeth into their throats.

But once Grumpet reached the fray, *Flad-rul* came alive, its fiery bite coming down harder and more painfully than the gnomes drove their teeth in the allies' flesh. The Sword of the South sliced through the flesh of the gnomes, chopping off limbs and spiking through their breastbones.

One by one, Grumpet cut down the fire gnomes, some squealing to their deaths. One tried to get into a duel with the burly human, but with a raised eyebrow, Grumpet chopped its head clean off before it had the chance to parry.

***

Aidan, of all the allies, had an easy time cutting through the gnomes' attack. With the double-bladed weapon, he twisted and turned his body to and fro, taking the sword and axe combination with him and not looking as he dismembered many gnomes. Soon they learned to stay away from the young dwarf, but that didn't stop him from coming to the rescue of his uncle as well as his comrades, slashing and hacking at the enemy with powerful swings.

Another gnome came at his right. He spun the blades twice through his hands before backhanding the gnome with the sword portion. Its head flew threw the air, and just for good measure, Aidan drove the axe through its gut.

"Just to make sure it was dead?" Yanos stopped and asked.

Aidan just grinned and fought on.

But Radamuck quickly caught everyone's attention.

"Me friends! Fight 'round me!" he yelled.

The allies complied, with Aidan swinging his blades in front of his uncle, while Yanos fought from behind. Grumpet and Jessica kept the enemy at bay on either side of Radamuck, chopping the oncoming fire gnomes.

"Dramin! Is this all yeh have to send at us? I expected more than simple gnomes when yeh wanted to destroy me people! Send somethin' that is worthy of bein' killed!" Radamuck yelled, swiping his axe down at the ground, gesturing to the dead gnomes that lay on the grass. "Better yet, send yerself and yer little highwayman down! I still have to teach that rascal a lesson about not touchin' me property!"

But then a foul voice came on the air, and Aiden recognized it to be that of the wizard.

"You say you'd teach him a lesson to not touch your property, Radamuck Rosar? Maybe I should teach you not to touch *my* property! The Chalice of Obloeron was mine before it was stolen by you!" Dramin screamed.

"It was the rightful property of the free peoples of all the realms, and yer evil sullied it!" Radamuck answered. "Send something worthy to be killed, Dramin, or me dwarves will come after yeh!"

"So be it," Dramin whispered, before he nodded to the orcs next to him.

Opening their mouths with a snarl, the orcs began to stalk in on the dwarves, their blades out and ready to fight.

***

Radamuck looked at the oncoming party let a grin flash through his beard.

The wizard is doing exactly what I want, he thought.

But then the grin turned into a frown, as several thousand orcs rushed over the hill and down toward the allies.

"Okay, methinks that wasn't a good idea," Radamuck said to Grumpet.

"Yeah, I'm in agreement with you. Bad idea," the human said as he looked at the approaching enemy.

The quintet of heroes grouped themselves together as the orcs approached, hoping beyond hope they wouldn't be separated from each other during the battle. Then Yanos sprinted forward, his little sword raised high above his head.

His little feet took him toward the enemy, and seconds later, Grumpet, Jessica, Radamuck and Aidan followed. They weren't going to let the halfling have all the fun.

As they ran after Yanos, they heard the telltale "swoosh" of elven arrows shooting from the summit of the mountainous city, sailing through the air and cutting through the slipstream and Kirkrik's rain shell. The arrows didn't stop until they found the chests of the charging orcs. One by one they fell, but more continued to walk over their dead.

"Ah ha, the elves take our kills! Can't let them out of the fight, can we?" Radamuck asked.

"Oh, they can have a fair few," Grumpet said, as he stopped to land a hard chop with *Flad-rul* upon a hapless orc that tried to knife him in the gut.

***

Grasping his sword two-handed, Grumpet parried chops and hacks by the orcs, reversing their thrusts with quick ripostes and turning their blades over. He then retracted his own blade, wound up and sliced through the orcs' arms and necks.

None of the orcs wore chain mail, which led Grumpet to believe that the evil wizard had more than enough to handle the dwarves and their human and elven allies.

A few of the fire gnomes were still mixed in with the orcs, fighting to the last. One stood toe-to-toe with Jessica, fighting her one-handed, getting her blade pinned before the gnome reached out with its right hand and grazed her skin, causing rivulets of blood to stream slowly out of the wounds. Jessica screamed and held her arm, before the fire gnome found its head detached from the rest of its body. Grumpet had cut through its neck with a powerful heave of his powerful word. He looked at his wife's hand and saw the cuts.

"Get back to the city and get yourself mended. I will deal with the scum of the wizard!" Grumpet ordered, and Jessica quickly complied, picking up her sword, which she had dropped.

When he saw her leave, he turned toward the oncoming orcs. He lifted Flad-rul above his head and gave a high overhand chop, splitting the orc's scalp, before retracting the blade and parrying a swipe from another. He leveled it by punching it in the face, his large fist breaking the orc's nose and twisting it into something unrecognizable.

The fire in Grumpet's eyes just added to his power: his wife had been hurt, and he held himself responsible for her injuries. He hadn't felt like this in months, when she had been hurt while defending Yanos from orcs back in Kayiko. He slashed and bobbed under the attack of an orc, before hopping up and driving his blade into its mouth and out through the back of its neck.

If anything worse happens to her during this fight, he thought, *I will never forgive himself*.

***

Fighting back-to-back, Radamuck and Aidan were the best compliment to each other. The two dwarves moved their weapons in perfect harmony, not letting an orc or a fire gnome find a hole in their defenses. As Radamuck chopped an orc down, Aidan slashed one, then spun his blades from right to left and speared one in the heart.

Yanking his blade free, the butt end of his axe collided squarely with the chin of a charging orc, dazing it slightly until Radamuck brought his axe across to the left, gouging the orc's back, severing the spine. It fell like a small tree, the thud barely heard over the din of war.

"You know, uncle," Aidan said, as he reflexively moved his sword back and forth, "if the wizard wants to win this fight, he's not putting much effort into it."

"I know what yeh mean, me boy. It's like he's toyin' with us," Radamuck answered, as he drove his axe deep into the skull of an oncoming fire gnome.

Then two orcs and a fire gnome came up to Aidan. The two orcs brandished their curved blades, while the fire gnome stood between the two taller creatures, awaiting an opening. Aidan showed two rows of teeth as he twirled his axe and sword through his hands, waiting for the orcs to attack. One lunged with his sword toward Aidan's right shoulder, but the dwarf parried its thrust with ease.

The other then tried to go for his gut, but Aidan shooed off the orc by swinging the axe back to the left. The orc got his arm out of reach just in time and sneered at the dwarf.

But as Aidan re-corrected himself and going after the orc to the right, the orc on the left charged in and timed his cuts with the other orc. Aidan worked hard to deflect each and every thrust by the orcs, pinning one orc's blade down to the ground, bending over to keep it down before giving a sharp kick to the partner's face.

And as he bent over, the shirt of silver rings rode up his lower back, exposing his tough flesh. That left an opening for the gnome, who reached in with his knife and cut Aidan on the lower back, a crease six inches long.

With a scream, Aidan reared back and spun his blades harder and faster, beheading the powerless orc before he swung the axe down and around forward, bisecting the fire gnome's heavy breast plate.

The gnome was only stunned by the blow. But Yanos Kingsfoil gave it a sharp pinch in its back, ripping apart its insides.

Radamuck came up to his nephew and place his hand on his shoulder.

"Come on, Aidan. Back to the city to get treatment for that wound. If yeh don't get that looked after, Prestillia will have me head on a silver platter!"

He and Yanos helped Aidan back to Lowbridge, while Madal Johannson, who fought nearby, cleared a path in front of them of orcs and fire gnomes.

"I heard you were coming before you knew you were coming," Kirkrik said to the trio, leading the injured Aidan to a clear spot underneath the battlements to the city. Above, elves continued to shower the attacking orcs with arrows.

The wizard had the dwarf lay down on his front, raising the ringed shirt enough to show where the gnome's sword had bitten him. It was bloodied and started to look like it was tinged slightly green, as if the gnomes' blades were all poisoned.

"Easily curable, my dear friend!" Kirkrik said with delight. "And there will be no lingering after-effects."

The wizard grabbed a flask full of white liquid as a ball of fiery pitch flew from above. Uncorking the flask, he poured its contents across the wound while waggling his fingers and muttering some well-chosen magic words. It bubbled and frothed until steam rose from Aidan's skin. If the onlookers thought it burned the dwarf, Aidan gave no indication.

But, as Radamuck and Yanos noticed, the curatives worked quickly: the blood had disappeared, and the cut looked healed and sealed.

"Up you get, Aidan. You're all better now. The cut has been healed," Kirkrik said.

Aidan got up to his knees and tried to take a peek around his back. He could see that the skin was again tan and that the cut from the gnomes' sword had been treated.

"How? How did you do that so quickly?" Aidan asked, amazed.

"Old family recipe," Kirkrik replied, "and if I were to tell you what's in it, my grandmother would come down from the Great Void Beyond and give me an earful, I can tell you that right now! But if you wanted, I could have done it with a needle and thread like they did in the old days, before magic. And that would have taken quite awhile, I can assure you. I can tell you a long story about when I was three years old—" he continued, but before he could relay his tale, which Radamuck thought would be long, he hurriedly thanked the wizard.

"Thanks for yer help, Kirkrik. We need to get back to the fightin' before Grumpet takes all me kills," the king said, grabbing the dwarf and halfling and scooting away from his wizard friend.

"Okay, well I'll tell it to you another time!" Kirkrik yelled after them.

When Radamuck was sure he was out of earshot, he muttered to Aidan and Yanos: "Probably wants to tell us of how he got his chin all cut up by ridin' across the sand and needed the needle to sew his head back up."

But just as he finished saying it, he heard the wizard yell after him again.

"Oh, so I told you the story already!"

Radamuck just shook his bearded head and laughed hard. Kirkrik's mind reading abilities never surprised him.

Chapter 13

Grumpet gave a powerful backhand to an orc with *Flad-rul*, cutting a straight line barely an inch above its voice box, when he turned toward the city to see Radamuck, Aidan and Yanos returning to the battle, the king chopping down a gnome that had slipped through the outer defenses.

But the sight of his three dear friends wasn't what caught Grumpet's attention.

The warrior looked past them, back toward the city. Semper Infidelius and his band of Imperialists stood there, swords drawn, not too far away from where Kirkrik treated Aidan for his wound. They stared out at the battlefield, whispering to each other, while Infidelius looked hard at the one looking at him from afar.

Grumpet scowled at them more to himself than anything; he hated that they let the others fight, even though they said they were here to defend the dwarven realm.

"The Imperialists lag behind," he said as Radamuck approached. "Perhaps they intend to watch us weaken ourselves in battle, or they intend to let us handle the mindless rabble before they take on the greater challenges that I am sure Dramin has cooked up for us."

"Aye, I thought that when I saw them. I am wary of this continued fight, especially if they turn on us and try to steal me chalice. Don't worry 'bout them, Grumpet. Worry 'bout cleavin' the heads off of orcs!" the king said, before raising his axe and dropping it in the head of an orc.

"I do worry about it," Grumpet said, almost at a whisper, and knew that back near the city, Semper Infidelius somehow heard every word.

The man nodded to Grumpet with a wide smirk.

Grumpet immediately thought Infidelius somehow had the same power as Kirkrik, but he quickly shook that thought from his brain. If Infidelius had that power, he would have been able to easily beat Grumpet in their sword fight.

He shook off the thought as he moved the great sword down, sweeping away the orc's blade. He plunged the tip of the flaming blade into its gut, its squeals dying on the bite of *Flad-rul*.

He looked back. Infidelius still grinned maliciously.

***

Above the fracas, Lord Baeron looked down upon the plains of Lowbridge, seeing the carnage before him, as wave after wave of orcs came rumbling down the hill that led to the dell before Lowbridge. He grimaced; he hated evil.

His elven archers continued firing their magical arrows at the orcs, connecting every time, not wasting a single arrow. Other elves managed the great war machines on the summit of Lowbridge. It was the elves evening the odds for their dwarven allies.

But then Baeron spotted something just over the grassy crest, and with his enhanced elven vision, he knew what it was before the dwarves knew.

Gargantuan and green, the beasts pulled heavy wooden structures forward, structures that were intent on destroying large amounts of the enemy.

And the beasts could also destroy the enemy, too, with one swipe of a club.

"Trolls! Trolls with war machines of their own!" he yelled, magically enhancing his voice so Radamuck could hear him on the plains below. "Prepare for whatever comes at you!"

He saw one of the trolls load a ball of black pitch onto the catapult, before an orc took a torch and set fire to it. As the flames danced along the cup of the catapult, the troll slammed the lever down. The fireball launched, soaring through the air.

Baeron watched as it flew, until he saw that the arc of the flaming sphere headed right at the elves!

"Move!" he yelled to his left, as elves dashed out of the way of the fireball. But some were unlucky, and some moved too slowly. Flames engulfed them as it crashed on top of the city. They died with a scream.

"We need to reposition our people," Baeron said to an aide, who stood to the elf lord's left. But before he could carry out

Baeron's orders, Kirkrik Dannell appeared next to the elves and laid a steadying hand on his elbow.

"Before you do that, my friend, I want to try something," the wizard said.

The elves stood back as Kirkrik closed his eyes, and Baeron watched as the wizard concentrated hard on the scene in front of him. He saw, in his mind, a troll loading a boulder onto one of the catapults. He saw it slam the lever down and saw the rock hurtling through the air.

With a few well-chosen words and a waggle of the fingers, Kirkrik flung his hands forth and a stream of energy flew from his palms. They rippled and buffered through the wind, coming head on with the boulder.

As the two forces met, the boulder stopped as the energy latched onto it, circling it in bands. Then Kirkrik chanted softly, and the elf lord saw the boulder slowly rotate counterclockwise.

Then, before anyone knew it, the boulder reversed course and collided head on with a troll. The troll couldn't move quick enough to get out of the boulder's way. A huge gash opened on the troll's scalp as it fell dead to the earth in a huge heap. The catapult, however, still stood, and more trolls hurried to reload it for another volley.

Baeron looked at the wizard in awe.

"You may keep your thanks, my friend," Kirkrik said before Baeron even mustered a syllable. "The less losses our alliance sustains will help us become victorious. I am only helping the only way I know how, and that is through magic. I am a wizard, and a powerful one at that. Here, let me demonstrate."

Kirkrik walked to the edge of the mountaintop and chanted loudly, before he threw his right hand forward. Baeron saw a bolt of light leave the wizard's hand and fly toward the battlefield.

The bolt collided with the lower backside of an orc, who leaped into the air, dropping his sword and grabbing his buttocks. That left an opening how a dwarf to plunge his axe into its belly.

Baeron whistled.

Chuckling to himself, Kirkrik continued to throw bolts at the orcs, each lowering their guard as the wizard shocked them. His hands flew back and forth, until one of his bolts went off target and hit Radamuck square in the rump.

"Oops!" Kirkrik said, before waving his hands in apology.

The trio on the mountaintop saw the black-bearded dwarf looking up at them, while shaking his fist at the wizard. He moved his lips, but they could not hear him.

"What's he saying?" the aide asked.

"He's calling me a silly ol' mage," Kirkrik answered, before he noticed the look of surprise on Baeron's face. Kirkrik's face then blanched. "Oh, I don't think I can repeat that."

Baeron just chuckled, before another ball of flaming pitch came out of nowhere, landing far behind where he stood.

"Oh no, no, no, that will never do," Kirkrik said, before he raised his hands to the sky, chanting yet again. A blue ball of energy emerged from his hands, and the wizard shot it forward with a quick lunge.

The ball spun as it flew, and it hit the catapult on the front of it. The blue ball exploded and surrounded the catapult in a bluish mist. The trolls tried to run, but they bounced off the bluish walls and fell down.

"Ah, I just love it when a spell goes right!" Kirkrik said with his high-pitched voice, clapping his hands together. Then, he raised his hands above his head once again, but this time, a pinkish ball appeared, and when it got to the size of a small boulder, he threw it skyward.

When it exploded, it cascaded down around the elves. They were now perfectly protected from pitch balls and boulders. The elves cheered.

"I'll stay up here with you, Baeron; just keep those archers firing! We need to help Radamuck's forces in any way we can!" the wizard said.

"Oh, like the way you helped him just a minute ago?" Baeron asked sarcastically.

Kirkrik just smiled.

***

Frampton and Dramin watched the battle unfold before their eyes. The spy saw Dramin's reaction to the pinkish glow over the dwarf city; the wizard had smirked, as if unsurprised that Radamuck Rosar had called upon another wizard to assist him in the fight.

Frampton eagerly awaited some dweomer of some sort from Dramin.

But as he saw, it wasn't coming. Dramin hung back, directing his troops a safe distance from the front line.

"Aren't you going to combat them with spells of your own?" the ghostly spy asked.

"I am waiting for the perfect time, my dear Frampton. When I used magic against them in our earlier battle, they found a way to combat it and defeat me. However, I shall use my magic when the orb instructs me. It has told me they will not be able to combat it this time."

Frampton knew the answer before he asked the question; he was the one who said they would trust the orb. But with the dwarf's wizard picking off the orcs and disabling the war machine with ease, Frampton had grown antsy.

But Dramin eased his fears.

"You overestimate the enemy," he told the spy. "They are too few, and our forces are killing as many of their warriors as they are killing ours. However, the wielder of the Sword of the South and his close friends still live. They are very hard to defeat. But I assure you, my friend, that I have yet to introduce my trump card. When I do, they are going to wish they never trusted *him*."

Dramin laughed hideously, one that resonated with hatred for the enemy. Frampton noticed that, and his spirit quailed with slight fear.

He had yet to see what the trump card was. Dramin hadn't told him about that part of the plan.

And somehow, Frampton wasn't sure he wanted to know.

***

Not worrying about what Infidelius and the Imperialists were up to at that moment, Grumpet concentrated on the fight at hand. The orc in front of him marked him, his sword held up to parry each and every swing Grumpet threw. But the orc didn't get any of its own swings off, and when Grumpet knocked its sword to the side, trouble registered on its dark face. Grumpet's left fist came off *Flad-rul* and came barreling in at the orcs' face. The punch connected with what served as the beasts' nose, sending its head flying to the left. The force of the blow made the orc tumble over, but before Grumpet drove the killing blow home, Yanos came over and stabbed the orc in the chest, his blade piercing the orc's heart.

"Taking my kills now, are we?" Grumpet asked.

"No, just taking care of this one so you can take care of the one coming at you from behind."

Grumpet turned and saw the orc coming at him. With the blade cocked over the orc's head, he bent over. The orc's waist collided with Grumpet's side, and the human reflexively lifted his left arm up.

The orc, as Grumpet raised his back, went flying over it, making a complete revolution in the air. It landed with a thump.

"There," Grumpet told the halfling, "you can have that one, too."

Yanos looked gleefully at the human. He then leaped onto the orc and stabbed away at its chest.

Grumpet grinned, and then went off in search of other prey.

He found it quickly, but the troll in front of him tried to take him down with an overhand chop. Grumpet ducked and rolled out of the way, coming up on his feet.

Nice try, he thought, as he then sped in behind them and sliced the back of the troll's legs with *Flad-rul*. The troll howled in pain, rearing back with the club. It fell over as it lost its balance, and Grumpet had to roll out of the way again, just in the nick of time.

Yanos and Grumpet both jumped on the troll this time, *Flad-rul* and a tiny sword stabbing and poking its flesh. It shook as the swords plunged deeper and deeper, and eventually gave a deafening roar as it knocked both the human and the halfling off.

Grumpet picked *Flad-rul* back up as he got off the wet ground, and the troll was up, too. It had pockmarked cuts on its chest, the result of Grumpet and Yanos' repeated stabbings.

And the duo clearly saw that it was not happy.

The troll opened its mouth and roared down at Grumpet, but it didn't see an axe fly in and lodge itself in the troll's head. The troll fell face first, the axe embedded deep in its skull.

Radamuck came over and tugged on his axe hard. It came out with a squelch, the odor of troll brains permeating the air as the head released the axe.

"Now you're taking a kill from me? Between you and the halfling, I won't have to worry about dirtying my blade!"

The dwarf laughed heartily, holding his belly as he chortled.

"Nay, yeh'll get yer blade dirty, believe yeh me, but I just wanted to throw me axe at a stupid troll. They never know its comin'. Now, if yeh'll excuse me, I have orcs to kill," the dwarf king said with a bow.

Grumpet nodded at both the dwarf and Yanos, before he went to check on Jessica, who busily fought an orc.

***

A hard thrust by Grumpet's wife ended up splitting the orc's scalp. Sidestepping the tumbling body, Jessica Paddymeyer raised her magnificent blade in front of her.

Black blood ran down its sharp edges, and Jessica's eyes scanned in front of her, looking for additional attackers.

Another orc came at her, its blade cocked back behind it, looking to swipe at her. It did, and she ducked out of the way and felt a breeze blow above her as the sword passed.

Despite it being too small for her, Jessica grabbed the sword of a fallen fire gnome and came up with it. With the two weapons, she gave herself a clear advantage over the evil one.

Jessica snapped the blades against her opponent, and with a cry she set the orc on its heels. She noticed its difficulty deflecting and stopping her swift attack that it dropped its weapon and fled.

She ran after it.

She quickly caught up with the orc, which tried to evade her through the swarm of dwarves and men. As it slowed, she tiptoed up behind it and tapped it on the shoulder.

It turned.

Her face had contorted in a grimace, and she had the two swords quickly behind her before the orc realized she had tapped on its shoulder. The blades flew in from convergent angles, and soon, the orc's head found itself separated from its body.

Jessica looked down at the beheaded orc, then up at another enemy, which stared daggers at her. She noticed that the one in front of her looked exactly like the one she just killed—it had the same ears and same lines over the eyes. Each had a little bit of its lip cut in the exact same place.

Again she went into her en guard position, both blades up in front of her. The orc attacked, but unlike the one she had just defeated, this one handled a blade rather well. It had first chopped toward her left, but her own blade moved down easily for the parry. It then spun and swung hard toward Jessica's right, but her borrowed sword, with a twist of her wrist, deflected that cut just as quickly as the orc had executed the move.

The orc snarled and shot blows with its sword, ones Jessica hardly believed she had blocked so smoothly. The attempts to get through her defenses were futile, having no luck with the swipes and slices.

Yet the orc took a breath as a left-left-center combination failed to strike a killing blow, and Jessica had readied herself for it. She quickly put the orc on the defensive, aiming chop after chop with the two swords.

She decided to quickly put this orc out of its misery. She chopped low on the right side, but the orc made to hop over the sword.

But Jessica feinted, a move the orc never saw coming.

Instead of going for the orc's legs, she stopped her blade mid-stroke, and instead of bringing it up, she brought her own sword, the sword she had sharpened, up and around from the left.

The sword sheared through the orc's right arm, before she righted herself and drove the tip of the orc blade into the chest of the enemy.

Tearing the sword from its carcass, Jessica saw her husband in a battle not too far away. She ran to him, first ducking the sword of an orc and driving her own blade into it up to the hilt. Another tried to hack at her, but the lithe female avoided the sword, backhanding her own blade across its throat.

"Good of you to come by," Grumpet said to his wife as he noticed her disposing of the enemy. "You really have improved, my love."

"All because of your training and watching you for so long," she replied with a smile.

"Well, I appreciate that," he said, bringing *Flad-rul* down and to the left to turn aside a fire gnome's blade, sending it flying away from Grumpet's size. "But you really have impressed me. You have proven that you can take care of yourself, especially among foes this great."

The smile on her face showed Grumpet that she wanted to kiss him, but they both knew the time wasn't right. The enemy was about, and they would have killed the lovers had they paused for the quick kiss they so desperately wanted to give the other.

But then, two dwarves jumped into the fray, axes spinning around them, cutting the enemy down. Radamuck and Aidan had arrived, slicing through orc armor and gnome shells quicker than a heated rod through earth. Aidan appeared to have finally broken a sweat.

"Just wanted to tell yeh, Grumpet," a sweaty Radamuck grunted as he hemmed down a charging fire gnome. "Yer friends from the south look like they are finally ready to fight for us."

Both Grumpet and Jessica looked immediately back toward the city. Semper Infidelius and the rest of the Imperialists from the southlands still had their swords drawn, but now they walked toward the battle with purpose.

For one, Jessica hoped the purpose was of killing orcs, and not starting trouble with her husband.

Chapter 14

Galloping as fast as he could, Rens Heider, a page in the House of Blen Duffel, the premier guild in Briskey Bucktooth, returned to the city astride his chestnut-colored stallion. Duffel, having seen lightning and flashes south of the city, sent Heider out in search of what Duffel was sure to be an approaching storm. He wanted to know how bad it looked.

Oh, he has no idea how bad it is, Heider thought as he remembered the guild leaders' words.

"Make way!" Heider yelled to onlookers and those in his way as his horse flew through the city at a healthy gait.

He made a left-hand turn onto Chenser Lane, scattering livestock and people. When he reached the front gate of Duffel's guild house, two pages younger than he came forward to grab the horse's reins, leading it off to the guild stables. Once inside, Heider walked with purpose toward Duffel's main audience room. As he walked, he kept his eyes forward, keeping his attention on the oak doors with the brass handles adorning them and not on Duffel's other prized possessions.

Heider was a fairly young page, with short-cropped black hair and a clean-shaven face. His posture was regal and his clothes had the necessary accoutrements of a warrior: squared shoulder armor, a flowing cape of crimson, and a steel sword for defending the guild master when outside of Briskey Bucktooth. His boots hardly made a sound on the marble floors.

He hardly waited for the heralds to announce his presence to the guild master. Instead, he crashed through the doors one-handed and didn't even notice the evening meal had Duffel otherwise engaged.

Duffel looked up as Heider barged in. The older man, dressed in the finest linens ever produced in Briskey Bucktooth, was in his fifties and was fairly portly around the middle. His hair was a mix of brown and gray, and his nose was sharp and only slightly rounded at the end.

With a chicken leg in his hand, the guild master rose from his chair, walked around the table and met Heider at the center of the large room.

The page dropped to his left knee and bowed his head in front of the legendary guild master.

"You may report your observations, my young page," Duffel said. "At what speed does the storm move?"

Heider took a deep breath and began.

"My lord, the disturbance over the skies to the south of our fair city is not what we originally believed. It is not a storm approaching. A party of orcs and trolls have attacked Lowbridge, my lord, but the dwarves are fighting back!"

Duffel dropped the chicken leg. Then he lowered himself to look the page in the eye.

"What did you say?" he said, thoroughly shocked.

"War has come to the doorstep of the dwarves, my lord. Orcs, trolls, and other ghastly, evil beings have attacked Radamuck Rosar's stone stronghold. But, from what I saw, the dwarves were ready for what approached. They are not alone though, my lord: humans and elves fight alongside our neighbors. And, my lord, they have a wizard. The wizard is the one making the lightning.

"But the orcs are many, the dwarves few," Heider said mournfully.

Duffel stood quickly and began to talk to thin air.

"Why wasn't I told of this war before this? Where are my seers and my mage! Send for them, and my generals! Immediately!" Duffel screamed, and from out of corners of the room, door wardens rushed out to do their master's bidding.

Minutes passed in silence, as Duffel paced. His slippers hardly made a sound on the floor, as he paced back and forth while the dilemma unraveled.

The doors flew open. Duffel's seers glided into the room, trailed by the archmage, Tiks Rinyard, and Duffel's assorted generals.

All went to a knee, except Rinyard.

"My lord, command us," they all echoed. However, Rinyard stayed silent through it all and looked unconcerned. To Heider's eye, he had a look of glee.

"War has come to Lowbridge," Duffel said, looking at each one of the assembled party. "My page, who rode hard through the wind to the very cusp of the war, tells us that orcs and trolls have attacked our dwarf neighbors to the south.

"I am of the opinion that we, the premier guild of Briskey Bucktooth, should not let the war against the dwarves to progress any further than it has; our army should stand beside our neighbors and fight the menace back. Lowbridge is our neighbor and, as long as Radamuck Rosar has been king, the economy of our city has been linked to the success of the Lowbridge mines. The products they create with their silver, swords and shields, have protected us in many battles," Duffel added, and Heider noticed the guild master made sure to have the complete attention of the generals when he spoke that particular sentence. "They trade weapons for goods throughout our district. It is only smart business sense that we go to their aid."

"But why haven't they called us for aid prior to tonight?" one general asked.

"Word of war had perhaps not reached your ears," Rinyard interrupted, "but it had reached mine. The dwarves' wizard contacted me before this; I told him I would relay their 'request' to you in time.

"It seems that the request slipped my mind."

To Heider, it looked like Rinyard had smirked when he said this.

Then the page looked at the guild master, who had suddenly gone red in the face. He stared at the wizard with contempt.

"You never let your master know about this? How dare you! You were instructed to inform me of anything surrounding us, especially as important as our neighbors to the south! What were you thinking, Rinyard!" Duffel bellowed.

To Heider's surprise, the archmage fired right back, in an equally bellicose tone.

"I was thinking of the state of your guild, my lord! I have consulted the orb; I know how dangerous this enemy is. I did not want your soldiers put in harm's way, I did not want your guild to crumble! You should be thanking me!"

"I will decide what is right or wrong for this guild, mage!" Duffel responded viciously. "I have decided what is right for this guild for years! We have not gotten where we are today by foolish decisions; my decisions are never foolish."

"I think helping the dwarves would be a poor decision, my lord," the mage began, but Duffel cut him off quickly.

"That is why it is not your decision. If helping the dwarves will help the city's economy stay steady, then by the gods, we will help the dwarves! Now get out of my sight before I decide your services are no longer needed."

Rinyard, taking a deep sigh through flared nostrils, turned on his heel and left the audience chamber.

Duffel then issued his orders to the remaining generals.

"We must arrange an army to go to Lowbridge. Heskin, arm the soldiers of this guild; tell them what they will be up against. Dinnen, alert the guilds in league with us to see who will ride. Tell them the economy of Briskey Bucktooth as a whole would be hampered should we not go to assist the dwarves. If you have to, tell them their personal wealth *will* be hampered should they refuse me. And then all of you, return here for further orders," he said, and the generals saluted and left.

Duffel turned to Heider.

"My young friend, I know you wish to take rest. You have ridden hard already, but I ask you to ride again for Lowbridge. Let the king know the armies of Briskey Bucktooth will be coming to their aid as soon as we are assembled; it may be that we will be en route to their realm when you arrive. If you succeed, wealth will be the least of your concerns and you shall have my gratitude and the gratitude of this great city. Make haste, my friend," he said, and Heider bowed.

He turned on his heel and walked out the same door, walked down the same hallway, before he ordered the two young pages to bring him a fresh mount.

When it was brought to him, he leaped atop his horse, pulled back on the reins, and kicked the horse into motion. The great steed reared on its hind legs, whinnied hard, before charging off through the streets of Briskey Bucktooth toward the dwarf kingdom to the south.

He hoped he made it in time.

***

With matching horizontal and vertical strokes, Grumpet cut a path through the orcs, making one for Jessica, Radamuck and Aidan to follow. Their swords were also in use, keeping any enemies from attacking Grumpet from the rear.

Then a flash of light came from the sky, drawing their attention, for just a split second.

The bolt of lightning came from the south, followed seconds later by a low rumble of thunder. Then the rain, which had abated slightly, came back in full force. It was a downpour that drenched the skin.

Radamuck and Aidan hadn't felt a rain like this since their walk toward Mount Bastine, which, to the dwarves and all they've been through, seemed like millennia ago.

With the rain pelting their faces, visibility waned. But that didn't stop Grumpet and the others from fighting.

They cut through platoons of orcs and fire gnomes, before they got up the hill, where they finally saw the rest of Dramin's army.

"By the gods!" Aidan yelled. "It will take forever to cut through that many!"

"Aye, I bet yeh're right, me boy. But we'll cut them down afore they make mincemeat out of me dwarves!" Radamuck answered, before a troll's club came down in front of the dwarf king.

Stunned by the near hit, Radamuck raised his axe to plunge in into its flesh. But before he did so, *Flad-rul* tore in from the right, severing the troll's left knee tendons.

It gave a blood-curdling howl as it reared back, trying to paw at the gash.

Aidan moved forward, spinning his axe and sword combo before he gave a quick one-two; the axe coming over first from the left and the sword flying in from the right, twirling the blades in between hits. The troll bent double as the dwarf hit it.

Jessica then sliced horizontally, cutting the throat of the beast, before Radamuck, who never let the axe drop after

Grumpet had his hit, drove the blade of his axe deep into the troll's head, cracking the skull hard.

The troll, with the king's axe still embedded deep in its brain, fell forward, with Radamuck reeling as it fell to the muddy earth.

Grabbing his axe and giving it a hard tug, it came free from the creature's head.

"There are more to fight. Let's stick together and we can inflict even more damage!" Radamuck said, and all rose their swords into the air with a mighty cheer.

They did stick together, despite having trouble with their footing. The grass, what was left of it, had grown slick and the dirt underneath muddied the soles of their moccasins. They knew that an overswing against an opponent as lethal as these led to disaster.

Grumpet matched a diagonal cut by an orc before the human twisted his wrists and turned the orc's sword over. He backhanded the beast with his left hand, before bringing *Flad-rul* back up to parry the orc's blade once again.

He got *Flad-rul* underneath it and turned it up and over, sliding the blade toward the orc's throat with a horizontal swipe. Blood poured out of the wound, and Grumpet added insult to injury by punching the evil beast with a powerful roundhouse right to the nose.

Grumpet then felt a shove from behind. He looked to his left and saw the fair-haired Semper Infidelius push past him to slash and kill the oncoming orcs.

Grumpet grew enraged; his nostrils flared, and he gripped *Flad-rul* so tightly that it felt like he had the strength to rub the handle away. But he kept his emotions in check and didn't strike out at Infidelius.

Without thinking, Grumpet got next to Infidelius and began to keep the orcs at bay, *Flad-rul* blocking everything the enemy had. He didn't even look at him, but Infidelius looked at him. He sneered.

Yeah, keep looking at me Infidelius, Grumpet thought. *You'll get yours soon enough.*

The other southerners, Grumpet noticed, hung back slightly from he and Infidelius. He felt certain they wanted to keep out of the way should their leader suddenly attack him.

But he was unconcerned with the matter. Radamuck told Infidelius he would let Grumpet finish the job he started several days ago.

The two continued to fight alongside one another, until Grumpet looked back behind the southerner. He saw the other Imperialists were otherwise engaged, when an orc came up from behind to get the drop on Infidelius.

The black-skinned being didn't get as far as he hoped, as with a yell, Grumpet moved his feet to the left, swung the great *Flad-rul*, and leaving a trail of fire behind the blade, beheaded it. The orc dropped like a stone, still holding on to its knife.

Infidelius, startled by the yell, looked behind him and saw the dead orc. He looked to Grumpet, staring hard at human, who looked equally hard at the dead orc.

When Grumpet raised his head and saw Infidelius staring, he knew the tumultuous thought that now enveloped the southerner's mind. He just put Infidelius in his debt, and knew how much that rankled the proud man.

But he decided not to say anything. This was not the time nor the place for conversations such as that.

"Keep fighting," Grumpet ordered instead, and he then walked off to find other prey.

***

Infidelius just kept looking at Grumpet's back, not believing Grumpet saved his life, especially after all the grief the southerner gave him when he had arrived in Lowbridge.

He did realize that he was now in Grumpet's debt; after all, if Grumpet's sword didn't slice the orc down, the orc would have killed him and he would not get the chance to return to the southlands.

He didn't see the orc coming, and that was what bothered him the most.

The growls of an orc shook Infidelius out of his reverie, which came at him with its sword raised. Infidelius parried, swiped the sword to the right, before he spun in the mud and drove his sword down to the right.

Infidelius's blade connected, severing the orc's knee, cutting swiftly through the bone and flesh. The orc went down with a squeal, before an arrow from the elves above, fired seconds before Infidelius's spin, lodged itself in the creature's throat.

The southerner looked up toward the elves and saw Arrol looking down. The elf saluted the southerner with two fingers to the brow, but Infidelius, unsurprisingly, did not salute back.

***

"Are you ready?"

"Yes, master."

Dramin's voice, however cold it had been since he murdered Danolf Jenson, did not sound as cold or hollow as the one that answered him. But the wizard was satisfied nonetheless with its reply.

He looked at the menace in front of him and smiled. He had taken this being, a being he had killed, and returned it to life so that it may cause incredible amounts of devastation on his enemies.

"Go forth and wreak as much havoc on the dwarves as you can! But a word of caution—leave the one with the flaming sword for me. If he dies, then you will risk my displeasure! I want to be the one to kill him, to exact revenge on him! The dwarf king, you may kill; I care for him not. Kidnap the woman, if you can. It will weaken Paddymeyer for me even more," Dramin said, and with a nod, the beast turned away.

Frampton, however, looked on at the scene with interest. He didn't like the trolls much, especially the ones created by the wizard for his deadly plans.

But he did have to admit it to himself: Dramin had it right this time.

"You approve of my decision, my friend?" Dramin asked the ghostly spy, shaking Frampton from his thoughts. The spy nodded.

"We consulted the orb for this, Dramin. It is what the orb said to do, and I trust the orb explicitly. You have outfitted our weapon in impenetrable armor. It will be tough to defeat. Even Paddymeyer will have his hands full with it."

"And are you prepared to do what the orb says for us, as well?"

Frampton looked at the wizard and smiled.

"I have never been more ready."

Dramin grinned, before laughing maniacally.

"I know you haven't, my friend. I know."

Chapter 15

When Heider and his horse splashed through the Stream of the Dwallows, he knew his journey was nearly complete. The near three-hour ride from Briskey Bucktooth to Lowbridge wore on the page, but he knew that, unfortunately, a rest at the end of it would be unlikely.

During his scouting mission, he knew the dwarves had held their own against the enemy. But that was nearly seven hours ago, and anything could have happened in that time.

And that worried him. He hoped that the dwarves and their allies continued the fight, knowing that the enemy had a 10-1 advantage over them.

But he knew who fought with Radamuck Rosar, and knew anyone who wielded that sword had to be powerful indeed. He didn't tell Blen Duffel this; he knew that the guild master would be even more cautious than Rinyard wanted him to be if he had that knowledge.

All of Heider's thoughts over the journey was the survival of not only Lowbridge and the dwarves, but also of Briskey Bucktooth. Duffel had a point: if the dwarves failed and the realm was destroyed, Briskey Bucktooth's economy would founder.

Being a resident of the city all of his life, he wanted to make sure the city prospered.

Heider dug his heels into the horse's flank, spurring it on further and faster. He held on to the reins as the horse sped up.

A few minutes later, the horse carried Heider over a small crest to the northwest of Lowbridge, and there he saw it: the war continued.

Things had changed, though. Where it had been green and lush, the ground was now brown and barren. The army of the enemy had torn up the ground as they fought against the allies, and, aided by the rain, made the going treacherous. Bodies, he saw, littered the ground with dwarf, human, orc, and gnome. Thankfully, most of the dead were of the enemy.

Heider also saw the pink bubble above the city protecting the elves, formed since he was last here, and also saw balls of fiery pitch flung from war machines on the enemy's side. Where the spheres landed, the grass ignited, and he saw dwarves running. The smoke rose and made the battlements on the façade of the city practically invisible.

He knew he made it just in time.

He heeled the horse into motion, moving toward the base of the city, where he hoped to deliver Blen Duffel's message to Radamuck Rosar.

As his horse began its trot, Heider noticed that many non-combative dwarves looked at him warily. Clerics worked on bandaging dwarves from injuries suffered during the battle, and some assisted the clerics in their tasks. Some kept an eye on the battlefield, keeping watch to make sure that none of the enemy's balls of pitch came toward them.

"Where can I find the king?" he asked, but he knew the answer before he asked the question.

"He's in battle, stranger. His steward is with the wizard, though. That way," a red-bearded dwarf said, pointing toward the main gate.

Heider nodded and trotted off toward the large, silver gate.

There stood a dwarf and a tall man, which, he knew just by the man's attire that he was the wizard of whom the other dwarf spoke. The wizard turned as he approached. Smiling, the wizard spoke first.

"I was thinking you and your people weren't coming. I take it Tiks Rinyard delivered my message?" Kirkrik said.

"No, my lord, he did not. I was sent by Blen Duffel to find out what was happening. I returned to him and relayed the situation. Our people should be en route to Lowbridge to aid you. Where should I help you while we await them?"

Fib Niosh came forward.

"We will take yer horse. Yeh may quickly sup, if yeh like, then join the battle. As yeh can see, our lines are holdin' fairly well, and the elves above us are keepin' them back with their arrows," Niosh said, before he clapped his hands.

Female dwarves came forward holding bread and water for Heider, but the page waved them off.

"Nay lord. I am weary, but I am able to fight. The survival of your city is essential to the survival of my city. I will fight now and eat in your wonderful halls later," Heider said, before dismounting his horse and watched as the dwarf women led it away. "Blen Duffel said that the army of Briskey Bucktooth may already be on their way when I arrive. They could be marching out of the city now, or have been on their way for two hours. They could be marching over the Dwallows now. I will help to hold the city up until they arrive." Heider drew his sword and rushed off to the battle.

Fib Niosh looked off after the man and turned to Kirkrik.

"The news that Briskey Bucktooth is on its way fills my heart with joy, master wizard. I just hope we can hold the enemy back before they can get here to join the fight," he said, looking up into the reddened face of the wizard.

"I think we will, Fib. In fact, I know we will. Once the men from the northwest arrive, it will change the face of the war. But what shocked me most was that the wizard trusted most by the highest guild master of the city refused to aid us. We may have to deal with him at another time, and he is powerful, indeed," he responded.

"We should be glad that at least one warrior came," Fib added.

"One helps, but it won't be enough. I must return to the summit, my friend. Keep the gates closed, and may the gods protect you from the enemy."

Fib bowed to the wizard, and Kirkrik disappeared with a swish of his robe, not appearing again until he reached the summit of Lowbridge.

***

"Quickly now, we must head to the ground! We need to repel the enemy from below! We must join our dwarf brethren and help them fight off the orcs! Bring your arrows and swords!"

Baeron issued his orders to the elves, and they readily complied. Arrol, who had come up to the summit an hour before, itched to get to back into a battle with his friends. He put his quiver on his back and led the elves to the entrance to the city.

Down the stairs they walked, walking briskly. The city had grown silent and practically empty, as Radamuck had ordered the women and children, except the young male dwarves, like Andrew Flibberstimmer, who wanted to fight, down into the lower reaches of the mines. It was there that Lady Rosar and baby Radasack were lodged, along with those who couldn't fight.

The enemy had no way of reaching them there, if the battle turned for the worse.

As they approached the gates, the Guard of the King saw them and immediately halted them. They looked at the elves curiously, before Baeron strode out to the front.

When the dwarves saw Baeron, they bowed low to the elf lord, knowing the relationship he had with their own king.

"Open the gates so we may join our allies," Baeron ordered.

The dwarves complied as quickly as the door would allow, and soon a stream of fair-haired beings from Bastine flowed from the city.

Unfortunately, Fib Niosh was in the way.

The steward saw the hoard of elves rushing through the gates, and his eyes grew wide as they approached. He tried to yell for them to avoid him, but instead he managed to tuck his arms in as they breezed by him. One accidentally bumped into him, sending the dwarf sprawling to the muddy ground.

Baeron, after all the elves had filed out, walked up to the steward and helped him to his feet. He brushed him off, but Fib began to brush him away.

"I can do it meself; I, unlike others, don't need elves to help me! I'm perfectly capable of taking care of meself!" the steward said rudely.

Baeron looked at the dwarf with a raised eyebrow, but decided not to worry about it. He left the steward to stew in his muddy clothes and went off to join his warriors defend his friends' homeland.

Even if that meant saving the life of Fib Niosh.

The elves rushed across the plains, their feet not making a mark in the mud. Some had their bows loaded and fired bolt after bolt at the enemy, plugging them down with all they had.

And some of the elves' quivers were magical, so there were no need to reload them when their arrows had appeared exhausted. By just saying the word "arrows!" the quivers reloaded themselves, and made all enemies in the area blanch.

Other elves carried bright swords and daggers, and they were not afraid to use them. As an orc approached, Arrol slung his bow around his back and, in the same motion, took out two curved blades on his hip.

Uncrossing them, he waited for the enemy to draw closer. The orc took a swipe at him, but he dodged that easily, jack-knifing out of the way. He then buried the dagger in his right hand into the back of the orc's neck, before another tried to come up from behind. He twirled the dagger in his left hand and, without looking, drove the weapon right between the orc's eyes.

Pulling the daggers out, he twirled them again and sheathed the deadly blades. He returned to his bow, pulling an arrow, nocking it, and stringing it. He measured his shot, lifting the bow just over the horizon, aiming for a troll that Kirkrik Dannell had long since imprisoned.

Pulling back on the string, he let the arrow fly. The arrow shot quickly through the air, and when it reached the blue bubble, it sped right through, catching the troll unawares. It embedded into the troll's heart, but it wasn't enough to take the massive beast down.

Seeing what he had done, he yelled to several of his cohorts and quickly told them to draw their bows and fire at the troll. Soon, one, two, three arrows zoomed away, all puncturing the blue bubble. They connected with the troll, and it staggered some more, but still did not go down.

Then, seeing what his elves had done to the troll, Baeron took out his own bow. Made of balsam, the bow was nearly as large as the elf lord. Carved into it were elven symbols, which danced along its length.

Baeron stared the troll down, before pulling an arrow from out of nowhere. The arrow looked to be as long as a tree trunk, but Baeron handled it with ease.

He pulled back on his string and, with his left eye closed, snapped the string forward. The arrow propelled itself through the air, twisting like a missile with dark red flames coursing behind it. It crashed through the blue bubble, plunging deep into the troll.

The troll exploded, but the arrow didn't stop. It went right through the troll and plunged into the war machine.

The war machine shook before it, too, exploded, sending shards of wood and silver flying through the air. Several orcs died from the blast.

Dwarves around him cheered, and knew that if the war were won, the dwarves would drink flagon after flagon to him for that one act.

Then he heard the largest, lowest growl that he had ever heard in his three thousand years, a growl that chilled him from ears to toes.

Baeron turned and did not believe what he saw.

It stood nearly ten feet high and looked stretched, perhaps with the wizard's magic, from its original height. Armor covered it, with none of the vital organs exposed. Its helm covered its face, except slits for the eyes and a wide opening for its mouth. It carried a tree trunk for a weapon, and immediately, the elves and dwarves who fought at Statuary Tower muttered something about another elemental.

But no, it wasn't an elemental.

Elementals need not be armored, Baeron thought.

Then he saw the beast's skin. It was green, and he saw it was a troll. An overlarge troll.

Baeron saw that it headed directly for Radamuck and his friends, and the elf lord said a silent prayer while his elves fired multiple arrows at it.

***

Growling again, the troll swung the tree trunk, taking both orc and dwarf out with it. Her victims went flying in different directions, all falling to the muddy earth a great distance from where they originally stood, coming down with a crunch or a crunch and a squelch.

Clerics rushed out to tend to the fallen dwarves, all bringing potions to numb them and their spell books to heal their injuries. Some looked to the mountaintop to find Kirkrik, but jumped back in surprise when the wizard appeared at their side.

"Easy now, lets try not to harm him further," the wizard said, as he closed his eyes and concentrated on healing the injured dwarves.

As he healed them, dwarves the clerics had already healed saw the giant troll and rushed forward to take it out. Even Caz Axewielder, who had been nicked repeatedly by fire gnomes, sprinted past the wizard, ready to gore the beast with his twin-horned helm.

Soon he had the first set of dwarves healed, before he saw that the armored troll had sent another three dwarves—one of which being Caz—flying with its makeshift club.

Sighing, he got off his knees.

"A wizard's healing is never done!" he said, before rushing off to begin more treatment.

***

Grumpet, Radamuck, Aidan, Jessica and Yanos stared at the behemoth troll with something resembling awe. Of the five of them, Yanos looked around and hoped he could stay out of the way of it: he liked to fight, but not something nearly thirty times his size.

Of the five of them, Grumpet, Radamuck and Aidan looked for ways to hurt it.

Of the five of them, Jessica worried that if Grumpet went after that thing, it would kill him. She wasn't concerned for her own safety.

The quintet saw the beast staring at them, and all five got their weapons raised, poised to do battle. They saw the beast coming as arrows skipped off her armor, swatting them away with her gauntlet-like hands. They heard Baeron order his elves off and aim for less armored creatures.

As it neared the heroes— and the heroine—they noticed her entire lower half of her body was armored, which would deflect the weapons of the dwarves.

But Grumpet, who was only shorter than the troll by four feet, would have the better opportunity to take the troll down.

Grumpet gnashed his teeth as the troll neared. He cocked *Flad-rul* back near his right shoulder, before he sprinted forward.

“Grumpet!” Jessica yelled after him, but Radamuck put a hand on her arm as she tried to run toward him.

“He has to do this himself, Jessica. Let’s wait,” the king said. Jessica had no choice but to watch helplessly. Semper Infidelius, fighting nearby, turned and watched Grumpet rush off, as well.

***

Even if Grumpet heard his wife, he didn’t acknowledge her. He was in the zone, concentrating on his objective. He looked directly at the troll, but occasionally he turned his attention to the ground and a semi-dry piece of turf.

Several feet away from the troll’s feet, he saw one. He concentrated on it, and didn’t see the troll raise the tree trunk, ready to strike once Grumpet was in range.

With the trunk cocked back, the troll let out another growl as Grumpet closed in. He now looked at the ground, and once he came within two steps of it, he put his feet together and bounced right on that spot.

The beast brought the trunk down in a swing to the left.

Grumpet sprang into the air, executing a double somersault. The ground propelled him high, just high enough to get him over the troll’s massive swing, which came across level with its waist. It missed him by mere inches.

Grumpet twisted his body and landed on both feet, looking right at the troll’s back. With *Flad-rul* cocked back again, he didn’t even wait for the troll to turn.

He swung hard, aiming for her just above her waist. The blade connected with her armor, not making a dent as steel met steel.

Flad-rul shook, vibrating in the man's hands. Grumpet looked up at the beast, his eyes wide. He took the blade away and twirled it in his left hand as the troll turned toward him. It roared hard, leaning toward him.

Grumpet gritted his teeth and made a decision. He looked at the troll, looking for its weakness. As he had already determined, anything from the waist down was off limits, as *Flad-rul* wouldn't be able to penetrate it.

But then he saw an opening, just under the shoulders. The opening was at the armpits. If he could get *Flad-rul* stuck in there...

He knew what he had to do.

Grumpet sped in, swinging his sword to the left with both hands. Instead of using the sharp edge of the blade, he adjusted the sword and slapped the flat side of it against the troll's forearms. The troll's arm moved slightly, but not enough from Grumpet to get his sword up under the arm. He swore.

Twirling the sword, he tried again, this time to the right. It moved again, but not by much.

He looked up at the troll, who looked amused by his efforts. It simply leaned in and roared as loud as it could.

Grumpet bent his arm and tried to stuff his sword into its mouth, but the troll, despite its size, was too quick. It leaned back just as quickly, before winding up and backhanding Grumpet thirty feet away.

***

Jessica's eyes followed her husband as he sailed backward, falling hard on his back, splashing mud everywhere.

There was no chance of Radamuck stopping her this time. She broke away before the king knew she was gone, rushing through the dwarves on her way to her husband's side. She had her sword out, and if any enemies came near her, she only swiped at them, not stopping to engage them.

Radamuck followed her, ordering Aidan to try to take out the beast. However, Semper Infidelius was quicker.

The king got his axe into it, chopping down opponents that had gone after the woman, before he threw his axe into the back of an orc that closed in on her. It fell to the mud with a thud, and he pulled the axe out before parrying an orc blade with the handle.

The troll walked toward Grumpet in an attempt to finish him off, but Aidan quickly caught up with it and stood in front of the troll, next to Infidelius. Spinning the blades in front of him, Aidan did his best to keep the beast away from his friend. Infidelius jabbed at the troll, trying to make an opening for Aidan.

It lunged at him with her hand, but the dwarf stopped spinning his weapon and jabbed the sword at it. It didn't hurt her, but he believed the troll realized this opponent would be a tough one.

Infidelius and Aidan stayed ever vigilant, keeping the troll at bay, while Jessica knelt next to her husband, getting him up from the muck and mire. Radamuck was there as well, keeping the orcs off their backs.

"Are you okay, Grumpet?" Jessica asked her husband.

"I'll be fine. Damn troll packs quite a wallop, but it's nothing to me. It'll need more than that to keep me down!" he said as he quickly got back to his feet.

Bending over to pick up a fallen orc's blade, he shrugged as much of the mud off his broad back before stalking in on the gargantuan troll.

He stood next to Aidan and whispered to the dwarf, "distract her." Infidelius looked over at the pair and saw an orc coming at Aidan from behind. Spinning on his foot, he reached over and sliced the orc's neck open. Infidelius brought his sword up in front of him, his eyes keeping watch for other threats.

Without noticing what Infidelius had done, Aidan nodded at Grumpet, all while grinning at the troll.

Spinning the dual sword-axe, Aidan let the handle of the axe side slide down to his hands. He then snapped the axe forward, trying to aim for the unprotected joint where her head met the shoulder.

The troll reared back in agony as the axe cut a deep gouge in its collar. Its arms flailed around as it tried to get the axe out, but by doing so, it gave Grumpet the opening he ever so desired.

Grumpet reached up with the orc blade, getting it into the troll's armpit. He buried it deep, trying to pierce the tough shoulder muscle above it. That set the troll in a greater rage, and it blindly slapped Grumpet aside again.

Seeing this, Jessica grew more enraged than the troll. Stealing Radamuck's axe from him—surprising the dwarf king in the process—Jessica wound up and flung the axe at the troll.

It connected, hitting the troll in the skull armor.

Stunned by the blow, the troll staggered after Radamuck's axe bounced away. Aidan backed away, but Jessica didn't. She waited for the troll to lift her arms again, and when she finally did, Jessica leaped and jabbed her own sword into the left armpit.

Instead of what Grumpet did, Jessica plunged the sword into the troll's body cavity. In doing so, Jessica's sword tore through a lung.

The troll continued to thrash around. With Jessica still holding onto the sword, the troll tossed her around, but she managed to get her sword out of the beast before it fell to the earth, covering those nearby with layers of mud.

It flung Jessica several axe-lengths away, her momentum rolling her away.

Dwarves suddenly swarmed the troll, and with their axes beheaded the monstrous being so that she would never cause harm again.

As the dwarves finished the beast off, Radamuck came over to Grumpet.

"Are yeh sure it couldn't keep yeh down?" he asked.

"I think after that one, she would have kept me down," Grumpet joked, laughing with his dwarf friend. "Where is Jessica?"

Radamuck suddenly looked around, not being able to find the woman. Then, he and Grumpet heard a scream, one that chilled the human's blood.

Two trolls had Jessica in their arms, and they carried her away; they had come in behind her undetected, as the dwarves had hacked the troll's former leader to pieces. Jessica's sword wasn't in her hands or anywhere near her.

Grumpet grew enraged, even more enraged than Jessica had been when he was knocked to the mud.

"Jessica!" he screamed, the yell echoing through the dell. Drawing *Flad-rul* once more from his sheath, he rushed toward her, but it seemed like the rest of Dramin's orcs had been released from their moorings. They swarmed the human and the dwarves, and the allies only hacked at the enemy.

Grumpet then heard, from behind the orc lines, a deep, maniacal laugh. He knew exactly who laughed, and what he laughed about. It was his worst nightmares coming true, all the nightmares that he had since before the battle at Statuary Tower. The simple fact that Jessica was in the evil wizard's clutches enraged him further, and his hatred for the wizard spurned him on.

Then a blur of dwarf rushed by him. Caz Axewielder lowered his helm and busted through the orc lines, taking several orcs out like a battering ram. Grumpet, Radamuck, Infidelius, Yanos, and Aidan followed the dwarf's lead, and fought through the legions of enemies.

As he swung his sword at the orcs, Grumpet felt a twinge in his back as well as in his sternum. With a scream he hacked at a nearby orc, spearing it through the leg with *Flad-rul*. Radamuck heard the scream and noticed Grumpet's pain. Grabbing the human, he ordered his dwarves to keep fighting, and with Aidan on the other side of Grumpet, he pulled his dear friend to safety.

Grumpet, however, wanted to fight, but Radamuck's grip was tighter.

"Nay, me friend. Yeh're injured in body and spirit. We need yeh healthy. Come with us," Radamuck said.

"Get back," Infidelius said. "We can handle it here."

At Infidelius's words, Grumpet finally relented, even though he gave a look of longing past the sea of orcs.

***

When Radamuck told Kirkrik Dannell how Grumpet had injured himself, he tried to lighten the mood of the friends.

"Well that's what happens when you have armored troll colliding with an unprotected human!" Kirkrik said cheerily.

They were back near the city's gates, Grumpet perched on a wooden table the clerics brought out for those of greater height than they. Kirkrik bustled around his patient, examining Grumpet's bruises and the slight fractures his ribs sustained during the fight with the troll.

"Personally, I think you were stupid to go up against someone like her, but since I was busy with the patients, someone had to do something," Kirkrik added.

Even though his mind was elsewhere, Grumpet smirked at Kirkrik's little jibe.

"If it wasn't for me, you'd be neck high in broken dwarves. One broken human is easier to fix than a broken dwarf."

Kirkrik nodded in acknowledgement, and then closed his eyes. He put his hands over his bruises and muttered some well chosen words of deep curative magic, and within Grumpet's body, healing began.

Except the injury to his heart; Grumpet knew he'd have to retrieve his wife before he could ever begin to heal that organ.

And he wanted to get her now.

"You need a few minutes rest before you go back out there, Grumpet—"

"But Jessica is out there in the clutches of that madman! You can't expect me to just sit here and do nothing!" Grumpet screamed, but Kirkrik's utter calm washed over him, and again, the wizard said a few soothing words, and Grumpet immediately began to calm.

"We will find Jessica and bring her back, and Dramin will pay for even thinking of touching her. And yes, my friend, you will meet him again in swordplay. However, I think that when you do, I will be there. I feel he has something up his sleeve for you, something we have yet to think about and account for, but I assure you Grumpet, we will not abandon Jessica. What we need is a plan, and a spy," Kirkrik said.

"What do you need me to do, Kirkrik?" Yanos said, wiping ale from his lips. His brown hair was slightly wet from the rain that had started to ebb.

"Yanos, you must sneak around the enemy lines and find where Dramin is keeping Jessica, then report back here immediately. Do not tarry; do not engage the enemy if you can help it. Just find her," the wizard said, and the halfling nodded.

Yanos then went up to Grumpet and put his hands on the table.

"I will find her my friend," he said. "She won't be gone long."

"Fare thee well, my friend," Grumpet said, feeling much better knowing that the halfling was on the job. He would have felt even better if he had been the one searching for his wife.

Then killing the wizard—again—for threatening him and his friends.

But before Yanos left, Kirkrik spoke to him again, in a little louder voice, a voice meant for all the friends to hear.

"Yanos, may I suggest going around to the south? You may not want to head around to the northeast, my friend."

"Why not?" the halfling asked, sheathing his sword.

"Well, if you go that way," Kirkrik said, "you'd be trampled by horses in a few minutes."

The quintet looked confused.

But then, Kirkrik's statement finally dawned on Grumpet. Radamuck, however, found his voice first.

"Do yeh mean—?"

"Yes, my friend," Kirkrik replied. "The armies of Briskey Bucktooth are on our doorstep. Our reinforcements have arrived."

Chapter 16

Nearly a thousand strong, the combined army of Briskey Bucktooth's most powerful guilds stormed out of the city as one, all on horseback. Blen Duffel, despite his weight, sat atop his trusted black stallion, leading the cavalry to war.

They turned south and rode for Lowbridge lightly, save their weapons. Like Heider before them, the journey to the dwarven realm would take three hours. They hoped there was plenty of battle left when they arrived. All knew the importance of the mission. All knew what was at stake—help the dwarven realm take out the enemy before the enemy took the dwarven realm out. It was that simple.

The army rushed silently past the Stream of the Dwallows, and as they crossed onto dry land, their horses sped up of their own volition. The men in the army knew of the reinvigorating powers of the river on the northern border of the dwarves, but had no idea it worked so well on horses. Soon, the army saw smoke rising near the city, saw the top of the mountain and its pink bubble created by Kirkrik Dannell.

At the head of the army, Blen Duffel pulled out a horn and blew it three times straight. A deep, bellicose toot emerged from it, and the Bucktoothians cheered. It would be a while before those fighting heard it coming. Duffel wanted any stragglers of the enemy to either get out of the way, or be trampled.

Minutes later, the army found themselves overlooking the battle, and several gasped in astonishment and awe. Some had never seen a group of orcs that size, and a great deal of them were already dead!

Duffel turned and, as one, the army of Briskey Bucktooth trotted down the slight embankment toward the battle, waiting to draw their swords until it was time. They picked up speed as they reached the bottom of the short hill, and as the sounds of hooves intensified, their enemies noticed them, and so did their new allies.

Once the horses were on the battlefield, the dwarves and elves ran toward the city, while the orcs ran toward the Bucktoothians. Swords drawn at last, the horses approached the orcs, and once the two forces met, the Briskey Bucktooth army ran over and trampled the enemy, slicing them down.

Cheers from the dwarves met the ears of the humans, but the humans weren't ready to accept the cheers just yet: they were in the midst of battle, and would not stop until they completed their task. Several orcs tried to run toward the city to escape their fate, but the swing of an axe sealed it just as quickly.

Several circuits around the battlefield the horsemen made, their swords cutting down foes and their horses' hooves running them down from behind. It appeared that the army of Briskey Bucktooth had annihilated the enemy within seconds, but those near the city knew there were still plenty behind the crest immediately opposite Lowbridge's outer walls.

There they stayed, for now.

***

With the enemy distracted by the arrival of Briskey Bucktooth's forces, Yanos took the chance to head south. His little feet carried him around the dead bodies of both dwarf and human, but he didn't pause in reflection of their lives.

Kirkrik Dannell had handed him a job to do, and by the gods, he would complete it or die trying.

He rushed toward the hill but instead turned right, for there was flatter land in that area and would make it easier for him to traverse it. With no enemies nearby, he kept his blade sheathed, yet he was on his guard.

No one saw him as he got down onto the ground to crawl on all fours. He continued in this fashion until he looked up and saw the orcs still had a sizable force remaining behind the enemy lines. At least four hundred of the filthy beasts remained, and he hoped his thoughts about the enemy's numbers found their way to Kirkrik's head.

Yanos continued crawling until he got far enough behind the enemy to turn left undetected. Luckily for him, brambles lay along the wet grass. He snuck behind them, staying low enough to stay hidden from evil eyes. With morning approaching and the clouds dissipating, the halfling utilized the feeble light and peeked through the thin branches. He saw a cage a great distance away, two hundred axe-lengths at the very least. Orcs tended it, poking swords through the bars to keep the person inside on her toes. And yes, inside stood Jessica Paddymeyer, who kept her feet moving away from the swords and the torment.

Yanos scanned the area. Around the cage were orcs and trolls, and walking around to the front... yes, the halfling knew, it was Victor Dramin, strolling out of the dark void into the torchlight that surrounded the cage.

But there was something different about him, Yanos noticed. He carried himself differently, the halfling noticed, which he thought peculiar. The hair was the same, even though he now sported a thin goatee. At Statuary Tower, Dramin's had believed no one had the power to defeat him. Now, Yanos saw that he appeared more cautious, which made the halfling shiver, a bead of fear squirrelling up his spine.

Trailing behind the wizard, he saw, was a ghostly figure in the shape of a man. Yanos couldn't make out what it was, but it wasn't at the top of his priority list to discover its identity. He watched as Dramin now paced between the torches, and it looked like he addressed Jessica. The misty being remained stationary. The orcs had stopped prodding her, and Jessica looked at the wizard. From Yanos' vantagepoint, it looked like her eyes had narrowed, as if with loathing.

He didn't hear anything, not even the drops of water plinking off what remained of the grass.

After a few minutes of verbal torture, Dramin turned and disappeared from the scene, but the ghost chose to linger. The orcs, usually subservient to their master, gave the ghost a wide berth. They stood off to the side and kept an eye on the proceedings.

Yanos wanted to rush the entire distance and engage the orcs, but not knowing what the ghost was, he bit his lip, keeping his emotions and desires down while he continued his stoic vigil.

He then saw the ghost try to reach in at the woman. He saw Jessica recoil, trying to get as far away as she could manage.

That did it: Yanos couldn't help himself. He stood and screamed.

"Noooooooooo!"

Four hundred orcs and one ghostly spy turned as one toward the brambles, and Yanos, gulping, knew they had his neck caught in a noose. He gnawed at the inside of his cheek until he tasted liquid metal. He looked toward Lowbridge, and knew that even if he ran now or chose to retreat later, he was as good as dead.

Without a better option, he sprinted as fast as his hairy feet carried him.

But he didn't run toward the city.

***

Snarls came at her from several different directions, but Jessica did not succumb to her growing fear.

She stood in a cage slightly taller than her own height, one wide enough for several people. Even though it was of wood construction, she tried to break through it, but a spell on the barricade had made it virtually impossible to destroy.

She was stuck in this prison, with many deadly orcs around her.

If the orcs attacked her, Jessica had no defense against them: she had dropped her sword, the blade she had lovingly sharpened before the Battle of Kayiko, when the two trolls had captured her. With the orcs' sharp claws and overlarge teeth, Jessica knew she couldn't keep them off her.

The minutes seemed to drag by as she slowly realized the extent of her incarceration. She felt miles away from her friends, especially her husband, as the enemy's minions surrounded her.

The orcs jabbed their swords between the wooden poles, trying to poke the woman, but she kept hopping out of the way, avoiding their incessant prodding. Deep laughter met her ears, as the orcs howled with sounded like amusement. The laughter continued until a menacing voice emerged from the darkness, stepping into the torchlight so Jessica finally saw the enemy close up.

"Enough!" a voice ordered, and at once the orcs put an end to their antics.

Jessica looked at Dramin with loathing. However, the wizard seemed to smile, almost sneering at the woman, as he knew he had her at his unscrupulous mercy.

"Welcome to this side of the war, Jessica Paddymeyer," he said. "Comfortable?"

Jessica didn't answer. Instead, she looked over the wizard's left shoulder and saw a ghost.

Her breath caught in her throat.

Dramin noticed her reaction and grinned ever so maliciously.

"I see your eyes have found the person that started it all. Jessica Paddymeyer, meet Frampton, the spy who stole the Chalice of Obloeron from under Radamuck Rosar's nose, and beat your husband in swordplay, as well," he said, and Frampton's spirit bowed as much as it could.

Jessica flared at Dramin's defamation of Grumpet and wished she had a sword; any sword would do at this point. If she had one and broke through the poles, she would try to take out as many orcs as possible before she made an attempt at killing Dramin, in as close a way as Grumpet had done him in.

Her lip curled and twitched.

Dramin chortled softly.

"I believe you'd like to know what I plan to do with you, don't you?" he said, pacing the front of the cage from left to right, leering at her from the side of his eye socket.

Jessica stood defiantly silent in the cage, narrowing her eyes, awaiting the wizard's announcement.

"You see my dear, your husband, the elves, and those pestilential dwarves caused considerable damage to myself," he said, pausing to feel the cuts on the sides of his throat, where Grumpet had beheaded him, "and my home of many years. I wish to pay them back for that incident. I have thought long and hard over the past few weeks, since I returned to the realms, how to get my revenge. I admit, the idea was outlandish. I wanted to get the chalice back, and thankfully, Frampton here saw to that shortly after the dwarves returned to their home. I took it from him, as well as his body. I needed his body to perform suitable magic, magic which created the army you helped hack to pieces.

"But I am not upset at that, my dear. The army had its uses. It weakened your husband to the point of exhaustion, and then, when I sent the troll forth, I gave it such weapons that would make it virtually impossible to kill. I hoped that he would see that and think it a challenge, and in the process, hurt himself. He has done so; he had to retreat after you were taken because he was hurt badly. He's not coming for you, Jessica. Get used to the idea. But if he does, I will be ready for him."

But as he turned, he paused and turned back.

"Actually, we will be waiting, Frampton and I. We will face him together, and this time, I will not lose!"

Dramin turned on his heel and left Frampton and the orcs with Jessica, disappearing into the darkness again.

Turning his head to see that the wizard had gone, Frampton smiled before his disembodied form walked toward the cage. The orcs, feeling his presence, stepped away from Jessica's prison, but kept their weapons close, keeping an eye on the prisoner.

"If I had my body back right now, I wouldn't wait for your husband. I beat him once, I can beat him again," Frampton taunted, his tone laced with pure acidity. "He wasn't as worthy to fight me as he thought, and with the power of Dramin behind my sword, I will kill him, and then the Sword of the South will reside by my hip! And just for good measure, if Dramin allows it, I may let you live!"

Jessica shuddered at the notion, the unclean innuendo lingering in the air as the ghost looked up and down her muddy body.

Then the spy reached into the cage with his right hand, trying to grab the woman's arm. Then a loud scream of "Nooooooooo!" pierced the air. Frampton and Jessica both jumped.

Both turned toward the south, as well as the legions of orcs remaining in the enemy army. There, standing among a row of brambles, was the dwarf's halfling, apparently performing an important reconnaissance for the dwarf king.

But there was no one else around him.

Jessica shuddered as she watched Frampton's ghost smile, and he turned to the orcs near him.

"Kill him. See to it that the little beast doesn't get back to the dwarves, unless it's as a corpse," he yelled, so that they and the rest of the army heard him.

Jessica watched helplessly as the orcs snarled and walked toward where Yanos Kingsfoil stood, with swords drawn in their hands and malice sketched in their eyes.

***

Trotting up to Radamuck, Blen Duffel dismounted and allowed the dwarves to lead his horse away. Bowing to the king, he offered his hand to the dwarf, who also bowed.

"Thank yeh for showin' up when yeh did, guild master. Yeh've got the enemy on the run," Radamuck said. "But we know there's plenty more where they came from. The wizard is a slippery devil; he'll have more in reserve waitin' for us."

"It was no problem, Your Highness. If we had received your summons earlier, we would have been here earlier. But our mage had decided to not allow us to interfere; he felt it was a lost cause."

"Tiks Rinyard is a powerful wizard, Blen Duffel, but he is a dotard. He doesn't see where he should think. You had it right: the stability of Lowbridge in turn ensures the stability of Briskey Bucktooth. Future ages of dwarves will remember Briskey Bucktooth and honor you all with poems and songs for coming to their aid in their darkest hour," Kirkrik Dannell said, as he held his hands in front of him.

"I can assure you that Tiks Rinyard will be dealt with when we return to Briskey Bucktooth, Radamuck. No wizard should hold back a realm from assisting their allies, especially those close to them," Duffel said, but Kirkrik interrupted before the dwarf king responded.

"My friend, you will find that Tiks Rinyard's treachery may run deeper than you can possibly fathom. Even now, as you stand here, he plots to overthrow you, and looks to gain the favor of many other guild masters while you fight here."

Duffel's eyes widened at the wizard's premonition.

"If it should come down to it, Blen, yeh'll have the assistance of the dwarves to take back what is yers," Radamuck said.

"You'll also have the assistance of the elves," Lord Baeron added. "Your bravery here today will not be forgotten by the land of Bastine. Any who are able to fight for you will do so."

Blen Duffel bowed to them all in thanks, even though his face twitched a bit in the corners of his mouth.

"We have greater things to think of now, my friends," Kirkrik said, gaining the attention of all. "Blen, when you arrived, we had just sent out our halfling, Yanos Kingsfoil, out to the southern reaches of the realms to spy on the enemy. He should be there now. You see, our friend Grumpet's wife was kidnapped while we were in the midst of the battle. We believe he is setting a trap for us."

"What are we to do then?" the guild master asked.

"We are to wait," Grumpet said, finally standing from his crouch. He had been deep in thought over the entire situation. "I would prefer not to; but Yanos Kingsfoil is Radamuck's best spy. He can slip in and out undetected and give us the information we need to set a counter attack.

"But if the wizard has touched a single hair on her head, then I will have to reacquaint him with *Flad-rul,*" Grumpet continued as he put his brilliant sword on his shoulder, gripping the handle hard, flexing his muscles as he rubbed his hands on it.

And when Blen Duffel and the other Bucktoothians saw the sword, they were in awe.

"The Sword Of The South has returned!"

Duffel quickly went to his knee, followed by the rest of his army. They held Grumpet in reverence, a fact that would have stunned Grumpet weeks ago.

Right now, though, as Radamuck plainly saw, he was too concerned with the state of his wife to worry about reverence.

“Yes, the Sword Of The South has returned,” came a voice from the side. Semper Infidelius walked up to the group, dirty from the battle. The other Imperialists followed him.

Grumpet lowered his sword, holding it in his right hand. His knuckles had started to whiten. He stared at the Imperialist leader. Radamuck tensed.

“My lord, I owe you a debt for what you did on the battlefield earlier. Please allow me and my men to go in search for your wife,” Infidelius said.

Grumpet smiled for the first time in hours.

“I’d be pleased to have you on the party. All the good men we can find would help. You are a noble man and a great fighter, Semper Infidelius. Anyone who says differently will taste Flad-rul.”

Infidelius then walked up to Radamuck and went to a knee.

“My lord, I apologize for my behavior when I arrived. My service to the kingdom of dwarves in repayment,” he said, bowing his head.

“Rise, Semper Infidelius. No harm was done; no apology is necessary. And if Grumpet misses with *Flad-rul*, which hasn’t happened yet, then me axe will be bitin’ the man that speaks ill of yeh!” Radamuck said, patting the man on the shoulder.

“So what are we to do then?” Aidan asked after Infidelius had risen, rubbing a scratch an orc blade had given him.

Kirkrik stepped forward.

“We are to wait until we hear from Yanos. Until he returns, we can not plan our—”

The wizard had gasped, his face ashen, the blood leaving in a hurry as his features grew set with fright. His eyes bulged slightly.

“Yanos,” Kirkrik breathed. “He’s in trouble! He’s been spotted by the orcs!”

Without thinking, Radamuck grabbed his axe and rushed toward the hill. Following quickly were Aidan, Arrol, and Grumpet, all three of whom had their weapons drawn and ready to go. The rest of the warriors, including Semper Infidelius, Blen Duffel, and the Imperialists and Bucktoothians, followed them.

The dwarves and elves saw their leaders in action and quickly drew their axes and bows. The second part of the war was about to begin, and they certainly didn't want to be left out. Caz Axewielder quickly replaced his helmet and began the charge.

***

If I am about to die, Yanos Kingsfoil thought, *I will do so with my sword in hand, meeting the enemy head on.*

When he noticed he only had one true option—running back toward Lowbridge was folly, as the orcs had a greater stride and would be on him in mere minutes—Yanos drew his sword and crashed through the brambles, hacking at the branches with everything he had. The thorns scratched him, but pain was a hazard he had to embrace right now: he was a few moments from the fight of his life against the remaining four hundred orcs, and he needed to concentrate on them. They charged fast with looks of hatred embedded on their ebony faces.

The halfling hardened his face. He set his jaw and furrowed his brow. He held the sword tightly in his right hand, and prepared for the worst.

Seconds passed slowly and the orcs advanced quickly, and soon they were there. Yanos shook.

The lead orc came in and brought his blade down low in an attempt to get the halfling in the gut. But Yanos was too fast, as he put both hands on the sword and swung to parry. As steel met steel, he turned his wrists and brought his opponent's blade over, putting the orc at a disadvantage. He retracted his blade and then drove it high into the orc's stomach. Not waiting for it to fall, he pulled the blade out and turned to his left, where he got his sword up to deflect an enemy sword in front of his face. The orc looked at him and snarled, but the halfling simply smiled, then swiped the blade away to the right before reversing his thrust and driving his own sword through the creature's neck.

He clashed swords with several orcs, before the opposition completely overwhelmed him. He prayed to his gods and hoped that they would take him quickly. A false move by the halfling would bring about his doom.

Surrounded, the enemy closed in and tried to make overhand stabs at him, but using his quick-thinking, Yanos hit his knees and crawled through the legs of the enemy. The enemy stabbed at thin air or themselves, and when Yanos got through, he looked up, snickered, then sliced at the closest orc's knees.

When the orc fell over backward, its tendons knicked, Yanos plunged his sword into its heart. Seeing that the orcs didn't notice one of their own missing, he leveled two more with swift chops to the back of the knees, then picked up a fallen orc's sword.

With the two swords, he moved in and began to cut down the orcs, first with the left and then the right, until they noticed the halfling had decimated the first wave of attack. One rushed after him, but Yanos bent over and the orc fell over the halfling, and he followed the trip with a knife to the throat.

Another came, and then another, until the orcs scrambled to find a way to defeat this one-halfling wrecking crew. They were unsuccessful, as Yanos effectively countered every attack: he got his swords up in an 'X' in front of him, stopping an orc from cutting a line down the front of his face.

Yanos forcefully uncrossed the swords, sending the opponent's sword flying backward. That left it defenseless, and soon found the halfling's right-hand sword boring a hole in its gut.

But seconds later, the orcs had Yanos surrounded once again, and it appeared he wouldn't get out of it this time. They all jabbed their swords in his direction, snarling and releasing low guttural noises from deep in their throats, when four arrows came from seemingly out of nowhere. Arrol and three other fleet-footed elves had sprinted up the embankment and fired their bolts into the backs of the enemy.

Yanos laughed a hearty chuckle before he caught the orc next to him asleep, slicing off its wrist and taking off its sword hand. It gave a horrid squeal, before Radamuck Rosar came up and drove his axe into its spine.

Yanos hugged his friend quickly, while Aidan and Grumpet came over and started hacking the enemy, with Aidan's blades spinning and twirling, while Grumpet criss-crossed Flad-rul in front of him, dazzling the opponent and confusing it all the same. He stopped his motions, before chopping low and tearing through leg bone.

Radamuck looked around and whistled, before looking down at Yanos with disbelief.

"Yeh did all this yerself? Maybe yeh should be the one to challenge Dramin!" Radamuck said, but Yanos just chuckled.

"There is no way I'm getting near the wizard. I'll just stay back here and keep any orcs from going toward the city," the halfling said. Then he noticed Grumpet. "Your wife is in that cage there," he said to the man, pointing toward the rear of the encampment, "and there is a ghost with the wizard. Use caution, my friend."

At these words, a flame erupted in Grumpet's hazel eyes and he saw the wooden cage. He gritted his teeth.

"Aidan!" he said, and the young dwarf fought his way backward toward the trio. Using a two-handed defense on his patented double weapon, Aidan parried quite a few blows, but once he spun the blades he clipped more orc throats and gashed more orc sides than Yanos did. "Let's go. Time to show Dramin he should have stayed dead."

***

Orcs came at all angles as Grumpet walked away from his friends, although Aidan followed to keep the enemy off his back. But none of them got close to Grumpet's body, as the pair's whirling swords parried and shunned the enemy's attack one by one.

It appeared as though Grumpet's ribs no longer hurt him, and the human silently thanked Kirkrik Dannell for healing him. There were no twinges as he extended his arms to execute two orcs at once with powerful one-handed swings to the neck.

Grumpet and Aidan turned the fight into a slaughter, as their weapons carved a burning path through the enemy that kept coming at them despite the trail of bodies they left behind.

Flashes of light followed the duo, distracting Grumpet. He looked back to the source and saw Kirkrik at the top of Lowbridge, hurling magical energy at the orcs, setting them alight, causing them to run into other orcs. Grumpet smirked as everyone got into the battle.

Semper Infidelius and his band of Imperialists followed.

With twirls and precision strikes of *Flad-rul*, Grumpet angrily killed many orcs. One-handed, he parried a thrust from the left, before flicking his wrist down to the ground to pin the opponent's sword. Then he spun and kicked the orc in the face, shattering its nose and dazing it. It dropped to the ground hard and never got back to its feet, especially after Grumpet drove the heart of the blade into the heart of the orc.

The battle progressing to near victory, the remaining orcs wisely ran eastward and northward, away from the dwarves and their powerful allies; some never made it, as the elves tracked them down and buried an arrow in their heads. With a great cheer, the dwarves celebrated their victory, but Grumpet wasn't worried about the victory. He continually scanned the area for more orcs or enemies, and all he saw was death and destruction covering the grassy vales, with turf pulled up and nothing but dead bodies and mud remaining in its place.

Seeing no enemies coming at him, he put *Flad-rul* at ease, and turned and walked toward the cage. Semper Infidelius and Aidan did, as well.

When he finally saw her behind the wooden posts, he saw a great deal of emotion on her beautiful face. Tears welled in her eyes and streamed down her cheeks, and that's when he felt burning in his own eyes. His own salty tears poured forth at the sight of her in captivity.

"Grumpet," she choked out, "it's a trap! Dramin and the spy are behind this whole thing! They kidnapped me to lure you into a trap!"

“It’s okay, there will be no trap. We’ve sprung it. Now let’s get you out of here,” he replied, as he tried to grab the posts that barricaded his wife from him.

But the powerful magic placed on it by Dramin kept Grumpet’s hands at bay.

“You won’t get her out that way,” came a soft voice from Grumpet’s left, and from out of the shadows walked Victor Dramin, although to Grumpet’s eye, it was a meshing of Dramin and Frampton the highwayman.

“The magic I have placed on the cage will not abate unless I remove it or I die, and since there is no chance of either happening any time soon, you might as well say good bye to your precious bride,” Dramin taunted, looking daggers at the human in front of him.

Grumpet stared Dramin down. He so wanted to kill the wizard, but knew Kirkrik Dannell wanted him to keep his hand steady until it was time.

“I have waited for this moment ever since we last met, Grumpet Paddymeyer, and this time, there is no chance of you escaping my blade. I have someone who has defeated you before—”

“He only defeated me by luck, and I can assure you, Dramin, I won’t get stuck this time,” Grumpet interrupted, his right wrist tightening, bring the sword straight up to be perpendicular with his waist. Semper Infidelius also had his sword up in the same manner, but he didn’t know how dangerous this opponent was.

Dramin looked over to Infidelius and smiled.

“You must be one of the rabble rousers from the south,” he said mockingly. “An Imperialist. A defender of the weak in place of no standing army or government. I think that after I’m done here with the dwarves, I’ll continue south and batter what remains of a once proud kingdom,” Dramin sneered.

With a yell, Infidelius raised his sword and charged; Dramin didn’t move.

But Grumpet moved, and moved quick. With his strong hands he intercepted Infidelius’s arms and held him there. He looked into the southerner’s eyes threateningly.

"Don't give in to your anger," Grumpet whispered. "He is trying to make you fight with anger. He taunts because that is his base offense in a battle of swords; if he gets you to fight with anger in your heart, then he has already beaten you. Clear your mind. We will do this together. He can't handle both of us, and I have beat him once prior. We will be victorious, just calm down and keep your emotions in check." He only let go of the man's arms when Infidelius took a deep breath to calm himself.

Turning back to Dramin but staying a feet away from Infidelius, Grumpet spoke loudly.

"And what makes you think you will get out of here alive, wizard? If you were to somehow strike me down, you'd have to get past a legion of dwarves, elves and men, and I can assure you the only way you'd leave then is when they bury you!"

Dramin gave a throaty laugh in response.

"Oh, I will strike you down, Grumpet Paddymeyer. And it will be with a bit of old magic that you should easily recognize!"

The wizard made a motion with his left hand, and from the shadows stepped the ghostly figure of whom Yanos had spoken. Grumpet knew from the features that it was the highwayman, Frampton, the one he had fought with inside the corridors of Lowbridge, before the spy's lucky escape.

He even thought Frampton's ghost looked like Dramin's twin.

Grumpet immediately thought that Dramin had erred, for he did not know what magic of which he spoke. He grew more confused when Dramin turned to face the misty being, raising his arms toward the heavens and chanted in a guttural, incomprehensible language. The winds immediately picked up, swirling through the valley, roaring in the ears of Grumpet. It picked up in speed and intensity that it knocked Grumpet and Infidelius off their feet, both landing in the mud: Grumpet on his back, Infidelius on his left side. Infidelius lost his sword as he fell, while Grumpet kept a hand on *Flad-rul*. Aidan also hit his knees.

He heard Dramin's voice over the gale, and both men had to squint through the wind to see the proceedings. It appeared as if a vicious, transparent cyclone twisted around both the wizard and the spy. Then Frampton's ghostly arms rose from his sides as he joined in the recitation of the wizard's chant. The ground then shook around them, finally knocking Jessica off her feet to the bottom of the cage.

It then all happened at once: the two beings, one solid, one spectral, walked toward each other, their arms outstretched. Black clouds reappeared over the dell, but instead of rain, powerful lightning bolts shattered the air, filling the surrounding space with electrical currents of many different magical proportions. The aroma of ozone filled the valley.

And then Dramin and Frampton collided, with the ghost of the spy stepping into the body Dramin had taken over.

A radical transformation transpired: the body shook as they continued speaking in tongues, the words coming from ancient magic that had never been heard in Lowbridge before this moment.

The magic ended a few long heartbeats later. The wind died to a breeze, the ground stopped quaking, and the black clouds dissipated as quickly as they had been formed.

Still on the ground, Grumpet looked up at the wizard, who now stood facing him, his head lowered and his eyes closed. The ghost was no longer seen, and the sun had just finished its initial rise over the eastern horizon.

Then, the wizard raised his head, and his eyes popped open.

And then, a voice from deep inside Dramin echoed throughout the valley.

"Thank you, master."

Dramin smiled, showing his yellowed teeth.

Grumpet knew then what had just happened, and unfortunately he had been powerless to stop it.

Dramin and Frampton had merged souls.

They were one.

Chapter 17

When the ground stopped moving under him, Radamuck felt confused at what had just happened.

"What in the name of Dausonne was that?" he asked, but Yanos Kingsfoil had no answer.

But just as he asked his question, the crystal amulet now burned in his pocket. Gingerly, he took it out and quickly opened it, revealing the wizard's face.

Radamuck turned back to the city, where he saw Kirkrik standing on the mountaintop.

"It was Dramin casting spells," Kirkrik said, "powerful spells that once casting begins, no one can stop them, not even another wizard. I saw everything, Radamuck: he and the spy have joined souls. It is up to Grumpet to stop him. Semper Infidelius and Aidan are there as well, and I'll be there quickly to support them."

And then Kirkrik closed the connection, the amulet winking out at the dwarf.

"What does that mean, Radamuck?" Yanos asked.

The dwarf king thought carefully before answering his diminutive friend.

"It means that everythin' changes, and we need to hope that Grumpet and Aidan can hold off the wizard. The southerner, Infidelius, is there, too. Three against two should be enough."

"Don't forget that Kirkrik said he'd be there, too."

"Nay, I'm not forgettin' that, me friend. And I'm not forgettin' yeh, either," Radamuck said, looking down at Yanos' arms. "Yeh're all scratched up! I'd take yeh back to the clerics, but there's no time."

Radamuck pulled out a silver flask from his belt. He opened it and handed it to Yanos.

"A little somethin' that should take care of the scratches, and maybe yer insides, too."

Smiling, Yanos accepted the dwarven curative quickly, and downed it in one sip. He tuttered and sputtered as the potion took hold of him, and within seconds, the scratches on his arms disappeared.

Then he fell face forward, splashing in the mud.

Radamuck chuckled at the sight, but then Yanos' head popped up, all covered in wet, brown muck. He then got up and wiped it from his face.

They walked down the hill, back to the battleground which had soiled the lush, green valley.

But then they stopped suddenly, for the most unlikely being imaginable blocked their way.

Fib Niosh stood there, looking at Radamuck with hate in his eyes. He carried a sword in his right hand, and he looked ready to use it.

***

Dramin stood motionless as Grumpet, Aidan, and Infidelius realized the foe had essentially doubled. He then drew a sword from a sheath on his hip, and its blade gleamed brightly against the rising sun.

Grumpet saw it and his eyes widened.

"I know that blade," he said.

Dramin seemed to laugh from deep within himself.

"Yes, Grumpet Paddymeyer. I'm sure you do. It was Frampton's, and he has since bequeathed it to me for our little... insurrection." He said it as a sneer, and he awaited the response.

Keeping the anger down, Grumpet twirled *Flad-rul* in his hand. He started to walk back and forth, keeping his eyes squarely on the wizard, awaiting the attack.

Dramin's next words weren't the attack Grumpet expected.

"Maybe I should tell you, Grumpet Paddymeyer, that there has been a spy in your midst for some time," he said.

Grumpet felt the blood rushing out of his face, only replaced by a littered trembling in his flesh.

"What do you mean?" he asked.

"Long before I attacked your pathetic village, I had a spy among the dwarves." The wizard paced. "A double agent, you may call it. I had flown to this very realm, Grumpet Paddymeyer, and put a powerful spell on a member of Radamuck Rosar's inner circle, to act on my orders when I called him to my service. During the spell I just performed, the spell that brought Frampton and I together," he said, which preceded a low laugh from the spy deep within, "also called my agent in Radamuck's circle to turn aside from the ways of the dwarves and join me. He is currently executing my plan. He will execute Radamuck Rosar!"

"No!" Aidan yelled, and then he turned and rushed back toward the city.

Dramin turned and raised his hand, firing an immense fireball at the back of the dwarf, a fireball so intense that Grumpet and Infidelius had to lean back and away from the scalding heat.

But the sphere of flame never reached the dwarf, as Kirkrik Dannell intercepted it the moment he materialized in their midst with a spin and a raised hand of his own. He practically inhaled the fireball with his palm, and a few well-chosen words obliterated the fireball into nothingness.

Kirkrik emerged from it without a mark on him. Aidan kept running.

Dramin, Grumpet saw, fired a sneer his way.

"So you are the infamous Kirkrik Dannell. Pardon my lack of manners when I say that I am not happy to make your acquaintance," the young mage said.

But Kirkrik didn't miss a beat.

"Think nothing of it, my friend. I already know that manners are completely beneath you," he said sarcastically.

Dramin's lip curled at Kirkrik's retort. Grumpet's grin went wide.

"Just because you have interfered with my affairs, protecting the dwarf scum, does not mean that he will protect his uncle. No, I believe that Fib Niosh will dispose of him, too," he taunted.

Grumpet swore.

Dramin turned and looked right at him.

"Yes, does that surprise you, Paddymeyer? Can not believe that someone so close to Radamuck Rosar, even one such as he that despises non-dwarves, would betray him like that? I can tell you it wasn't easy to convince Fib Niosh to do my bidding, but he fought until he succumbed to my control! Once I defeat you and he defeats Radamuck Rosar, then I, Victor Dramin, will have complete control over the southern realm."

His eyes flashed as he spoke, as if lightning struck inside his brain.

But Grumpet just looked at him and laughed.

"You thought you would rule the northern realm, once upon a time, but you seem to forget that it was I who ended that fantasy!" he said, raising his voice. "It was I that ended your dream, your rule, and your life! And if I have to do so again, then so be it!"

He raised *Flad-rul* up in front of him, holding the handle with both hands. Semper Infidelius copied him, cocking it back toward his right shoulder.

Dramin spat his derision on the mud.

"I have planned my revenge against you, Grumpet Paddymeyer, for many weeks. We will not need the excess baggage," the evil sorcerer said, before hurling a bolt of lightning at Infidelius.

Ready for it, Infidelius swung and batted the bolt harmlessly aside. Then he went after the wizard, prepared to strike him down.

He chopped toward Dramin's right flank, and the wizard effortlessly parried the attempt, swatting the sword to the side. Grumpet came in from the left and tried to go high for Dramin's head, but the wizard spun and deftly avoided Grumpet's attempt.

"So be it; two on one. Or two on two, I should say. Since I created the spell, I seem to have inherited Frampton's knack of escaping," he taunted.

Without pausing to respond, Grumpet quickly chopped again, this time at Dramin's knees. A split second later, Infidelius attacked, again at the flank. With unbelievable quickness, Dramin deflected both attacks, parrying both with a one-handed sweep to the right.

It seemed impossible to Grumpet that Dramin had turned into an improved fighter with just a simple spell. It had to be a complex one neither he nor Infidelius understood. Both would have to work together and in harmony to defeat the wizard and spy combo.

Without thinking, Grumpet sprang and somersaulted twice in the air. Dramin tried to swipe at him, his first offensive move, but Grumpet swung *Flad-rul* down to parry before he dropped to the earth, landing on both feet.

Growling, Dramin moved his sword back and forth, deflecting the advances by both men, getting his sword over in time to meet the thrusts and swipes they made.

Infidelius then tried to give an overhand chop to Dramin's scalp, but the wizard turned his wrist, batted the attempt to the left and backed out of danger, getting both Infidelius and Grumpet in front of him.

***

"And what do yeh think yeh're doin', Fib Niosh? Get out of me way!" Radamuck bellowed, not knowing the seriousness of the situation.

Fib just looked at him as if looking through him.

Fed up at his steward, Radamuck tried to walk past him. But Fib's sword stopped him, as Fib flicked his wrist and placed it against the king's breast.

Sensing trouble, Yanos took his sword out and immediately poked it against Fib's stomach. The steward removed the blade from the king's chest and swung at the halfling, steel connecting with steel, the sound reverberating throughout the vale.

Radamuck was purely incensed, and he let his anger get the best of him.

"How dare yeh attack him, councilor! Yer job is to protect these lands when the king is away, not to attack the king and his advisor! Now get back to the city and stay there until I return!"

Fib Niosh just laughed. Radamuck did not like the sound of it.

"Yeh order me, do yeh? If yeh were to think of me followin' it, it would be the last order yeh'll ever give! I have sat around long enough while yeh cater to the likes of this insolent halfling and the elves you call 'friends.' Or the northerner who is supposedly the heir to the south kingdom! After Dramin is done with him, he will be the heir to a shallow grave! Yeh're a sorry excuse for a dwarf, Radamuck Rosar! This is where yeh'll meet yer end, and I will be the one to lead the dwarves to greater times, like yer forebears intended!"

Then Radamuck realized the importance of the moment when Fib Niosh raised the sword in his hand above his right shoulder and tried to slash down at Radamuck's neck.

Showing incredible agility for a dwarf his age, Radamuck rolled to his left, tucking into a ball and picking up an orc sword before coming up to his feet behind the steward. The weapon felt peculiar in his hand, having never used one, but it didn't matter. Radamuck swiped at Fib Niosh's head, and the steward got his sword up to parry.

Radamuck retracted the sword and praised Dausonne, the dwarf god of war, before attacking again. He wished he had more moves like Aidan or Grumpet, but his rudimentary knowledge of swords would have to do in this situation. The two matched strokes, both with crossing strikes in front of them, before Radamuck spun awkwardly in the mud and landed a solid kick in the other dwarf's gut.

Fib staggered, losing his balance and nearly toppling to the ground. Radamuck didn't attack just yet, allowing time for his formerly faithful steward to catch his wind.

Instead of attacking, Radamuck fixed him with a stare and said words he hoped neither he nor Yanos nor Fib would ever forget.

"Fight the curse that did yeh in, Fib. Fight the durned dweomer hard; yeh're a dwarf of the Rosar clan! Yeh're strong deep inside, and yeh were poisoned in the mind. Fight it off!"

But Fib appeared in too deep now. He caught his breath again and then charged, rushing toward the king with both hands on the sword. He struck low, and Radamuck nearly had to bend all the way over double to defend himself, parrying the attack before raising himself up and slashing at the other dwarf's left shoulder.

Instead of slapping the dwarf's shoulder with the flat side of the sword, Radamuck changed the angle of the blade slightly. He cut the dwarf, and a bead of crimson blood oozed out and ran down the muscle. Fib responded with a flurry of chops and slices, all of which Radamuck stopped breathlessly.

He pushed hard with his sword, and Fib pushed just as hard, and with swords crossed in front of each other, the two faces were inches apart.

"Yeh can't stop Dramin, Radamuck; he's bigger than the both of us!" Fib spat.

"Oh really?" he replied. "I was under the impression I already stopped him once. I think we can do it again. I tell yeh one more time, Fib Niosh: fight off what the wizard has done to yeh, and this will be forgotten. But if yeh attack one more time, I will be forced to kill yeh, and the gods won't be blessin' yeh, me old friend."

It appeared as if Radamuck had finally gotten to his old childhood playmate. A mist formed in the steward's eyes and a grimace appeared on his face, as if he battled internally against the wizard's spell.

Radamuck looked at his friend with pity, knowing deep inside Fib Niosh fought the dweomer with all he had. He had known Fib Niosh a long time and knew he was a tough dwarf, but he didn't know how much fight he had against such a terrible power as Victor Dramin. But as soon as he thought it, he saw Fib's eyes widen and his brow furrow. The dwarf screamed, twirling the blade around his head and attacked the king with everything he had.

Radamuck knew it had come to this before he realized it, and he brought his sword up to fight off the powerful strikes from Fib Niosh. He parried multiple times, before Fib Niosh threw the sword away and punched Radamuck in the nose.

Radamuck dropped the sword he held, too, and fell to the ground. Fib then leapt onto the king and grabbed at his throat with both hands. He squeezed with all the strength within him, but before he did further harm, Yanos leapt and drove his sword into his lower back.

Fib got off Radamuck and belted the halfling with a backhand, sending Yanos to the ground.

Then they all heard a bellow from the hill.

Aidan stood there, his dual sword-axe in his hand.

***

Aidan saw Radamuck laying on the mud and Yanos opposite him, and Aidan felt his anger welling. He dampened it down and walked down the hill, the weapon in his right hand. He immediately knew Fib was Dramin's agent in Lowbridge.

Aidan picked up his pace as he reached the bottom, and without asking questions, began his attack, driving the sword down from the right.

Fib, sword in hand again, parried the sword effortlessly, but jack-knifed out of the way as the axe came flying in from the left.

He sniggered at the dwarf, but Aidan's face showed no emotion as he circled the steward. He didn't speak; he preferred to let his weapon do the talking here. Again he lunged in with the sword, this time chopping low. The chop was a feint, a feint that Fib Niosh fell for. The steward swung low to parry, but hit nothing but air.

Aidan turned the blade over and swung perpendicular to the ground, with the axe coming around from the rear. It met Fib's left elbow, shearing it off.

Fib screamed in agony as his left forearm and hand fell to the earth, followed by his sword. He grasped the stub to try to stop the pain that rushed from the extremity, his nerve endings surely set aflame. He tried to back away, but he immediately fell backward as his feet hit a body. He had tripped over Yanos Kingsfoil, who had stayed still throughout the entire battle. He moved out of the way after the dwarf toppled over him.

Aidan stalked in, swinging his blades over his head. He looked down at the steward with hatred.

Fib Niosh looked up without fear.

"If yeh're going to kill me, kill me now! But believe this—Dramin will have his day, and he will sit on the throne of Lowbridge!" he screamed.

Aidan twirled his blades again until the sword portion of his weapon pointed toward the ground. He stepped up and stood next to the steward, and was ready to drop the blade into the dwarf's heart.

"No!"

Aidan looked to his uncle, now on his feet. He walked over to his nephew and grabbed the weapon. He looked down at the steward with a Rosar stare that made the steward blanch.

"I told yeh that if yeh attacked me again, I would kill yeh. This is the end for yeh, me old friend, and for Dramin's supposed rule in me kingdom. Good bye," Radamuck said, closing his eyes and driving the point of the sword deep into Fib Niosh's chest.

The steward gasped as the sword pierced his heart. He died quietly, not speaking a word of remorse as the light left his eyes.

Radamuck pulled the sword from his old friend's corpse, handing it back to his nephew.

"I had to do it, me boy, not yeh. I said I would do it if he attacked me again, and by the gods, he did it. It hurts me heart to kill me friend. I didn't want yeh to have that pain, me boy."

Aidan nodded his head.

"I understand, uncle. When I heard what Dramin said, I had to rush back to your side. I can't believe it was Fib Niosh, though."

"Me either, Aidan. It is a sad day for all of Lowbridge, when a dwarf has to kill one of its own."

Aidan looked into the wide eyes of the steward, which were now devoid of life. The dwarf king and the halfling joined him, and prayed to their gods.

Even though he became an enemy at the end, he was still one of their own. They prayed long and hard, hoping his spirit would find its way to the halls of their gods, to live forever.

***

Grumpet looked for every entrance past the wizard's defenses. So, too, did Semper Infidelius.

Neither had much luck.

Dramin met each and every swing, each and every thrust, each and every chop. He parried everything, even going so far as to spin and block identical swings by the two warriors.

Grumpet took his sword away from the fray, but Infidelius didn't. He wanted to take out the frustration he had boiling in him when Dramin threatened the southlands with a reign of terror. Grumpet, grimacing, had hoped the southerner would have seen him back out, so they could put their minds together and execute a plan.

Surprisingly to Grumpet, Infidelius did just that once Grumpet thought of it, and then caught Infidelius's casual nod. Smiling and twirling *Flad-rul* through the fingers, Grumpet wound up, stepped up, and swung with everything he had, just as Infidelius did the same thing.

They were aiming for Dramin's waist, Infidelius going for the left, Grumpet for the right.

Their blades inched closer through the air, and Dramin turned back and forth and grabbed his cloak and spun in place. As the two swords crossed where Dramin should have been, they only met air and a gray cloud.

The two skilled warriors stood astonished as they looked at the area between them, where they should have cleaved the wizard in two equal portions.

Scratching his head, Infidelius looked up at his northern counterpart.

"Nothing's left," Grumpet said. "He's gone."

Infidelius nodded, then turned his head back toward the city to see if there were any signs of his Imperialists.

"Grumpet!" Jessica screamed.

Grumpet spun to find Dramin standing right behind him.

The wizard had his sword raised and ready to strike when Grumpet got *Flad-rul* back up in the nick of time to parry, a two-handed deflection on an angle over his forehead.

The sounds of steel brought Infidelius back to reality, and he ran to Grumpet's aid.

Dramin looked down at the human with fire burning behind the eyes, sweat pouring down his face, and his mouth turned in a fierce scowl.

"I have you beaten, Paddymeyer. Time to meet your maker!"

But Dramin didn't get the sword away before Grumpet turned his wrists, then his entire body, bringing Dramin's sword up and around to the right. In his spin, Grumpet backed to the right to allow Infidelius to come in. The two traded cuts with the wizard, who held the sword one-handed as he deftly parried each, before sending a jab toward Infidelius.

Infidelius barely jack-knifed out of the way as the sword came rushing toward his stomach. Grumpet responded with a flurry of moves, a right-left-right chopping combination the mage blocked before rolling forward into a somersault. Before he came to his feet, Grumpet turned and sped off, winding up and dropping the fiery blade toward Dramin's head.

Dramin ducked and backed away, getting his sword up to swipe at the brown-haired northerner. He extended his wrists and tried to cut at Grumpet's shoulder.

But Infidelius was there to knock the sword away.

Grumpet looked briefly to Infidelius, and nodded. Infidelius nodded, too. The debt was repaid.

Dramin took advantage of the dual distraction and yelled, before he started to make two-handed cuts and swipes, knocking their blades out of alignment. He then ran off, before the two men rushed off in pursuit.

When he felt they were right behind him, the wizard turned and immediately swung back and forth, hitting one sword and then the other. He started walking backward as he swung, the swords connecting with each other with a harsh clang.

The wizard then spun to the right and leveled Grumpet with a kick to the head. Grumpet saw it coming and tried to back out of the way, but Dramin clipped him on the left temple, sending the big man sprawling to the mud. Grumpet shook his head to try to clear the cobwebs, and his eyes went wide as he groaned with pain throbbing in his sinuses.

It was just Dramin and Infidelius now, and the two combatants swung hard at the same time from opposite directions, the blades colliding in between them. The pair continued to battle, each trying to gain the upper hand with backhanded swings and uppercuts, twisting their wrists and extending their arms.

Infidelius screamed and circled his sword over his head once before crashing it down toward the wizard. Dramin sidestepped the blow and immediately brought his own blade down with his left hand.

The sword snapped through Infidelius' right wrist. He screamed as his hand fell to the muddy ground, blood pouring freely from the wound.

Dropping the sword and grabbing at the stump of a wrist with his left hand, he turned back to Dramin, and noticed the wizard stalking in, preparing to make the killing blow.

Infidelius ran, but that didn't keep Dramin from walking faster. The sorcerer had a devilish smile on his face, as if he were enjoying himself. With a crooked grin, Dramin pulled the cloak around him and spun on the spot. Again he disappeared from sight.

Infidelius looked behind him and didn't see the wizard. He had stopped twenty axe-lengths from where Grumpet lay. He then felt a piercing in his gut. He gasped, then felt a change inside of him.

At this moment, Kirkrik Dannell's head shot straight up and looked over at Infidelius, who looked frozen in place. There was no one around him, yet he wasn't moving. Something held him there.

Then a being re-materialized in front of the southerner. Infidelius looked down and saw that he had been stabbed, before he looked up into the face of his attacker.

There stood Victor Dramin, a wicked look on his face. It was full of glee as he laughed in Infidelius' face. Then, as his laughter abated, the features froze as he pushed his sword up into Infidelius' chest, clean up to the hilt.

Chapter 18

Kirkrik helped Grumpet to his feet. The man was still groggy, but because of Kirkrik's aid, he was better than he had been when Dramin leveled him.

Grumpet then looked over toward Dramin, and looked past him to see the prone, dead form of Semper Infidelius. It dawned on Grumpet he was now utterly alone in this fight against two potent warriors, two warriors who shared the same body.

But Kirkrik laid a friendly hand on his shoulder.

"You are not alone, Grumpet Paddymeyer. You have me to help you in this fight. We won't let the wizard best us," he said. "We will have to work together, just as they are. The exact same way."

Grumpet looked at Kirkrik, and just from the look he received in return proved that Kirkrik was serious about this.

"You could die," Grumpet said, but his words rebounded right back at him.

"And you could, too," Kirkrik answered. "We have to take a chance. It is the only way to save ourselves, our friends, and your wife."

At that last, Grumpet's eyes smoldered. While he fought Dramin with Infidelius, Kirkrik had worked over at the cage.

"It is very powerful magic that we would be fiddling with, but Dramin has done it, too. We need to kill him in order to counteract the dweomer on her prison. There is no way to get her out unless he lets her out or he dies. We both know the former is a matter to laugh at. We must do what we have to do," the wizard continued, looking hard at the young man.

Grumpet looked over at Dramin, then looked to his imprisoned wife with longing. He saw her standing there, in her magically protected prison, and knew Dramin had done all of this to get back at him, for what he had done at the Tower.

Attacking Lowbridge was about Radamuck's utter defiance of Dramin's rule of the northlands as well as the stealing of the Chalice of Obloeron, that much was clear.

But the kidnapping of Jessica, making it impossible to free her, was all about revenge for killing him.

And that was too much for Grumpet to stand.

He turned back to the wizard and said, “Yes. Let’s do it. I’m going to need all the help I can; your stamina is high and I am weary. Thank you, Kirkrik.”

Kirkrik smiled and waved off the thanks.

“Don’t mention it. You’ll give me a big head, and Edison would never let me hear the end of it if my head doubled in size,” he said, winking.

“Ready?”

Grumpet nodded.

“Ready as I ever will be.”

Kirkrik smiled again, before he closed his eyes and concentrated. His lips started to move slowly, as he spoke an ancient spell that would set a wall of flame around them. That wall would protect them while Kirkrik prepared to rip his soul out of his body so it could join with Grumpet’s.

Grumpet felt the sweat roll as the heat from the flames tickled them, but each maintained incredible poise and concentration throughout the transfer. Kirkrik chanted louder, reciting an incantation few knew. This incantation pulled Kirkrik’s soul while leaving his body intact and in a deep sleep. Dramin, who had been bodiless, used lesser magic to pull the soul from a living body and allowed it to float through the void.

This, however, was different: Kirkrik’s full living energies would meld with Grumpet’s and his own body would not be subjected to the torment Frampton endured.

A swirling wind surrounded both Grumpet and Kirkrik, blowing their hair around as the spell took form and effect. Both men looked to have total concentration on their side. Kirkrik’s incantations grew louder, and suddenly, he threw his hands into the air. A white light flashed from his hands, causing the flames to go ever higher.

Then the wind stopped, and neither Grumpet nor Kirkrik opened their eyes. Kirkrik’s arms lowered and came to rest at his sides, and it appeared that his upper body drooped. A ghostly figure emerged from Kirkrik’s body at that moment. It was if Kirkrik’s body had cloned itself, but wasn’t solid.

He walked forward, before he tuned around to look at his own body. Seeing that he did the spell properly, Kirkrik smiled lightly, before his ghost fell backward, right into Grumpet's body.

Grumpet's eyes flew open as Kirkrik's soul merged with his. He looked around as his eyes adjusted to the light again, then saw Kirkrik's apparent sleeping body on two feet away from him.

He knew he would have to draw Dramin away from Kirkrik's body so that it would not be harmed in the upcoming fight. He looked toward Dramin and saw him pacing near the flames.

Then he heard Kirkrik's voice, as if it were coming from his belly.

"Grumpet, you must be on the defensive first. Let him expel his energies. When he attacks, let yourself move with him. It will be like letting yourself fall, and you will feel like your defenses are buffering you to the ground."

Grumpet nodded inward, then drew *Flad-rul*. The flames surrounding their bodies disappeared at once, and the fight resumed in earnest. He immediately ran out to the right, and Dramin followed, making a cut from the left which Grumpet easily blocked with a flick of his wrist. The wizard snapped off a variety of moves, chopping and slicing and swinging hard, and the warrior, with Kirkrik's magical aid, deflecting each. Infidelius' blood flew from Dramin's blade with every swing.

The northerner moved backward, keeping his feet moving as Dramin pressed. A mélange of vertical and diagonal cuts followed as Dramin's face showed incredible anger and determination.

Then, Grumpet heard Kirkrik's voice.

"Now Grumpet! Turn the tide!"

Winking at the evil one in front of him, he blocked another swing by Dramin, before twisting his wrists, bringing Dramin's blade up and around while he moved behind the wizard. Now Grumpet was on the attack, and did he let the wizard have it.

With hard chops that came from above, Grumpet hacked at the wizard's sword, with Dramin getting his sword up in time to parry, but just barely. Grumpet continually drove the wizard backward, his chops hard. A misjudged parry by Dramin, though, brought the two blades together near the hilt of his sword. Grumpet shoved him backward hard, and Dramin lost his balance and fell to the mud.

He moaned as he hit the ground, splattering mud into the air. He dropped his sword, but scrambled back to it, grabbing the handle. He got the blade up horizontally as Grumpet brought an overhand chop down upon him. Dramin swung and knocked the blade away, before he got up quickly and spun to his right, bringing his sword around. Grumpet jack-knifed out of the way before giving a jab toward the wizard's midsection. Dramin dodged it, before the pair spun in sync, one to the left and the other the right, the two swords meeting in between with a shrill clang.

Grumpet pushed his blade up, sending the wizard's sword up as well. He then backhanded Dramin with his right hand, before the wizard threw a punch that landed squarely on Grumpet's jaw. He staggered and nearly fell.

Dramin then went to the offensive, swinging from three different directions, it seemed. His cuts came left, right, and from below. But it was Grumpet's excellent swordsmanship, aided by Kirkrik's magical abilities, which kept the evil wizard at bay.

A slight backhand by Grumpet followed the multitude of cuts by the wizard and put the two on even footing, if for only a split second. Grumpet fired back, sending stabs and thrusts Dramin would never have stopped had Frampton's soul not been inside him.

Circling the blade above his head from right to left, Grumpet brought his sword down toward Dramin's shoulder, but Dramin rolled to his left before the stroke fell. Coming out of his somersault with his back to Grumpet, he swung his blade up and behind him.

His timing was perfect, parrying Grumpet's blade, as Grumpet had turned and tried to sever Dramin's spinal cord.

Frustrated with the wizard's luck, Grumpet spun again and tried to swing low, but Dramin had leapt over the sword and flipped away from Grumpet.

Dramin smiled as he looked at Grumpet from two full axe-lengths away.

"Come on, Paddymeyer," he taunted, but in the voice of Frampton. "Come after me and give it your best shot. You couldn't beat me when I stole this," pulling the Chalice of Obloeron from Dramin's belt, "so what makes you think you can beat me now?"

Grumpet saw the chalice for the first time in nearly a month, and his eyes widened at the sight of the golden object, which shined brighter than the sun, which was high in the sky.

"What are you doing, you fool!" Dramin yelled at the soul inside himself. "Put that thing away!"

Grumpet heard the words and, without prodding from Kirkrik, chose the time to strike.

He raised *Flad-rul* and rushed in, his legs driving him forward through the sloppy turf. He took the wizard by surprise.

Instinctively, Dramin dropped the chalice to the mud, but it wasn't Dramin who had done it; Frampton's soul, in an obvious attempt to defeat Grumpet, had dropped the chalice to get the sword up to deflect Grumpet's attack.

That brought a long scream from the wizard.

"You idiot! Get the chalice!" Dramin yelled, but Frampton's soul had clearly taken over in this fight and hadn't heard his master.

Grumpet, seeing the chalice on the ground, swung hard, pushing the duo away from the magical object, keeping himself between Dramin and the chalice.

Then there was a change in the fight, as Frampton swung at Grumpet with his right hand, while Dramin tried to stretch with his left hand. Grumpet, keeping a two-handed grip on *Flad-rul*, batted the sword away to the right, before spinning hard. He brought *Flad-rul* over his head as he turned and dropped it down, both hands still firmly gripping the handle.

Dramin's left hand, still reaching for the chalice, was left undefended. Frampton couldn't get his sword over to parry Grumpet's.

Dramin's wrist fell away from his body, severed in a flash of flame.

With a scream, Dramin held up the stub of his wrist and tried to bring the right hand over to stop the pain, but

Frampton's determination overrode him. He kept fighting, chopping at Grumpet awkwardly with a look of pure hatred on his face.

Grumpet went on the defensive, parrying Frampton's thrusts with both hands on his sword. He then swung hard, knocking Frampton's sword aside with an equal amount of force. He then laid a swinging kick at Frampton's knees, getting his heel behind the spy's left kneecap, dropping him down.

Frampton tried to get back up, using the stump of a wrist as leverage. But Grumpet was there in a flash.

Grumpet pointed his blade at the left side of Frampton neck, right at the decapitation marks from when he first took off Dramin's head.

Frampton swung and batted the famous sword away, then got up to his feet and then backhanded the man with the sword. Grumpet backed away with a lean, watching as the point of the blade passed within two inches of his face. Grumpet responded with high and low chops, turning *Flad-rul* over and down, with Frampton hard-pressed to meet each swing. The spy had started tiring, while the northerner worked off his adrenaline; his muscles flexed taut as he swung, extending his wrists.

Panting hard, the spy tried to take in air, but the thorough pounding Grumpet gave him had taken its toll. He had nearly lost against the powerful man what seemed like years ago, and it looked like there was no escape this time, as Grumpet forced him backward.

Keeping his feet moving forward, Grumpet powered ahead, before springing forward into a roll.

Frampton tried to plunge his sword into the man, but he was too slow: instead he drove the sword into the mud, and the one-handed spy could not pull it out.

Grumpet got to his feet and immediately swung *Flad-rul* to his left, stopping it as the blade was pointed at the spy's chest. Frampton immediately took his remaining hand off the blade and spread his arms wide.

He looked at Grumpet with pure loathing.

"It's over. Set my wife free or I will make sure you never walk the realms again," Grumpet said.

But Dramin remained defiant, the same taunting voice coming through with a raspy breath.

"You'll have to kill me then, for I will never remove that spell!" he said, wheezing. "Forever she will be my prisoner, unless you run your sword through me. But I know your mind. You can't do it with the wizard holding you back!"

Grumpet's brow furrowed, and, without waiting for Kirkrik to say anything, he stepped forward and placed the point of *Flad-rul* just under the wizard's breast bone.

"I've done it once," he said, before pushing it through the skin, "and I'd do it again!"

The sword plunged deep inside the wizard and the spy, and a pair of quick breaths blistered the morning air. Both Dramin and Frampton took in air, Grumpet's flaming sword searing their combined innards and souls.

Grumpet looked down into the face of the defeated duo and saw the pain written in their eyes. Their eyelids fluttered, then the eyes rolled back into their head as the body drooped.

Kicking it off *Flad-rul*, Grumpet looked down and felt relief wash over him as he saw the corpse looking up into the morning sky. He sheathed his bloody sword and breathed a tremendous sigh of relief.

"At last, it's over again," he said, and he then heard another voice coming from within him.

"Grumpet, pick the chalice up, then bring me back to my body, then free your wife. I believe Dramin's spell has been lifted," Kirkrik said.

Without thinking, Grumpet ran toward Jessica's cell, reaching down for the Chalice of Obloeron as he ran, grabbing it by its jeweled brim. It left the mud with a squish. He made it seconds later to Kirkrik's side, and without the windy conditions that joined them together, the spirit of Kirkrik rejoined his own body.

"That has worked; we were victorious! The victory belongs to you again, my young friend. Without your skill, Dramin would have defeated our alliance handily," the wizard said.

"If it wasn't for you, Kirkrik, I would have been dead. There was no way that after Dramin nearly knocked me out I would have beaten him," Grumpet replied, trying to give Kirkrik a majority of the credit.

But Kirkrik wasn't having it.

"You did it all, my friend. I was just along for the ride, to make Dramin think that by having my soul inside you, the flooring would be somewhat level. You know it from experience: Dramin loves having an uneven floor, mainly one leaning to his advantage."

Grumpet blinked his confusion away.

"So what you're saying is," he asked, adding it in his head, "once he saw you do the spell to merge with me, we threw him off his game?"

Kirkrik nodded.

"Essentially, we called his bluff. He knew that if the ground was level, if there was any chance you could keep up with him and his ally, the fight would be long. And it was. A long fight against one so powerful will always go to the side of good, Grumpet. And, once you tired them, their combined brain had different purposes: Frampton wanted to beat you, while Dramin's only concern was the chalice. We achieved our ends, and the realms are now safe again.

"And speaking of safe, I think it is time for you to make sure someone you love is safe, too."

Grumpet's head snapped to the side, looking at his beloved wife again and knowing that the spell was done. He looked at her with longing, and quickly rushed to free her.

With two hands, he gripped the wooden poles and tugged. They came loose in an instant, and Jessica leapt into Grumpet arms. She wrapped her armed around his neck, burying her face between his pectorals and cried.

"Shh, it's okay Jessica. I'm here. Nothing will happen again, you're safe."

Jessica looked up at him, her eyes streaked with tears.

"I knew you would come for me, my love. Is he?"

"He is dead," Grumpet finished for her, nodding. "He will never hurt you again."

Lifting his wife out of the god-forsaken cell, he brought her over to Kirkrik, who bowed to her. He pulled a cloth from his robe and handed it to her.

"I'm sure you need this more than I do," he said, pointing toward her eyes.

But Grumpet touched his arm to get his attention.

"What should be done about Dramin and Frampton? We can't just leave them there," he said.

Kirkrik closed his eyes in concentration. Off to the right, where Grumpet had fought the pair, flames ignited out of nowhere, seemingly consuming the body.

When Kirkrik opened his eyes, he smiled again.

"There is no need to fear. I have... taken care of them. There will be no more need of worrying about Dramin or Frampton. They will not come back to life ever again," Kirkrik said with absolute finality.

Grumpet grinned and wrapped his arms around Jessica. Pulling her close, he closed his eyes and prayed silently, thanking the gods for the strength he showed throughout the war, and for returning his wife to him.

He said a longer prayer for that.

After a few minutes, Grumpet, still holding the chalice, led Jessica and Kirkrik back to Lowbridge, retrieving Jessica's sword as the flames that consumed the bodies of Dramin and Frampton continued to burn.

Chapter 19

Radamuck ordered his dwarves around as they prepared funeral pyres and collecting downed weapons, when he saw Grumpet, Jessica and Kirkrik walking over the crest that overlooked the dwarven realm.

The dwarf king gave a mighty shout, which drew the attention of the dwarves and elves around him. They dropped their tasks and, once they saw the trio, gave hearty exclamations of welcome. Grumpet lifted his wife's left hand in victory, which received a larger ovation. But then, looking at Radamuck, he raised the Chalice of Obloeron in his left, and immediately the dwarves gave a greater cheer than ever before.

Grumpet handed it over to the king.

"The wizard and the spy are dead," Grumpet said, and again the cheering started. "Victory is ours!"

The cheering continued, this one larger than the previous.

"Unfortunately," Grumpet added, "our friend, Semper Infidelius, was killed by the wizard. His body is still out there. Someone will have to retrieve it."

At this, the Imperialists bowed their heads mournfully.

Radamuck was initially saddened by this news; he knew Infidelius had come around at the end. But, despite his grief, he had his eyes on the chalice when Kirkrik came up to him and placed his hand on his right shoulder.

"I think it is time you did what you wanted to do with it in the first place, Radamuck," he said. "It is time that none fear for their lives when they hold this object. It is time to destroy it."

Radamuck nodded without thought. It had been this object that had killed many dwarves, humans, and elves, and it was a great reason why the plains of Lowbridge were no longer green.

Calling Aidan, Yanos, Grumpet, and Jessica to his side, he marched back into the city while the dwarves outside hugged each other in celebration.

They all walked together to the mines, where Lady Rosar, Prestillia and baby Radasack waited, along with the rest of the women and children. Several members of the Guard of the King guarded the room, and when Radamuck approached, they all went to attention.

Nodding to the guardsdwarves, he walked passed them and through the passageway. He was met with a round of applause by the townsfolk, and his wife immediately rushed up to him, embracing him tightly.

Prestillia also rushed forward and ran to Aidan, who immediately grabbed her and held her for what seemed to be an eternity.

Radamuck looked to see Radasack, sitting in the lap of a handmaiden, gurgling to himself happily. Radamuck nearly cried at the sight. He never thought he would see Radasack again, if the war had turned bad.

"Me friends, Grumpet Paddymeyer has once again served the people of the dwarves well," he said. They cheered for him. Grumpet blushed. "He has once again proven his worth as the heir to Krampel Paddymeyer, by doing away with the evil wizard Dramin, and his slinkin' highwayman, the one who stole me chalice!

"But it is time that the chalice be destroyed, and it will be done so here in Lowbridge. Me word is law, and no one better try to stop me. Grumpet may look tired, but he will still draw that sword on me command!"

He turned back to his wife and whispered to her, "I'll be back, me love. Take Radasack to our chambers, and I'll join yeh when I'm finished with this," Radamuck said, heaving the chalice.

Aidan pulled himself away from Prestillia, and Grumpet asked Jessica to stay with Lady Rosar and Prestillia, while he, Aidan, Radamuck, Yanos, and Kirkrik all went deeper into the mines to destroy the chalice.

The group waited until the entire room had emptied, before they marched to a passageway on the far side of the room. This passageway went even deeper into Lowbridge, and that was where the great fires were kept.

They walked down the narrow causeway until they came to a flatter concourse, which had many furnaces lining the walls. Radamuck stopped at the first one.

Opening the door, he saw the remains of a fire that had been put out before the war started. With a look to Yanos, the halfling fetched a pail of coal, which he lifted and dumped into the furnace.

Radamuck spread the coal around so that it covered the entire bottom, then nodded to Aidan. The younger dwarf fetched wood, and handed the pail to his uncle. Radamuck placed the wood inside, and then nodded to Kirkrik.

The wizard began to hum to himself, and soon the humming turned to an incantation. As his incantation ended, he threw his hands forward, and powerful flames flew into the furnace from his palms.

"Show off," muttered Yanos, which earned himself a slap to the back of the head by Radamuck.

With the flames burning at such a great intensity, Radamuck raised the Chalice of Obloeron up above his head and, with a few well chosen words, whispered a prayer to the dwarven gods. When his prayer ended, he placed the chalice into the fire.

Under the furnace was a holding vat where all the gold fluid would go. When it had cooled, Radamuck would take it out, melt it again in a larger vat, then dip his axe into it, like he always knew he would.

The group watched as the flames licked around the Chalice of Obloeron, and soon the fire had grown so hot that it didn't take long for the chalice to melt.

Radamuck looked at the melting chalice and began to breathe easier. No one would be on his back, seeking him out to take the chalice away from him.

An hour later, after the chalice had fully melted, Radamuck removed the vat of molten gold, and the group left the furnaces as one.

***

After the cleanup of the surrounding valley, Radamuck invited all of those who helped with the defense of Lowbridge into the city: the Imperialists, the elves, and the army from Briskey Bucktooth, for a celebratory meal and houseroom.

Radamuck stood on the dais of the great hall, with Lady Rosar, Grumpet, Aidan, Yanos, Kirkrik, Duffel and Lord Baeron next to him. A space was left open for Semper Infidelius; the Imperialists didn't request it, and the king knew they looked at the open space with heavy hearts.

Grabbing a flagon of mead, Radamuck held it aloft. Those on the floor also stood and raised their mugs.

"Me friends, our celebration is smaller than it should be. Pray to the gods that our departed friends find their respective halls and live in harmony forever."

After a moment of silence, Radamuck ordered the party to begin, and flagons of ale and mead were passed around, along with a great feast that lasted for hours.

There was laughter and great cheer, as dwarves and elves and men drank and ate together.

***

When the party had died down, some seven hours later, Radamuck walked the corridors of his great city alone. He passed dwarves lying on the floor, next to empty flagons filled at least twenty times next to them. He snickered at his subjects' drinking, and remembered he had quite a few flagons, too. He walked easily through the halls, and soon he came out to the middle battlement, where he found Kirkrik Dannell standing there, overlooking the scene where the great battle took place.

"Party over?"

"Aye, me friend. 'Bout an hour ago. When did yeh leave?"

"Two drinks in. I don't like a lot of spicy drinks, except the altodium rum in my cellar. Plus, I had to make sure Edison was okay; he doesn't like being in enclosed spaces for very long."

Radamuck had a small chuckle to himself, as he thought of the wisecracking bullfrog stuck in the beautiful house which had been the size of a small stone throughout the war. But then the dwarf king looked to where Kirkrik had his gaze, and from the vantage point they had, Radamuck finally saw the truth of the war.

Where green used to flow easily, the land was broken by great chunks of brown. The enemy war machines still stood, and Radamuck knew that under them there was still grass, hopefully.

"Look at all of that, Kirkrik. Just look at it. Me sires would be disappointed in me," Radamuck said, but then the dwarf felt a hard whack on the head by Kirkrik.

He looked up at the wizard while rubbing the sore spot. The wizard's gaze was furious.

"Your sires would be pleased that you fought with all you had and protected your people! That is what they will praise you for! A war of this scale had to come sooner or later, whether you had the chalice or not. If you think that Lowbridge was safe from an attack during your reign, then you have another thing coming, Radamuck Rosar! Comfort leads to complacency, and it was only a matter of time before someone said, 'Hey, let's attack the dwarves!' You have your dwarves well trained, which leads back to your training, long ago. Your sires are proud of you, Radamuck. You kept their homeland safe, and if it were not for your great friends, this city would be overwhelmed by orcs, and all that you hold dear would have been destroyed.

"Your place of honor in the halls of your sires is not tarnished, my friend," Kirkrik concluded with a soft word.

Radamuck smiled at his friend's scolding, then looked back out over the plains.

"Grass will never grow there again. Radasack won't know what it is like to live in beautiful splendor."

The next crack filled the hallway and filtered deeper into the city.

"Are you listening to yourself? You don't sound like a victorious general! Don't you realize you have people here in your kingdom right now with some gardening ability?" Kirkrik said, puffing out his chest importantly.

Radamuck gave a weak smile, remembering back to his visit to Kirkrik's chateau after the Battle of Statuary Tower, where Kirkrik showed him his plants. At that thought, he immediately thought of crazy plants growing in place of grass, and didn't want to tell Kirkrik that he didn't want that in his front yard.

But Kirkrik laughed and said, "No, my friend. I wouldn't dream of burdening you with my type of plants; I don't think the dwarves would take too kindly to them. I have already started the process of growing new grass. In the spring, grass will be where it once was, and it will be just as lush and green!"

Radamuck looked back out over the expanse, expecting grass to magically appear on the fertile plains of his kingdom. But he wasn't disappointed when the grass didn't appear.

Kirkrik simply chuckled and said, "The grass will come, my friend. I have spent the last few hours working my magic to plant millions and millions of grass seeds along these plains. We must let nature take its course; accelerating the process can be disastrous."

After a few seconds, Lady Rosar appeared at the opening of the battlement. She had brought him his long stocking cap.

"Radamuck, it's time to sleep. There is no use thinking about everything that happened over the past few days. You have to see the armies away in the morning, you'll need your sleep," she said.

Knowing his duty—and not wanting to cross his wife again—Radamuck nodded and walked away, but turned to the wizard one last time.

"Yeh did a good job, Kirkrik Dannell. I'm sure I don't say it enough, but thank yeh for everythin' yeh've done for me people."

Kirkrik smiled.

"No thanks are necessary, Radamuck. Just doing what I can to save the realms!" he said happily.

Radamuck chuckled, then turned and followed his wife to their chamber, while Kirkrik continued working his magic over the fields.

***

The next morning came, and bright sunshine reflected off the façade of the city. The armies which fought alongside the dwarves were about to leave, and Radamuck was there to thank them and wish them farewell.

Again, Arrol Goldleaf departed with the Bastine elves, and again there were many tears and handshakes when he left. Radamuck and Baeron shook hands as the two leaders said their good byes.

"Thank yeh again for everythin', Baeron. I'm glad yeh came when we needed yeh," Radamuck said.

"We know you would have done the same for us, Radamuck, and would have done so at a moment's notice. We are always proud to stand beside you, wherever it may be."

Baeron bowed low to the dwarf king, and Radamuck did likewise.

"See to your other guests; there is no need to see us out, my friend," Baeron said, and patted Radamuck on the shoulder.

Radamuck then turned and extended his hand to Blen Duffel. The larger man grasped it and shook it.

"I thank yeh for comin' to our aid, and if yeh have problems with that mage of yers, give us a call and we'll come to help yeh get rid of him," Radamuck said with a smirk.

Duffel laughed heartily.

"I don't think we will need that assistance, but thank you anyway, Radamuck. We had to come to help you. We in Briskey Bucktooth are glad to have you all as allies," Duffel said.

Before he could mount his horse, Radamuck held out a sword. It was Heider's, who dropped it when killed during the battle.

With tears welling in his eyes, Duffel nodded.

"Thank you, Radamuck. I will make sure this weapon has a place of honor in my guild house, and no one will ever wield this sword again, save his kin."

Radamuck bowed low, and backed up as Duffel's stallion was brought forth.

As he mounted his horse, Duffel turned to the king.

"We will call you if your assistance is necessary!"

"We will answer that call immediately!" Radamuck answered, and Duffel led his army through the gates, all on horseback.

When the last horse departed, Radamuck followed them outside to see them off.

And the scene that greeted his eyes made him take in a great deal of breath.

The grass had returned to the plains, as if overnight, and Radamuck stood speechless. There were no more spots of brown mud, and the grass looked as high as it did when Radamuck returned home from his quest nearly a month and a half prior.

Tears started to fill his eyes, and at once he yelled for Kirkrik Dannell.

But Kirkrik didn't answer his summons.

"Where in the name of Dausonne did that dratted mage run off to?" Radamuck asked.

"I think he left before the dawn, uncle. He said he wanted to leave it a surprise." Aidan smirked. "I guess he surprised you."

"That he did," Radamuck said, laughing. "I would have loved to see him again, but I'm sure we'll see him soon enough. He said we should let things take its natural course and let the grass grow on its own. He said it would be disastrous to accelerate the process.

"I guess he changed his mind."

Aidan laughed, and then looked at Yanos, who then looked to Grumpet, who stood behind them all with his hands behind his back. It was obvious he held something.

"Well Radamuck, if you know anything about wizards is that when they speak, they speak in riddles. The grass seed he used was fast-growing grass seed. It grew in less than five hours! He couldn't accelerate it any quicker than that!" Grumpet said, then holding out a leather sack full of the fast-grow seeds for everyone to see.

Everyone laughed heartily, and as Lady Rosar brought Radasack to Radamuck, Radamuck could only chuckle at the wizard and his fast-grow solution.

"That silly ol' mage," he said, "getting me thinking that there would be grass in the spring! Wait until I see him again!"

"Well, there is grass now, and there will be grass in the spring, too!" Aidan said, and everyone laughed harder.

Radamuck looked out at his front lawn again, and heard the unmistakable sound of Briskey Bucktooth's horns blowing off in the distance. The elves of Bastine soared past the city as the horns blew out of the north, and Radamuck smiled at the elves' departure.

He looked down at Radasack and kissed the baby's smooth forehead, as the child saw the grass outside Lowbridge's doors. He cooed and pointed at it happily.

"Aye, Radasack. Look at all that grass! There'll always be grass there for yeh to play in, mark me words."

As the horns faded and the army of elves disappeared from sight, Radamuck brought the baby outside, followed by Lady Rosar, Aidan, Prestillia, Yanos, Grumpet, and Jessica. They all enjoyed the sunniest day in Lowbridge for what seemed like weeks, with little thought to the war that had just passed.

TO BE CONCLUDED

Like what you've read? Sean Sweeney has something for every member of the family: check out more books and stories!

For young adults:

Zombie Showdown

For adults:

The Jaclyn Johnson, code name Snapshot series
Model Agent: A Thriller
Rogue Agent: A Thriller
Double Agent: A Thriller
Promises Given, Promises Kept: A Jaclyn Johnson novella
Federal Agent: A Thriller
Literary Agent: A Thriller
Jail Bird Jenny: A Jaclyn Johnson short story
Travel Agent: A Thriller
Chemical Agent: A Thriller
Ticket Agent: A Thriller
Scouring Agent: A Thriller

Redeemed
Royal Switch: A Major League Thriller
An Invitation to Drink… and to Die
The Lone Bostonian
Freedom (with David Wood)

The Ricky Madison series
The Long Crimson Line: A Thriller
Persuaded By The Reflections: A Thriller

The Peg-Legged Privateer: A Tattered Sails novel

The Alex Bourque Small Town PI series
Cold Altar
Voir Dire

Beach Blanket Bloodshed

The Obloeron Saga
The Rise Of The Dark Falcon
The Shadow Looms
Krampel's Revenge
The Quest For The Chalice
The Return To Lowbridge
The Fall of Myrindar

Short stories
Belief Debt: Paid In Full (Part of Christopher Nadeau's Not in the Brochure anthology)
C is for Coulrophobia (Part of the Phobophobia anthology)
Red Christmas (Part of the Bump in the Night 2011 anthology)
Refugees: A short story of survival

Writing As John Fitch V

One Hero, A Savior
Turning Back The Clock
A Galaxy At War
The Mastermind: A novella

Short stories
Sidetracked
Amber Twilight
Vuvuzombie

Writing as D.L. Boyd

Scollay Love: A Romance

The Glorious series
Glorious Slip
Glorious Rise (coming soon)

Visit Sean online:

www.seansweeneyauthor.com

Join Sean's mailing list and get updates on his work straight to your email!

Email Sean!

seansweeneyauthor@yahoo.com

www.ingramcontent.com/pod-product-compliance
Lightning Source LLC
La Vergne TN
LVHW091157150826
845672LV00005B/1183

* 9 7 9 8 5 6 0 7 0 9 0 4 4 *